Out of Her League

Samantha Wayland

Also by Samantha Wayland

Destiny Calls
With Grace
Hat Trick Book One: Fair Play
Hat Trick Book Two: Two Man Advantage
Hat Trick Book Three: End Game
Crashing the Net
Home & Away

Out of Her League

Dedication

For Lauren.

Welcome to the family. We're not exactly the Morrisons, but I promise we will love and look after you as well as they love and look after their own.

Acknowledgements

I've been extraordinarily lucky to be able to work with the same editor for all my books, and from that professional relationship has come a friendship I cherish. I cannot begin to express how grateful I am to Meghan Miller for all she's done, and does, and probably will do to not only make each of my books possible, but keep my life in some semblance of order. I swore in a previous book that I just needed to find a way to get her to move to Massachusetts and install her on the couch in my office so that all would be perfect.

Having done so, I can attest it's better than that.

I also must thank my patient cover artist, Caitlin Fry, for putting up with me on this book. As a rule, I defer to her in all things cover-design related, but for some damn reason I had *ideas* I just couldn't let go of on this one. Fortunately, she's still speaking to me.

A huge welcome and so much gratitude to the newest member of Team Wayland — my copyeditor, Cindy. She jumped in on this at the very end and made it infinitely better by catching all the little things my eyes could no longer see.

Many thanks to Stephanie Kay, for being the best cheerleader/ass-kicker a writer could ask for. And to my generous and thorough critique partner, Victoria Morgan, who has been on this journey with me the whole way and hasn't given up on me yet. To Darth, for giving me access to all the inspiration a girl could ask for. And Rosie, for talking me off more than one ledge.

Finally, of course, I thank my family. If I listed all the ways they make this possible and bring me joy, it would cost too much to print this book.

Chapter One

"Holy shit, I just met the Queen of England."

Michaela burst into laughter at the wild look in Callum's eyes. In all the years they'd been friends, she didn't think she'd ever seen him look more freaked out.

"She's nice," Michaela offered, having met the Queen before with her parents. Granted, the first time Michaela had been too young to remember it, but the second, she'd been eighteen and far too clueless about, well, *everything*, to appreciate what a great and rare gift it had been.

She didn't expect to ever have the honor again—the price of a misspent youth.

"You met her yesterday, Cal," Michaela said with another chuckle. "Why are you freaking out now?"

"Because it's easier than freaking out about the fact that I'm going to walk down the aisle in ten minutes?"

Well, that was honest, anyway. Michaela was more surprised Callum wasn't standing at the door, trying to barrel through it to get to Rupert and the boys.

"You getting cold feet?"

Callum shot out of his chair. "Of course not!"

Michaela smirked. She hadn't really thought so, but at least Callum didn't look nervous anymore. He looked pissed.

"Put it away, Grumpy," she said unsympathetically. "Yelling at your best man-lady-person won't help."

He grinned at Michaela. "You're my best woman. Accept it."

"Maybe. It's not like we all get to choose what people call us, do we, Countess?"

"Don't call me that," Callum grumbled, his cheeks turning pink.

"Why not? You're marrying an earl in" —she checked her

9

watch— "seven minutes."

Callum gulped audibly. "Holy crap."

The thing was, that while Callum might have been a mess of nerves, Michaela didn't have a single worry about today. Planning the bachelor party had been way more stressful than having to get Callum to the back of the chapel in a few minutes. She looked out the windows at the clear blue skies above Woodcock—the seat of the Weckfordham earldom and Rupert's childhood home—and thought how very far they'd come.

A year ago, Callum and Michaela had been pretending to be in love, letting the world—and more specifically, the press— wonder how long it would be before they married. It had seemed like an ideal setup, allowing her to finally quash the rumors that no man would have her, while also easing the scrutiny from Callum, who was exhausted after a decade of pretending to be straight for the benefit of his NHL career.

In hindsight, she should have known that when they stopped "dating" it would probably be a shit storm. But Callum was in love. Stupidly, head-over-heels, sappy in love.

And for that reason alone, Michaela wouldn't change any of it.

She squinted at a black dot hovering in the sky, her ears straining to hear the rhythmic whump of helicopter blades, her heart not beating right until the bird dipped to the left and disappeared into the trees.

She shook her head and turned back to Callum. He and Rupert had hired a top-notch firm to handle the security for this event. And what neither groom knew, or needed to know, was that Michaela had then paid that firm to triple whatever they'd had planned.

She knew her role in today's festivities was adding to the press melee surrounding the entire thing. It wasn't every day an NHL star up and retired in order to marry his boyfriend and raise their children together. It only added to the insanity that the already infamously disgraced woman, the woman had pretended to be said NHL star's girlfriend for five years, was to stand in as best man-lady-person.

She refused to be called the best woman. It just didn't fit.

"Ready to go?" she asked, hooking her arm through Callum's.

"Yes," he replied immediately, if a little hoarsely.

She drew him out the wide french doors in the study and across the lawn toward the chapel. The path was lined with a riot of flowers to celebrate the perfect June day. The smell of roses wafted in the air, both from the grounds and the nosegay of blood-red buds in Michaela's hand.

She wore a simple dark blue strapless gown that skimmed the gravel and tugged at the grass edging the path. A bright swath of the green, blue, and red Morrison tartan was draped from her shoulder to the opposite hip, matching Callum's kilt.

It was a shame so few men had an excuse to wear skirts anymore, because that look really worked for Michaela. She was very happily anticipating seeing the rest of the Morrison clan in their finery, and Rupert and the boys in the bright red of the Macalister colors.

Rupert had complained they would look like a Christmas pageant gone wrong and had suggested he and the boys could wear morning suits instead. Callum wouldn't hear of it.

Apparently, Michaela wasn't the only one really into men wearing their skirts. She knew Callum was her best friend for a reason.

The doors to the chapel opened as they climbed the stairs, and there stood Callum's five brothers, all grinning at the unusually pale Callum. Michaela's eyes sought out Kieran's, and he nodded.

Rupert and the boys were ready.

The rest, as she'd known all along it would be, was easy.

The wedding was beautiful. Lachlan had never seen his brother look happier, even as the tears rolled down Callum's cheeks. Lachlan tried very hard to be subtle as he rubbed at his own eyes, but failed, if the amused and affectionate look from his sister was anything to go by.

At least he wasn't as bad as Alexei Belov, the very large Russian goalie manfully weeping into his handkerchief in Rupert's family pew.

Callum clung to Rupert's hand, their two boys standing between them, part of the ceremony instead of just standing up for their dads. Michaela Price was Callum's best woman, while Reese Lamont stood up for Rupert. The rest of the ushers—a.k.a. Lachlan and his legion of brothers—sat with their parents and sister.

The ceremony was short and, frankly, unbearably sweet. If Lachlan hadn't been so busy trying not to cry, he might have been rolling his eyes.

The reception, on the other hand, was a little bit like Lachlan's version of hell on earth. Standing around in a skirt, making small talk, and eating canapés was not his idea of a good time. Well, okay, the skirt thing didn't bother him in the slightest. Sure, his usual khakis and a button up would be more comfortable. Or possibly even his hockey gear, sweaty jock and all. But it wasn't like this was unfamiliar territory. His brother Kieran's wedding had contained many of the same elements. Kilts. Handsome husband staring at one of Lachlan's brothers like he couldn't believe his good fortune. And lots of beautiful women decked out in fancy clothes, trying to flirt with Lachlan— only to discover they'd have more luck conversing with the statuary in the hedge maze just down the hill.

He watched his brothers with envy as they moved through the crowd. Easy smiles, big laughs, and the ability to put virtually everyone, from Rupert's sour-faced aunts to the catering waitstaff, at ease. The only one who remained reserved, even a little, was Angus. But he was young and even he, when needed, could employ whatever magical Morrison gene blessed the rest of the clan with social skills.

The gene Lachlan was missing.

He knew perfectly well that standing in the corner, eyeing the door of the tent for a possible escape, wasn't going to save him. But it still made him feel better. Forcing himself to look around, he saw the moment Callum noticed him there and cupped Michaela's elbow to pull her toward Lachlan.

Honestly, Lachlan thought bitterly, how did Callum think this was going to work?

Lachlan was reserved with strangers, had little interest in small talk with people he barely knew, and could more often be found listening rather than contributing to conversations, even among the people who he knew and loved best. But nothing turned him into more of a jabbering idiot than being faced with a beautiful woman and being expected to actually *converse*.

And *Michaela fucking Price*?

Forget about it.

Lachlan darted his gaze to the door again, longing for escape but knowing it was too far away. Then he searched the crowd for Rhian, one of his sister's two partners, and Lachlan's good friend. Rhian would bail him out. More than any of Lachlan's brothers, Rhian seemed to understand how to help Lachlan navigate tricky social waters.

He was also, apparently, one hell of a dancer. If he, Savannah, or Garrick thought they were fooling anyone in this tent, they had another think coming. Their half-blind great-uncle Milton could probably guess the three of them were *awfully* good friends.

Was that Garrick's hand on Rhian's…? *Oh geez.*

"Lachlan!"

Callum's voice jerked Lachlan out of his amused fascination with Rhian's gyrations and back to the problem at hand. *Shit.* The most beautiful woman Lachlan had ever laid eyes on was standing right in front of him, smiling warmly and making an alarming amount of eye contact.

Of course, there wasn't any amount of contact—of any variety and involving any body part—that Lachlan *wouldn't* find alarming.

Jesus Christ, she was gorgeous. Almost as tall as Callum, so only a couple inches shorter than Lachlan's six foot three, with long brown hair curling softly around her bare shoulders and down her back. He had to be imagining how her skin glowed from the fairy lights strung up in the support beams.

Lachlan's tongue stuck to the roof of his now hideously dry mouth.

This was why he'd skipped the bachelor party. This was why he skipped *all* the parties.

"Lachlan, this is Michaela," Callum announced, as if perhaps Lachlan had been living under a rock. "Michaela, this is my brother Lachlan."

"Hello," Michaela said, her voice smoky and low.

He blinked at her stupidly. Her smile warmed, which he wouldn't have thought was even possible. Her shoulder moved and he had a terrible, terrible suspicion that she was holding out her hand for him to take. Should he shake it? Kiss it? What was the etiquette here?

Forget that. He should stick with the basics.

Hi. That was what he should do, he should say something like that. *Hello. Howdy.* Some fucking greeting. He didn't have to be fancy. He didn't even have to bust out anything as basically sociable as *nice to meet you.* Just fucking say *hello.*

He swallowed and forced his mouth open.

No sound came out.

Michaela looked at Callum, who stared at his brother with obvious consternation.

She clung to her smile and pulled her hand back from where it had been left hanging, mid-air. She pressed it instead to her stomach as the silence stretched on, and on, *and on,* until she was lifting her foot with the intention of kicking Callum. For

14

Christ's sake, couldn't he help his brother out? Callum had warned her his brother was shy, but this was ridiculous. The man looked like he was about to have a stroke.

"I know your name," Lachlan blurted.

Michaela blinked and dropped her foot back to the floor. It wasn't exactly what she'd been expecting as an opening line, but it was something, so she nodded, as if this were perfectly normal.

"Yes, well, I guess a lot of people do," she offered, and good god, now she was as awkward as he was. She should have just said, *"Yes, I'm infamous. Have you seen my sex tape?"* and made this as painful as humanly possible. They weren't far off anyhow.

She gave into her earlier urge and clipped Callum in the shin with her very pointy shoe.

"Lachlan," Callum said, suddenly and a shade too loudly, "Michaela is going to Harvard in the fall. I thought it might be nice if you two knew each other, since you'll be neighbors." He smiled encouragingly at his brother.

Lachlan's eyes widened with horror. "You're moving to Trowbridge Street?"

"Um, no?" she replied, not sure if she should be insulted. The expression on his face could hardly be called flattering. "I think I'm going to buy a place on Massachusetts Avenue."

Which was not something she should be sharing, but she felt the instinctive need to set the poor man at ease.

He didn't seem to have any response to her comment, anyway.

She was caught in a conversational train wreck and she couldn't look away. She stared into Lachlan's wide, bright green eyes, the exact same color as Callum's. They also had the same shape face, but that was where the similarities ended. Lachlan's nose was still straight and unbroken, and his mouth was wider. His hair a lighter brown. And he was taller, leaner than his brother. Just as handsome, but in a different way. Or, he would be, if he weren't turning scarlet and starting to sweat.

Eventually he had to blink, didn't he?

15

Callum, the useless jerk, was doing nothing to end the stand-off. He was still staring at his brother like he'd never seen him before, head cocked to one side, eyes almost as wide and horrified as Lachlan's. She considered kicking him again.

"Mass Ave," Lachlan said, apropos of nothing.

"Pardon?"

"It's called Mass Ave. That's what people call that road. The one you're going to live on. In Cambridge."

"Okay, um, that's great. Great information. Thank you." Now *she* was stuttering. It was like Lachlan was a social skill black hole, sucking the ability to make small talk right out of her.

"You're welcome," he said sincerely.

Okay, well, this had been a nice, if totally ill-conceived idea, but she was done. She wasn't going to keep torturing this guy. It was starting to hurt to look at him. She wanted to put her hand over his eyes and *force* him to blink.

"Callum, I think Rupert needs you," she said, nodding to where Callum's smiling groom was paying absolutely zero attention to them.

"What?" Callum's head whipped around, homing in on Rupert instantly. "Excuse me."

Callum ran off. Which had been her plan exactly, except the idiot flew across the room to his husband's side and *didn't take her with him.*

Honestly, what was the matter with these men?

She smiled kindly at Lachlan, whose mouth was still just sort of hanging open. She'd had a lot of people react to meeting her a lot of different ways over the years, but this was definitely a first. The longer the silence stretched, the more nauseated he appeared.

"Well, it was very nice to meet you. I guess I'll see you soon," Michaela said, taking a slow step back.

"What?"

"In Cambridge," she reminded him. "Perhaps we'll run into

each other on campus. Though I'll be at the law school. I don't think that's on the same campus as your office and classes."

"No."

Right. *No.* Well, maybe that was for the best.

Lachlan watched Michaela's retreating back, his stomach a jumble of knots that had been twisting tighter and tighter for the past five minutes. That had gone even worse than he'd expected. *Awesome.*

He briefly considered pulling his sgian-dubh—the ceremonial knife in his right sock—and stabbing himself in the eye with it.

"So, that looked painful."

Lachlan jumped, then turned to see Rhian smiling at him with some combination of sympathy and amusement. "*That* was excruciating."

"Nice. But just think, now that you've gotten one of the most famous and famously beautiful women in the world out of the way, maybe everyone else will be easier?"

Lachlan let out a bark of laughter, wincing at how bitter it sounded. "I doubt it."

"Come on," Rhian said, tipping his head toward the bar. "I see a glass of scotch with your name on it."

"Funny, I see the whole bottle."

He didn't, in the end, drink the whole bottle. Getting loaded just because he'd humiliated himself wasn't really his style. Also, he'd be drunk all the damn time if it were. No, becoming even more introverted and tucking himself further and further into the shadows at the corners of the tent was more his speed.

Rhian didn't let him get away with it as much as he might have unchecked, but no one really gave him a hard time. His family didn't understand him, but they loved him and accepted that he would always be the odd duck in these situations. Rhian, sadly, accepted nothing of the sort. Lachlan was oddly grateful *and* resentful about that. At least with Rhian prodding him along, all of Lachlan's aunts got another spin around the dance floor.

Whenever Rhian allowed it or was sufficiently distracted, Lachlan ducked into a quiet spot to watch the party rage around him. He did enjoy seeing his family so happy, the kids running around and the older guests huddle up with their tea and coffee to catch up on years of life. Most of the very few people on earth he felt completely comfortable sitting and talking to were there. It made it bearable.

A flash of color and a bright laugh drew his eyes, again, to Michaela.

He didn't think he was imagining the way that, if she stood still long enough, everyone near her seemed to shift, slowly turning to revolve around her. Or that she was, at some level, aware of that, given the way she rarely stopped moving long enough to let it happen, and if she did, it was to deflect attention back to where it belonged—on Rupert and Callum.

She obviously adored them both, and their children, whose hands were often found clasped in hers. She danced with them, or other members of Lachlan's family, all night. And no one else.

His parents clearly liked her, too, their smiles wide and genuine when they spoke, his father's cheeks pink the one time he spun her across the floor. She had that bizarre ability to flirt outrageously with his father and only leave his mother beaming at them with approval.

How the fuck did anyone even do that?

And she was moving to Cambridge.

Fuck his life.

Chapter Two

Moving sucked. Moving to a new apartment, in a new city, in the depths of August when the humidity was so thick the air tasted heavy, and with no help other than the movers, sucked *a lot.*

Michaela's brothers had offered to come up, but they had lives and jobs in New York, and she'd wanted to move in on a weekday when there were fewer people around to witness it. She'd make a point of introducing herself to her neighbors in the coming week, but for now she was careful to stay out of sight while the movers lugged all her belongings into the elevator.

Her new doorman, Mike, seemed surprised when she came up to introduce herself and then stood by his desk chatting, keeping an eye on the flow of men and stuff. She hung out there for a while, until he was joking with her about the sheer number of boxes labeled "clothes" and she'd discovered that his niece was also due to start law school in a week.

By the time she went upstairs to supervise the placement of the big pieces of furniture, she thought she had a good sense of who Mike was. His quick humor and big smile were hard not to like. And she even felt a small ray of hope that she could trust him. It was probably foolish. She'd liked her doormen in New York a lot, too—but that hadn't stopped them from selling reporters and photographers information about her comings and goings, and letting them paw through her mail.

She was, as had been proven time and again, a terrible judge of character. But hey, maybe this time she'd get lucky. There was, after all, a first time for everything.

Clinging to that optimism, she looked around her new home and smiled. She'd liked this apartment when she'd seen the listing online, and had made an offer as soon as she'd seen it in person. It wasn't huge, but it was more than big enough for her, including a spare bedroom for her exercise equipment if it turned out the gym in the basement wasn't a good place for her.

She was used to people taking her picture, but she'd defy anyone to look good after a hard slog on the elliptical machine. Those were always the shots at the checkout line, announcing her descent into drug addiction or the latest in a series of mental breakdowns. If the *Weekly Inquisition* was to be believed, she was up to number forty-seven. Or was it forty-eight, now? She'd have to check with her brother Damon. He liked to keep track of these things.

He was such a help.

So, yeah, spare bedroom. Check.

The best part about the apartment, though, was the light. She was used to the high rises in New York, but for all that her last place had been twenty floors higher up, the windows had looked out at the buildings across the street. This place was on the top floor of the tallest building for blocks, and the windows and skylights were huge, bathing the open floor plan in unobstructed sunlight. Even better, off the kitchen there was a large rooftop terrace, which begged for a potted herb garden. She was trying to learn to cook, which wasn't really going very well, but she had a refined enough palate to know fresh herbs were better.

And she probably couldn't poison anyone with an herb. Which was more than could be said about her first attempt at chicken piccata. Damon had sworn he'd never sit at her table again.

Shaking off that memory, she ran down to the underground garage, grimacing when she heard the high-pitched barks echoing against the cold cement walls. She cast an apologetic look at the man striding past her car, ignoring his startled recognition. She focused instead on Fang, who had apparently been working on his best Rottweiler impersonation for anyone who dared to walk nearby.

She sent him a supremely unimpressed look through the back window and popped the door open.

"Are you done?"

Liquid brown eyes stared up at her, his whole body

quivering with joy.

Michaela rolled her eyes, but her heart melted, as always, when five pounds of mutt flung himself against her chest. She could only hope her new neighbor found his ridiculousness as endearing as she did, and wouldn't tell anyone about the stream of baby talk falling from her lips.

Tucking her little monster under her arm, she bypassed the elevator—preferring the eight flights of stairs to the company of her unknown neighbor—and ran back up to the apartment. She set Fang down to explore and went to work dragging boxes and smaller furniture to different places to see what she thought, and, once decided, putting stuff away. Her mother had suggested she hire someone to do this, but she didn't like the idea of strangers going through her stuff. She'd been nervous enough about the moving company, wondering if her shit would end up for sale on the internet rather than in Cambridge.

Callum's sister, Savannah, had offered to come help her get settled, which was really sweet. Michaela hoped they'd get to know each other better over the coming months, but as of now, she didn't know her that much better than the complete strangers her mother had proposed.

And, of course, Lachlan hadn't offered to help at all. Which, really, was for the best all around.

The brief and evil fantasy of innocently asking Lachlan to unpack her underwear drawer drifted through her mind, and she smiled momentarily before scolding herself. She felt sorry for the guy, and as much as a good prank could make her whole day, she didn't have any smelling salts.

Then she considered how bad it would be if he found the box under her bed, unlocked. 911 worked the same everywhere, right?

Grinning, she set up her speakers, chose a playlist, and bopped her way into the kitchen to start working.

Lachlan thought it had to *suck* to be Michaela Price.

Standing in Out of Town News, just a few feet from his office and in the heart of Harvard Square, he frowned at the wall of magazines before him. Normally he wouldn't spare them a second glance, but it was hard to ignore the glossy, full-color covers when they featured his own brother.

America was currently obsessed with the story of the Olympic-medal winning professional athlete who had left it all behind to marry the man he loved and raise their two adopted children. Add in that Rupert was an earl and it was the stuff of romance novels—or so Lachlan's mother had attempted to explain.

It all seemed like a lot of hooey to Lachlan. It was just Callum and Rupert. They were good people, trying to raise more good people well. Lachlan knew and loved them, and was one hundred percent certain their lives didn't really resemble the crap he was looking at on the newsstand.

Michaela, on the other hand, he didn't know, but his bullshit meter was still stuck at full tilt. She was on more than half of the covers, too. And in two cases, she got the big picture, and his brother and Rupert had been relegated to the little box in the corner.

Scorned again! declared one particularly busy headline. *Did she know?* asked another.

She had known. She'd known Callum was gay almost the entire time they'd been friends. And certainly for every minute they'd pretended to date. Lachlan had never understood why either of them had thought *that* was a good idea, but he'd been able to *imagine* why his brother had believed being an openly gay man and an NHL star hadn't been possible. Lachlan absolutely couldn't fathom why Michaela had done it. Hell, she'd been the one to *suggest* it.

Lachlan didn't know shit about society or celebrities, but even he knew Michaela was both. He'd heard someone once call her a celebutante. The daughter of a wealthy and powerful family, blessed with a symmetrical facial structure and a lot of shiny hair, meeting the current standards for beauty seemingly without much effort, thanks to genetics making her tall and slim.

So what.

None of this explained why people wanted to know so much about her. And why they didn't seem to care if what they read was the truth or not. Callum had been sick with worry about how his coming out and marriage would affect Michaela. She'd insisted that he not worry about that, about her, and make himself happy.

And he had. With her blessing and support, even though she'd known full well that this crap would be the consequence.

To Lachlan, that was the story that readers should care about, though mostly he thought people should just mind their own damn business. She'd thrown herself to the media wolves so her friend could be happy. That was interesting. *That* told him something about her. But people didn't care about that.

What they cared about appeared to be—Lachlan leaned closer to the rack of magazines, embarrassed to even be looking at this dreck—a sex tape.

Lachlan jerked upright. *A sex tape?*

"Did you hear Michaela Price is enrolled this semester? I read she's working on her PhD in psychology."

Lachlan glanced at the group of undergraduates to his left. The one who'd spoken picked up one of the magazines featuring Michaela, front and center, on the cover.

"Must be nice to be able to buy your way into any school you want," said another with a sneer. "Think we'll recognize her when she hasn't had herself Photoshopped?"

Lachlan wondered if they actually thought she'd *volunteered* to be on the cover of a magazine decrying her inability to keep a man happy.

"She's probably a bitch," another announced.

Lachlan's hands curled into fists, his lunch souring in his stomach. He fled the newsagent and walked briskly back to campus, his shirt sticking to his skin in the humidity.

23

When he arrived back at his office, he closed the door firmly and sat at his desk, staring at his computer for a long time.

There was a right and wrong here, and he wasn't sure where the line lay. Michaela had a right to her privacy, regardless of his curiosity and the fact that he could violate it, easily and thoroughly, via the internet. But he also wanted to know more.

He decided it was safe enough to pull up her Wikipedia page. Even someone as clueless as him knew that those were almost always carefully managed by a publicist or someone else with an equally weird job. His two more famous brothers' pages certainly were, given how they were presented as the perfect angels they only wished they could be.

Actually, scratch that. Neither of them wanted to be angels. But their publicists sure wished they were.

Michaela's too, apparently.

She was his age, more or less. Private schools, Columbia, Summa Cum Laude. Pretty impressive stuff. His eyebrows didn't lift, though, until he saw that she was now the Chairwoman of the Price Foundation. Given that both her parents were still healthy and relatively young, and Michaela wasn't the oldest child, it was interesting that she'd taken the helm already.

Lachlan's fingers hovered over the keyboard, then finally gave up and entered *Michaela Price* as a search term in Google.

The latest news was exactly the same drivel he'd seen on the newsstand, and her Wikipedia page was greyed out as already viewed. Then it got…a lot more interesting. And by interesting, Lachlan meant alarming.

He closed the browser window and picked up his phone. Maybe he could get a more truthful, edited-down version from his sister. He wasn't foolish enough to consider asking Callum. He strongly suspected his brother would blow a gasket if he even brought it up.

"Hi, Lachlan," Savannah said after two short rings.

"Uh…" How did one go about asking their sister if their brother's best friend had a former career in the pornography industry? *New plan needed.* "Is Rhian there?"

"Yeah, sure. He's right here. You have his number, though, don't you?"

"Yeah, sorry. Can I just talk to him?"

There was a series of thumps, then Rhian came on the line. "What's up, Lach?" Rhian asked in his best—and yet, still terrible—Bugs Bunny impersonation.

"Do you know anything about Michaela Price's sex tape?"

His question was met with long silence. "Pardon?"

Lachlan huffed and rubbed a hand over his face. "I don't even know why I'm asking, but I saw all the articles today and I read something about a tape and I met her at the wedding and was surprised, I guess, though really, who am I to judge one way or another, and I was just curious what the deal was there. So I called Sav and then thought maybe I should ask you instead. I guess."

His uncharacteristic doubt of verbal diarrhea was met with yet more silence. Then, "Hold on a sec."

The sound of a door closing came through the phone. "Okay, I'm in the office," Rhian explained. "Just like you don't want to ask your sister about this, I *really* don't want to talk about it when she's within earshot."

Which seemed fair.

"So, was she a porn star?"

Rhian laughed, more of a surprised sound than an amused one. "Uh, no. And let me start by saying that I don't know much about this, since it all happened when I was too young to be aware of this kind of shit. But it's sort of a big deal? Like, if I heard about it later, how the hell do you *not* know about this stuff?"

Lachlan shrugged, even though Rhian couldn't see him. "Not really my area of interest."

"Not really your area of..." Rhian trailed off with an annoyingly fond huff. "Okay, well, I can tell you what I know. The internet can probably tell you a lot more."

25

"I don't want to see it."

"What? The video?"

"No. Yes—that, or all the bullshit. I'm hoping you can distill it for me."

"Um, let's see. She was barely eighteen and her boyfriend, Blake Whelton, taped them having what I've heard is pretty...uh...gymnastic sex, then sold it a couple years later because she was famous and she'd just dumped him. I've never seen it, but I think I'm pretty unusual, to be honest. It got around, a lot, before her lawyers shut it down, and by then it was too late. The internet is forever—and that was *before* Blake's acting career took off and gave the tape new life."

Lachlan swallowed back the bile rising in his throat. "That's awful."

"Yeah. Seriously," Rhian agreed sadly. "The worst part, I hear, is that at the end they're cuddling, and she's obviously in love with this creep, and he's winking at the camera that she clearly doesn't know is there."

Lachlan rubbed his hand over his eyes. "That's really, really awful."

If he'd been put in a position like that, Lachlan didn't think he'd have left the house again, ever, let alone gone on to run a major philanthropic trust and—*shit*—enrolled in law school, just a few blocks away from where he sat now.

Michaela walked across campus, head high, her laptop and notebooks bouncing off her hip in their new messenger bag. Her first class of her first semester was set to begin in just a few minutes and she was more nervous than she could remember being in years.

This had been a really stupid idea. How had she not figured out before today that this was a really, really stupid idea?

She marched on, eyes forward, and tried to ignore the looks cast her way. They weren't unusual, of course, but she realized with a sinking heart that she hadn't really thought about what they would mean here. This wasn't just random people on the street in a huge city she could get lost in. This was a campus. A large one, but still a closed community, and she was the outsider in their midst.

She could guess what they were thinking. That she'd paid her way in. That she didn't deserve to be there. They saw themselves as the best and the brightest, and viewed her as something else entirely.

And maybe they weren't wrong. But she *was* here to learn just like everyone else. She didn't want special treatment, and would readily refuse it if it were offered. Her time here wasn't supposed to be about her name or her notoriety. She'd gladly leave both behind if she could.

Her sole purpose here was to learn everything she could to help grow and protect the Price Foundation. Her brothers were both in business, MBA'd up to their eyeballs and capable of making money in their sleep. They were responsible for managing the Foundation's funds, and they did an amazing job.

Between Michaela and her two brothers, they'd more than doubled what the foundation gave annually over the past five years. With that came a lot more contracts, negotiations, and responsibility. This, more than anything, was what kept Michaela moving forward and had brought her here.

Her parents didn't really understand why she felt a law degree was necessary. They'd handed the reins over to her years ago and were delighted with how things were going. Michaela thought they could be going better.

Her brothers, at least, understood. They'd been on her case for years to get out and do *something*. To get a life. Going back to school, as far as they were concerned, was as good a place to start as any.

They were kidding themselves, of course. She'd never have a normal life, no matter how much she wanted to be a regular student, stuck with hours of homework and freaking out about exams. Her undergraduate studies had ended as a circus, the scandal breaking right before the start of her senior year. She could barely remember how she'd gotten through those last two semesters. Her friends, who'd been happy to party across the city with her, using her name and fame to get into places most students could never dream of accessing, had abandoned her. The faculty and staff had made it clear they had no interest in her being at their school. The press chasing her across campus.

It was a miracle she'd finished school at all.

She looked at the groups of students sprawled out over the lawns and each other with raw envy. She'd had that once. But she'd blown it. And there was no way to get it back.

She wished, briefly, and not for the first time, that she could go incognito. But the press had gotten wind of her enrollment months ago, and people clearly knew she was here. Any hope that her fellow students wouldn't notice or care, that they might just *ignore* her, was futile.

As usual, her name and her reputation had preceded her. She'd contemplated going full-on Legally Blonde and just embracing the attention—garnering more of it, even. That way, at least, the stares would make sense. Would be expected. And if people weren't subtle—which they rarely were—she could pretend it was how she wanted it.

Most times it was a lot easier to be who people expected, rather than who you truly were.

She'd coped with unwanted attention that way for over a decade, and it had worked for her. Mostly. Her notoriety had brought a lot of attention, and through that, donors, to the Price Foundation and the charities it supported.

But she was also exhausted by it.

So today she was marching across campus in jeans, a t-shirt, and sandals, her hair in a pony-tail, much the same as everyone else. It felt a lot like going to war without her armor. Or maybe to sea without a boat. How hard would she have to keep swimming just to keep her head above water this way, alone in an ocean of fellow students who saw her as "other"?

Worse come to worst, she supposed, she could always bust out the pink suit, kitten heels, and Fang on his rhinestone leash in a week when she cracked.

Chapter Three

Lachlan looked out over his Philosophy 101 class and sighed. He *hated* these general education classes, crowded with freshmen who'd had grand ideas when they'd signed up for this class from the comfort of their mother's kitchens over the summer. They'd soon realize that they didn't really give a shit about philosophy, let alone at nine o'clock in the morning.

He clapped his hands together once, loudly, giving all appearances of being enthusiastic about handing out the syllabus and detailing what the homework would be.

Lachlan *was* excited about philosophy. It was his passion. His *calling*, even. It was just hard to believe he'd also been called to bore eighteen year olds out of their skulls.

At least half the class was nodding off, and that one poor kid in the front row was actually drooling down his own chin, the dark spot growing on his wrinkled, probably slept-in, t-shirt. Lachlan walked past and caught the familiar scents of smoke and stale booze. This kid was clearly settling into campus life quickly. Lachlan contemplated tapping his shoulder, but he was secretly impressed the kid had managed to remain perfectly upright, not even flinching at the sound of Lachlan's clap.

He wished there was a subtle way to reach for his phone and snap a picture. His brothers and Savannah would crack up.

Mentally scolding himself to stay on task, he scanned the room. Every year, Lachlan hoped that there would be that one spark. One bright light who he'd see nodding along instead of nodding off, who would email him questions about the reading and write interesting papers that showed real thought and promise.

It was early days yet, but he wasn't holding out a lot of hope. He knew one thing, though—it *definitely* was not going to be the drooler.

His teaching assistant, Anna, caught his eye and smirked. Lachlan turned his back to the class long enough to control his answering smile and hide his eye roll. The one bright spot in this year's schedule was that Anna was able to be his TA. Five years ago, she'd been that one spark. Now she was on her way to her PhD, and understood as well as he did why these classes were torture for all involved.

Lachlan had once wondered, foolishly aloud, if it were possible to interview incoming students to determine if they were suited to the subject. This was, of course, met with a great deal of scorn from his colleagues, many of whom still hoped that their presentation of self and subject would be *so charismatic* they could convert anyone to their passion.

Lachlan had no such illusions about himself. Or philosophy, for that matter.

On that depressing note, he dismissed the class and told himself not to take it personally that everyone, including the drooler, fled the building like it was on fire.

He and Anna followed at a more sedate pace, chatting about their plans for the new semester.

"Lachlan!"

Lachlan froze on the wide granite front steps of the Emerson Building as every single person on the green turned to stare. Not at him, but at the woman jogging their way and waving.

Anna's eyes widened. "Is that Michaela Price?"

"Fuck. I hope not."

Anna giggle-snorted at his side.

"Hi!" Michaela said with a wide smile when she reached them. "I'm so glad I found you."

"Uh," Lachlan stuttered, "what?" *Why?*

Michaela's smile didn't falter, though her eyes did narrow a little. Lachlan's palms and forehead went damp. He locked his knees but that only made him sway dangerously on the rock-hard stairs. Shit shit shit. He did not want to do this in front of Anna. He was her advisor. He was pretty sure that meant he was supposed to look intelligent in front of her. Or at least *coherent*.

Unfortunately, these thoughts were not helping the cause.

31

Anna looked at Lachlan, her eyebrows drawn together, then back at Michaela with a hesitant smile. "Hello, I'm Anna. Dr. Morrison's TA this year."

Michaela shook her hand. "Michaela Price," she offered, in case Anna lived under an even bigger rock than Lachlan, "I'm a friend of the Morrison family."

Anna's mouth opened and closed a few times before she muttered, "Callum Morrison."

Michaela immediately looked contrite, glancing at Lachlan as if to ascertain just how badly she'd fucked up.

"It's not a secret," he blurted. And wow, he'd managed a whole sentence relevant to the discussion. Woo.

Michaela's shoulders dropped several inches. "Okay. Phew." She turned back to Anna. "Callum suggested I look up Lachlan once I arrived and I'm just getting a chance to now." She glanced around at their gathering audience. "Though I guess I should have called ahead. I just figured I'd catch you after class."

When he wasn't expecting it. She was clever, he'd give her that. He stared at her, his brain buzzing louder and louder as the murmur of voices around them grew, and Anna and Michaela continued to wait for him to say something. Anything. His legs shook with the desire to just turn and walk away. He might have done it, had Anna not been there.

"We were just headed back to the office," Anna said helpfully.

Michaela smiled at her gratefully. "Can I walk with you?"

"Sure." Anna sent Lachlan another concerned look. "It's just this way."

The crowd parted as they moved down the stairs. Lachlan didn't think he was imagining hearing his last name repeated from a number of directions. He'd never made any secret about having two brothers in the NHL, one of whom had pretend-dated Michaela Price, but he hadn't exactly advertised it, either.

Not that he wasn't proud of his brothers. He was. Very. There were plenty of idiots on this campus who would find little to respect about professional hockey players, but there were many more who understood the brains and commitment that took. Lachlan had long ago consigned the former to the very large of pool of people he didn't give a shit about and happily ignored.

"So, do you have another class today?" Michaela asked.

Silence stretched before Lachlan realized she was speaking to him. "No."

"Great," she said, her smile not slipping an inch. The small part of his brain that wasn't totally useless right now could admire how hard she was working at this. "Do you have time for a coffee? Or lunch?"

He almost said no again, but bit his tongue just in the nick of time. He was socially challenged and objectively a total nerd, but even he could see the desperate hope in Michaela's eyes. He worried, suddenly, that something was going on with Callum.

He tried to say, "Okay," but it came out more like, "Nhghgn." Fortunately, he had retained the capacity to nod, so Michaela understood him.

"Great. Do you need to go back to your office first?"

"No, he doesn't," Anna said brightly, tugging the box of extra syllabi from his arms and leaving him feeling even more exposed. "I can take these, and you two can go on ahead." She smiled up at Lachlan. "I'll catch up with you later."

Lachlan frowned, trying to make sense of Anna's face. Then his stomach clenched, because oh, holy hell, was Anna *matchmaking*?

Anna winked and his face went hot with mortification. Oh, Christ, *she was.*

"Ready?" Michaela asked.

He nodded, not even bothering to try speaking aloud. He jerked his hand to the left in an attempt to find his manners and steer them toward the nearest gate and out onto the streets of Cambridge. Hopefully there, at least, they wouldn't be surrounded by so many curious faces.

He didn't have a destination in mind, but Michaela's earlier suggestion of coffee sounded good and it was something to focus on. He led them toward the Square and the massive Starbucks in the heart of it. With each step, he wondered if she was going to say something. If she was waiting for him to say something to her. He tried to be subtle and glance over quickly to gauge her expression, but she was always looking back at him, a small smile on her face.

At least she didn't look appalled. Or alarmed. That was good, right?

Five minutes into their walk, Lachlan stopped worrying about what he was expected to say, gratefully accepting that Michaela was content to remain silent.

This did, however, leave Lachlan plenty of opportunity to notice how many people were watching them as they entered the bustle of Harvard Square. Some people were even taking pictures of them. Or her, really. Lachlan suspected he could be walking along in a clown suit and no one would notice.

"Oh, they'd notice. They'd take it as a sign I was finally cracking up. Or cracking up *again*, depending on who you asked."

Lachlan hunched his shoulders in. "Did I say that out loud?"

"The clown suit thing? Yeah."

"Sorry," he muttered, wondering if this wouldn't be less painful for all parties involved if he simply took a hard right out into traffic.

He walked a few more feet, turning over what she'd said again and again, before curiosity trumped his nerves. "Why would my wearing a clown suit be a sign that *you're* cracking up?"

Her face remained neutral, but her shrug was weary. He appreciated that kind of eloquent non-verbal communication. He appreciated *all* non-verbal communication in social situations, now that he considered it.

It didn't, though, answer his question. He thought about asking again, but pressing her to speak when he could barely manage to string a few words together seemed hypocritical.

He opened the door to Starbucks and held it for her, waiting. She seemed momentarily surprised, but he held on. Some women didn't appreciate this kind of thing, which he understood and was fine with, but he was horrible at figuring out who did and who didn't. Rather than question it to the point of paralysis, he'd long ago decided to go with what his mother had taught him.

Who said he couldn't learn a social skill?

Michaela nodded, a silent "thank you", and slid past him into the cafe.

Michaela stood in line, staring at the menu as if she hadn't ordered essentially the exact same thing for the past decade. She was trying to give Lachlan time and space to settle. She didn't think she was imagining that the silence stretching between them was becoming increasingly comfortable. Well, okay, maybe increasingly less *uncomfortable*.

It was a start.

Callum had claimed that Lachlan was "shy" around women—and theorized the more beautiful the woman, the worse it was. Michaela had seen shy before, lots of times, and this wasn't that. Also, Callum's assertion didn't hold true. Lachlan was perfectly able to chat with his frankly stunning TA, Anna. So why could he hardly say a single intelligible word to Michaela? Except the clown suit thing, which was just weird.

Michaela ordered, then stepped aside for Lachlan to do the same, ready to run interference if he struggled with it. He didn't. His smooth, deep voice washed over her, pushing back the buzz of the crowd, his polite smile completely transforming his face.

The young man behind the counter blinked up at Lachlan, wide eyed and pink cheeked as Lachlan made all kinds of eye contact and used appropriate and articulate *words* through the course of their transaction.

The cashier wasn't the only one struck dumb by how compelling and gorgeous Lachlan was like this.

Lachlan turned, still smiling, and Michaela quickly paid for their drinks, pleased when he didn't protest. Of course, that might be because he couldn't speak in her presence, but whatever. She was taking it as a win. As far as she was concerned, going for coffee at all was a win.

Lachlan took his cup from the barista and gestured at the stairs to the large seating area above them. Michaela raised her eyebrows and looked around at the dozen or so pairs of eyes on them—three of whom were holding up their phones to take pictures or video to record this stunningly mundane transaction for the internet—then looked back at Lachlan.

"Let's walk," he said quietly.

Maybe that was the trick to getting him to talk, she thought as she held the door for him. She just had to shut up and wait for it.

They wandered through Harvard Square, listening to the street performers and dodging roving bands of excited underclassmen, then started up Brattle Street. The houses were old and well-maintained, the estates increasing in size and grandeur until the neighborhood felt more like a park, the street shaded by trees and lined with cast iron gates and fences.

The city noises fell away, but the silence between them continued. It was nice, actually, not having to say much. She spent a lot of time alone these days, especially in the two weeks since she'd moved here. That was why she'd finally given in and looked up Lachlan's class schedule. Fang didn't really satisfy the basic need for human companionship.

She'd previously believed she needed to *talk* to someone to get that, but it turned out it wasn't strictly necessary.

After about a half hour of walking, she realized Lachlan had circled them around the worst of the bustle and brought them to the other side of the Square.

"I live just a few blocks from here," she said, waving to their left.

He immediately changed directions. "I'll drop you at your door."

Huh. Were his manners so ingrained that falling back on them made speaking in the process easier? She considered how polite Callum was, even when he had been in full-on grumpy bastard mode back in Denver. Then she pictured Lachlan and Callum's parents, Mary and Bruce Morrison.

She strongly suspected the manners thing was true, and felt triumphant that she'd figured something out about Lachlan. Too bad it didn't explain why he couldn't speak the rest of the time.

When they drew up in front of Michaela's building, Mike appeared at the door. He immediately made eye contact with Michaela, eyebrows raised. She smiled, both to reassure him she was fine, but also because she really, really appreciated how protective he was of her. He'd become something of a pit bull since a photographer had been caught trying to "deliver flowers" to her neighbors.

"Thank you for the walk," she said to Lachlan.

As always, he appeared a little alarmed when she looked directly at him, but he nodded.

Michaela decided to push her luck. "I hope we can do it again."

His mouth opened, but nothing came out.

"We don't have to talk," she added quickly. "Just—it's nice to have company, you know? I don't..." *What? Get out much? Have any friends? Trust that I can hang out with people I don't know because I'll constantly be wondering if they've been watching me have sex?*

Crap. What if Lachlan had seen it? Maybe that's why he couldn't speak to her, because he—

Frowned down at her. "Yes."

"Yes?"

"Yes. Two o'clock tomorrow?"

"Sure," she said, her head spinning.

*****

The next day, Mike greeted Michaela the moment she stepped out of the elevator. "You've got a visitor."

She looked around the lobby. "Where is he?"

"He wouldn't come in. I thought you'd be okay if he did, since you were with him yesterday, but he said he'd wait on the street."

Michaela smiled. "He's shy."

"Really? Didn't seem like it to me," Mike commented, then held the door open for her, his smile falling away to give Lachlan a stern look.

Michaela wanted to roll her eyes and hug Mike at the same time. Instead, she introduced the men to each other, amused to see how they sized each other up. Both were in their uniforms— Mike's a dark suit with a subtle nametag, Lachlan's an Oxford cloth shirt, khakis, and a pair of worn Oxfords on his feet.

She considered cracking a joke about Lachlan's academic taste in clothing, but decided she'd rather stay silent now and hold out some hope that he would be able to speak to her this afternoon.

They started out towards the Square, a healthy gap between them, and were soon stepping into Starbucks again. Michaela wondered if coffee was to become part of their walking ritual. That is, if she could convince Lachlan to do this again. Given his absolute silence and how he looked everywhere but at her most of the time, she wasn't going to hold her breath.

Once they had their coffees, they turned as if to follow their path from the day before, but then Michaela saw the bright yellow shop on the corner.

"Can we duck in here?" she asked.

Lachlan frowned, but only shrugged and followed her into

the Curious George store.

He looked hilariously out of place in his spot in the corner, stoically watching while Michaela looked around. The manager of the store did a terrible job of surreptitiously taking her picture, and the sales clerk practically fell over herself to greet Michaela. Then she kept reaching out to touch Michaela's arm and elbow, under the guise of helping her with her selection.

It was nothing new, so Michaela put up with it all, more interested in how Lachlan's expression got increasingly puzzled with each glancing touch or photograph. He clearly had no idea what to make of it.

Finally, Michaela decided on a few things for Callum and Rupert's son, Oliver, and went to the register. Lachlan came to stand at her side, silently glaring at the manager and her phone until she dropped her hand and turned back to her work.

Michaela hid her smile, politely keeping her attention on the clerk in front of her. As soon as they left the shop, though, she grinned, pleased with her purchases and tickled by Lachlan's protective behavior. She should probably warn him that it was the equivalent of peeing on a forest fire, but it had given her another glimpse into who he really was, beneath his stony exterior, and she found she was hungry for more hints.

They walked slowly through the Square, then farther onto the quieter streets.

"How do you stand it?" Lachlan asked, out of the clear blue nowhere.

Michaela almost tripped, she was so surprised to hear his voice. "Stand what?"

"All those people looking at you. Taking pictures."

She shrugged. "I guess I'm just used to it."

He looked over at her, and, for the first time ever, caught her gaze directly and held it. "No, you're not."

Michaela arched one eyebrow. "What makes you say that?"

"I can tell you see them—you look around a lot more than most people do. Especially New Englanders. But like a New

Englander, you don't make eye contact with anyone."

She sighed. "I hope it's not obvious. I'm not trying to be rude."

"Oh, no, you're not." Lachlan's cheeks turned a dull red. "I didn't mean to—"

"It's okay. I didn't think that's what you meant. And you're right." She frowned down at her coffee cup. "I *should* be used to it, but I don't think I ever will be. It's not as bad as it used to be, right after—well, there was a time I couldn't go out without worrying someone would feel the need to condemn me to hell, loudly, in front of a large audience. I guess it's made me a little wary."

Lachlan actually *laughed*. Which seemed kind of rude, and would have pissed her off, except the sound was so new, so *rich*, it actually made her shiver. She'd never tell Callum, but Lachlan was the *way* better looking brother when he was like this.

"*A little wary?*" Lachlan repeated incredulously. "I'd have become a shut-in."

She didn't think before she said, "I thought you *were* a shut-in."

For the space of a second, Lachlan stared at her and Michaela cursed her big mouth. Then he grinned, his expression pleased and exasperated all at once. "Callum is an idiot. He's always on my ass about getting out more, like I'm locked in my house all day, reading philosophical treatises and yelling at kids to get off my lawn."

Michaela was almost delirious with the sound of his voice. Whole sentences, strung together in a row without a stutter, even. "That's pretty much what he had me expecting," she admitted.

"Idiot," he muttered, but it sounded affectionate, and was said with a warm smile still hovering on his face as he turned to look ahead of them.

"I considered it, you know," she said, apparently having adopted Lachlan's talent for non-sequiturs.

"What's that?"

"Being a shut-in. Not going out ever."

"Really? You don't seem like you'd enjoy that," he said, his deep voice serious again.

"Yeah, but..." She tried to figure out a good way to explain the enormity of it. There was no graceful way, so she just went with the bald truth. "Every time someone looks at me, recognizes me—whether it's one of my professors, my neighbors, strangers, a priest, a shop clerk—I wonder if they've watched me having sex."

Lachlan came to an abrupt halt. "Jesus fucking Christ."
"Yeah, him too."

Chapter Four

The walks became a thing. They weren't every day, some were longer than others, and the routes shifted with each outing, but they were consistent in one significant way: Lachlan made less and less of an ass of himself. Sometimes, he even spoke in complete sentences.

He was quite proud of this accomplishment.

This morning they'd already spent almost two hours together, mostly silent, but comfortable now with his awkwardness. They'd started to gravitate closer to each other, too, often brushing arms or bumping hips. It still made him nervous, but not like before. And under that nervousness was something else. Something he wasn't ready to think about.

Today Lachlan had suggested they visit the Harvard Museum of Natural History, in light of the rain outside, and because it was a strange and wonderful place filled with taxidermy and dinosaur bones and intricately crafted glass flowers.

He didn't really think about it before going into tour guide mode, blathering on about the anecdotes and unusual history he'd learned over the years, even going so far as to confess he'd spent many hours wandering the halls of the museum when he needed to think.

Michaela didn't laugh at him. Mostly she even seemed interested. And very kindly did not ask a lot of questions, allowing Lachlan to get through the entire time without stuttering or clamming up once.

Maybe that was why, as they perused the geological samples, he decided now was the perfect time to stick his foot in his mouth.

"Why are you hanging out with me?"

Michaela blinked up at him. "Pardon?"

Lachlan grimaced. "I mean, you must have a lot of friends. People to spend time with. Why are you here with me?"

Rather than answer, Michaela started wandering through the display cases again, her lips pursed. Lachlan couldn't tell if she was thinking, or annoyed, or what.

Social cues: Not his thing.

"I don't have any friends here." She spoke quietly, for his ears only, but still he wasn't certain he'd heard her correctly.

"You don't have friends?"

"Not here," she agreed with nod. "Back in New York I have some. My cousins. Brothers. But not up here."

"Why not?" he asked, knowing full well he was skirting the line between interested and fucking rude.

She shrugged. "Remember that problem I had about wondering what people are picturing when they look at me?"

Lachlan nodded—he'd thought about that a lot, actually. He couldn't fathom bearing up under that kind of scrutiny. Let alone with the constant, unfailing grace she wore like a cloak.

"I haven't made a lot of new friends since it happened," she said. "Only two, in fact, who I trust completely."

"Callum?" he asked.

She nodded. "Yes. He was the one exception, until recently."

"Until recently?"

"Well, I thought I had another exception," she said, smiling up at him.

"Oh. Oh, well, that. I—you mean—" Lachlan closed his mouth and took a deep breath through his nose. After several attempts, he managed a slightly strangled, "Yes."

Her smile could light up the entire damn city.

Lachlan promptly lost the ability to speak coherently, probably for the next hour. At least. Michaela seemed to understand and left him to gaze blankly into a glass case of not-at-all-interesting rocks for a few minutes.

After a while, Michaela drifted closer to him again. He caught her studying his profile, like she was checking for something there. Whatever it was, she must not have found it, since she ambled back down the aisle, apparently content to continue examining the massive collection without his tour guide assistance.

Then she came back again, this time catching his eye deliberately. "You done or do you need more time?"

He stared at her stupidly.

"Okay, more time it is," she said easily, smiling as she wandered over to a massive amethyst geode.

Did she just bust my chops? The laughter dancing in her eyes said yes. Lachlan couldn't understand why this, of all things, made something loosen inside of him. Maybe it was because in all the years he'd been humiliating himself in public, she was the first person to ever call him on it like this. Tease him about it, even. And somehow manage to do it kindly.

She caught his gaze and arched one eyebrow, daring him to say anything. And really, what was his defense going to be here?

His own lips twitched and her smile turned into a full-on toothy grin, the tip of her tongue caught between her teeth. His heart did something funny in his chest, but somehow he managed to retain control.

"You're something else," he said with a hoarse chuckle.

She snorted. "Then I guess we make a pair."

Michaela slid into her seat at the back of her Business Law class, nodding and smiling faintly at the people around her, most of whom had settled regularly into these same seats over the course of their first two weeks.

Three of her classmates had their heads together and kept casting her looks. She recognized them from several of her classes, but she'd never introduced herself to them. Or to anyone, for that matter.

They glanced over at her again. Michaela sat a little straighter, her shoulders tight.

Please please please don't let this be weird.

The professor called the class to order and everyone faced front. If anyone sent any more looks her way, she was stoutly unaware of them, her focus absolute on the lecture. Or, at least, she was doing her damndest to give that appearance. These were probably some of the worst notes she'd ever taken, which sucked since she'd come to class desperate to hear what the sadistic bastard was going to say to help her make sense of the reams and reams of reading he'd assigned.

She was distracted enough that the end of the lecture snuck up on her. She quickly shoved her things back into her bag, keeping her head down, but saw the moment her three classmates stopped in front of her desk.

She looked up reluctantly.

"Hi," said the woman. She had short, dark hair in a pixie cut that suited her face and features really well. Her smile was wide and earnest, her gaze direct as she stood flanked by the two men. "I'm Sadie."

"Hi, Sadie," Michaela said automatically, "I'm Michaela."

One of the guys—who looked like he shopped exclusively at his country club, a type Michaela knew too well—snorted, but Sadie's elbow in his ribs cut him short.

"*What?*" he asked, rubbing his seafoam green polo over the spot Sadie had nailed.

Sadie rolled her eyes. "This is Tanner. He's an asshole, but we forgive him because he takes exceptional class notes."

"Gee, thanks," Tanner said dryly, then offered Michaela a polite smile and nod. "Nice to meet you."

"And this is Eric," Sadie continued, pointing to her other side.

Eric nodded and smiled weakly, making eye contact for a second before looking back down at Michaela's desk. Unlike Lachlan, Eric was the kind of shy Michaela had seen countless times before and understood. He was wearing beat-up jeans and a black t-shirt, his backpack over one shoulder proudly bedecked with a rainbow flag and a NoH8 button.

45

"Nice to meet you, Eric," Michaela said with a smile.

Eric nodded again, faster, flashing her another quick smile, his cheeks turning pink. He was kind of adorable.

She looked at Sadie. "What can I help you with?" she asked, hoping her lingering dread wasn't apparent.

"Are you doing the Business Law program?"

"Uh, yes?" Michaela answered, not sure if being honest was wise. Then again, given the number of classes they all shared, it wasn't like they couldn't figure it out. Still, her stomach tightened, her nerves climbing. She didn't like the way Tanner was watching her through narrowed eyes, as if expecting her to do or say something wrong.

Sadie, though, smiled even more widely. "Great. Then we were wondering if you have a study group."

Michaela blinked. Because—*what*? "What?"

"A study group." Sadie gestured at the last of their departing classmates. "Most of the rest of the class has split up into groups, and the three of us were talking about doing the same, but we could really use a fourth. We didn't see you talking to anyone else in class, so we thought we'd ask."

"Oh, I—I don't know. I hadn't really thought about it. I didn't realize..." Michaela trailed off, having run out of things to say. She'd never once considered anyone *might* ask.

Sadie's gaze stayed direct, waiting. Eric continued to study the desk. But Tanner's mouth twisted into an ugly, knowing smirk.

"Don't worry about it. We can find someone else."

"*Tanner*," Sadie said sternly. "Cut it out." She turned back to Michaela. "Just think about it, okay? I mean, we should get started soon if we're going to do this, but if you want to get back to us, that's cool."

"Uh...okay, thanks."

Tanner rolled his eyes, then pushed his friends along the aisle. Eric sent her a tentative goodbye wave as he was shepherded out the door.

Michaela heard Tanner's not entirely subtle, "I told you that was a dumb idea," clearly from the hallway.

And Sadie's biting, "Shut up. She's just another student like us."

Michaela couldn't hear what Tanner said in response, but she could certainly guess.

Lachlan was sitting in his office, thumbing through this month's issue of *Philosophy Now*, when his door burst open. He dropped his magazine, stunned, as Anna dove into the room and shut the door behind her.

She'd never once entered his office without knocking first. No one did. And as if that weren't strange enough, she appeared even more nonplussed by her own behavior than Lachlan.

He carefully placed the magazine back onto the stack waiting to be read, giving them both a moment to recuperate.

Finally, when the silence had stretched on too long, he asked, "You all right there, Anna?"

"Yes, yes, I'm fine," she said quickly. "Shit, I can't believe I just did that."

"What exactly did you do?"

Lachlan was somewhat alarmed to see the usually very professional and cool-headed Anna blush.

"I told Dean Chomelsky that I didn't think you were in your office, when I knew perfectly well that you were, then I ran up here to warn you before he could come check."

"Warn me of what? You know I like Dick."

Anna clapped a hand over her mouth and giggled helplessly.

Lachlan mouth dropped open in shock, even if on the inside he was cringing at the unfortunate phrasing. "Anna, what is the matter with you?"

"Oh god, I'm sorry. I don't know what I'm doing. I think it's adrenaline. I'm never this sneaky."

"Do you want to tell me why you're being sneaky now?" Lachlan asked again, his patience fraying.

"I just, I really like being your TA and think of you as a friend, sort of, and I had to come see you before *he* got here."

Lachlan didn't know what he was supposed to say to that. He liked that Anna was his TA, too. She was the best student in the program, and she didn't get nervous around him. At least, until now.

"Why do you think I wouldn't want to speak with Dr. Chomelsky?" he asked, avoiding using his boss' first name in an attempt to keep the conversation moving forward without more hysterical giggles.

Anna looked at what she held in her hands and frowned. "Have you read the *Crimson Gossip* this week?"

"Uh, no? That's not really my thing," Lachlan said, wondering why on earth Anna would ask if he'd been keeping up on a blog that was universally reviled by the university's administration. The anonymous students who ran that website were very good at creating a fervor, and terrible about confirming anything was actually true before they posted it.

No doubt they all had promising careers in mainstream journalism ahead of them.

Anna held out the print-outs in her hand. "You should see this. I'm pretty sure Dr. Chomelsky already has."

Lachlan's heart sank, and not just because his dean was apparently reading shitty blogs. He took the pages and stared in bewilderment at the half-dozen pictures of him and Michaela together, including one of them grinning at each other in the museum the other day. All this was under the headline: *A New Beau for Michaela Price? Go Dr. Snorrison!*

Lachlan winced. *Dr. Snorrison?* Ugh. He'd never heard that unfortunate play on his name before.

The article was what one would expect, if one ever expected to be the subject of tabloid fodder—which Lachlan most decidedly did not. He did, though, have a sudden and startling insight into why Michaela had fake-dated his brother for so long.

Anna stood in front of his desk, wringing her hands.

He smiled at her reassuringly. "Thank you for bringing this to me. I had no idea we'd generated a stir."

"You didn't. Those idiots did," she said, gesturing at the papers with a frown. "I wish I knew who wrote that crap so I could tell them to mind their own business."

"Not to mention check their facts," Lachlan muttered.

Anna's eyes widened. "It's not true?"

If it was, or wasn't, didn't seem like anyone's business, but Anna had done him a favor by dashing up here, and it was nice that she thought of him as a friend. She was still his TA, and he still advised her on her graduate work, but he supposed they could be friends.

Friendship was a subject he'd given a great deal of thought, recently. Michaela hadn't made more than a few friends in years, and with very good reason.

So, the question remained, what was *his* excuse?

"We are not dating," he said at last, shoving the papers into his desk drawer and hoping he never found them again. "She's a good friend of my brother's and doesn't know anyone else in town."

"Oh, okay. Well, that's nice of you, to show her around and stuff."

Lachlan shrugged. He hadn't really done it on purpose. Or to be nice.

"So, what are you going to tell Dean Chomelsky?"

He frowned. "The truth." Though why it was any of Dick's business to begin with was a mystery to Lachlan. He rose to his feet. "But you know what? I'll have to do that later. I just remembered I have an appointment."

"I just bet you do," Anna said with a sly grin. She darted back to the door and waved him over. "Grab your stuff and I'll check the hallway to see if the coast is still clear."

Chapter Five

Michaela dodged into the lobby of her building, soaked to the skin by the torrential rain that had come out of nowhere halfway through her walk home. She should have ducked into the nearest shop or café, but after a long day on campus and in the library, she just wanted to curl up on her couch in her slouchiest clothes with her dog and some homework in her lap.

Mike looked up from his desk, his eyes widening. "Are you okay, Ms. Price?"

"Please, call me Michaela," she said for possibly the thousandth time. Not that he'd listen this time, either. "And yes, I'm fine. Just damp."

"You call that damp?" he said with a chuckle, grabbing something from his desk and one of his handy mops from the discreet closet hidden behind him.

She frowned at the puddle forming around her. "I'm sorry, I'm getting your floors wet."

"They're your floors, and I don't mind. That's why they're marble and I have a job. Here, this is for you," he added, handing her a piece of paper.

She unfolded the sheet and frowned at the phone number written on it. "What's this?"

Mike checked to make sure the lobby was empty before answering. "Your professor stopped by. The one you go on the walks with? He asked me to give you that. Said it's his phone number."

"Oh," Michaela said, more than a little shocked. And possibly unduly elated. "He came by? Was he looking for me?"

Mike chuckled. "No. I mean, I asked if he wanted me to call up to see if you were home, but he just looked freaked out and said no. He only wanted to leave you that."

"Did he say anything else? I mean, did he seem like he wanted me to call him?"

Mike pursed his lips, obviously trying not to laugh. "In my experience, Ms. Price, people rarely leave someone their number if they don't want them to use it."

Michaela laughed. "Okay, it was a dumb question."

"If you don't mind me saying so…"

"Go ahead," she prompted, though sentences that started that way rarely worked out well for her.

"I guess I just wanted to say that he seems like a nice guy. And I like the way you smile when you see him."

Michaela blinked, then lost all self-control and sense and hugged her doorman, right in the middle of the lobby and in full view of the front windows. "Thanks, Mike. You're the best."

Mike made a weird choking noise and kept his hands to himself, but when Michaela released him, his smile was enormous.

Michaela's eyes widened in horror. "Oh, my god, I got you all wet!"

He just laughed and waved her off. "I'm fine. Now go warm up. You feel like a block of ice."

She thanked him again and practically ran to the elevator and back into her apartment. Fang barked happily at her arrival, dancing in frantic circles until she picked him and kissed the top of his bulbous little head. She popped him out onto the balcony to take advantage of his patch of grass, and pulled out her phone.

It took ten seconds to add Lachlan to her contacts, and an embarrassingly long time after that to decide what to do next. She settled, at last, on a text message.

Thank you for your number. Here's mine.

Fang's sharp bark to be let back inside prevented her from staring at her phone all night waiting for a reply.

Rolling her eyes at herself, she took care of Fang, then went to her room to strip off her wet clothes. She had a ton of reading to do tonight, but when one of her sneakers thunked against the box under her bed, she paused, her thoughts stuck on Lachlan.

An orgasm *would* be nice. She hadn't had time to open the box even once since she'd moved, and it wasn't like her vibrator, or Mr. Big, or any of the toys she kept safely locked up in that box could feel neglected, but...

No. She had way too much to do. Shaking her head at herself, she decided she'd take a shower and get settled down to work.

Her plan failed. The hot water did warm her up, but it also, along with the tickle in the back of her brain, the faint hum in her veins, brought a flush to her skin. She ran her hands down her chest, her palms rubbing over nipples now stiff from arousal instead of the cold.

God, she'd been so busy. And it had been ages. Well, only weeks, really, which was long enough. Too long. But with school and moving, she hadn't been in the mood to take care of things. The thought had crossed her mind, a few times, but she'd easily shoved it away, knowing that the relief would be temporary, and that when she crawled back from the bliss, the ache for someone *else* to touch her would only be greater.

And not just sexually. At least in New York and Denver, there had been her family. Callum. They hugged her and held her hand and leaned against her on the couch while they watched TV. She'd been in Cambridge for almost a month, and in that time the only person she'd hugged was Mike, just a few minutes ago, and that hadn't even begun to assuage her need to be *touched.* By someone. *Anyone.*

Lachlan's image floated through her mind again.

Okay, so yes, there was someone in particular who, more and more, she wanted to be touched by. And in ways that she hadn't allowed herself to contemplate in a long, long time.

She wouldn't act on it, of course, and not only because Lachlan would probably drop dead at her feet if she so much as suggested it. It was too dangerous. The risk of the press getting wind and having a field day with it was no small thing. That he was Callum's brother would only make the media shit show that much bigger. And while she was past the point of caring most days, Lachlan would *hate* it.

52

She liked him too much to do that, and it wasn't like she had any delusions that he'd want her like that, in any case. There was no one more ill-suited to cope with the disaster that was her life than a quiet, shy man like Lachlan Morrison.

So, no, Lachlan was unattainable, but that didn't mean she didn't wish otherwise.

She stepped from the shower and dried off slowly, enjoying the brush of terry cotton against her skin, taking the time to squeeze as much water as possible from her hair before pulling it up into a messy knot on top of her head.

She left the lights off, the cool glow of the gray day outside creeping around the edges of her curtains just enough to see her bed, her hand reaching unerringly for the box beneath. It didn't matter that she'd only been in this apartment, with this arrangement of her belongings, for a few weeks. Some things didn't change, no matter where she was.

She punched eight buttons in the correct sequence to release the lock and smiled reflexively at the faint click. Kneeling by her bed, she looked down into her treasure trove of goodies and tried to think about what she was in the mood for.

She pictured Lachlan again.

For reasons she probably didn't want to look at too closely, she reached for Mr. Big, and a few other things besides, her pulse thudding heavier as she crawled up on the bed.

Over the years she'd often had prolonged periods of celibacy, but she'd learned to redefine what that meant. She hadn't been with many people—and she'd kept those encounters *strictly* vanilla—since Blake "the douchebag" Whelton had sold that video to the entire fucking world, but that didn't mean her needs weren't being met. Truth was, she had stopped being shy about her body and her desires long before the video was released. That was part of why it had made such good viewing. But in the years since, she'd explored further and gotten goddamn creative with it.

All by herself.

Lying back on her bed, she settled against the soft comforter, letting the cool air prickle across her still-damp skin. Just before it got to be too much, too cold, she ran her hands over her hips and belly and closed her eyes.

She didn't often start from scratch like this. Usually she'd be lost in a book or a movie and get to a particularly hot scene before the thought occurred to her. Whatever had fired her imagination was often incorporated into whatever fantasy she then built, but tonight it all started with a single face. One man.

What would he do?

Realistically, he'd probably go dead silent and run from the room. But fantasies were fantasies for a reason. This wasn't about being realistic.

She skimmed her palms over her nipples again and sighed. The silent thing, though. That could work for her. She liked the way he could focus on something, focus on *her*, his gaze intent, his attention absolute. She shivered at the idea of being the center of that focus in a more intimate setting. Of lying still as he looked her over, his expression thoughtful, his gaze hot along her skin.

He'd want to learn the details, she'd bet. Maybe run his hands over her shoulders or into the dip of her waist. He had big hands, like Callum's, only softer, less scarred. He'd probably been raised playing hockey like his brother, but had left it behind to continue his schooling. She could imagine the smooth drag of his fingers over her ribs, cupping her breasts and studying the peaks carefully before bending his head and sucking one into his mouth.

She whimpered, her fingers pinching and pulling, her eyelids fluttering as she imagined looking down and seeing his dark head bent over her, his lips working against her on one side. Then the other.

Her legs moved restlessly against the covers, her knees falling open, welcoming him closer, asking for more.

Would he find her brazenness enticing or alarming? She smirked, suspecting it would be the latter, but hoping for the first. She slipped her fingers down her belly and stopped to stroke the coarse hair and soft skin, teasing herself a little. Lachlan probably wouldn't do this. Tease and make her wait. He seemed far too straightforward for that.

He'd dive right in, she thought as she arched her back and slid her fingers along the just-damp folds of her labia, then zeroed in on her clit. She bent her legs and spread her knees wide as she took up a slow but steady flick with one fingertip. Each brush shot a zing up her spine, her toes curling into cotton, her chin tipping higher.

This felt good. He'd know it, but he wouldn't take it farther. Not at first. He'd keep her hovering there, almost floating above the sheets, as she swelled against his touch, her body silently begging for more.

God, would he give her more? Would he have any idea what she wanted? Needed?

Her desires were not simple. They hadn't been at eighteen when the douchebag had taped them fucking like rabbits, and they'd only matured and expanded since then. She wasn't particularly kinky, she just wanted much more than she would allow herself to do with another person since the douchebag exposed her to the world.

She slid her hand down, moaning as she sank her ring finger deep into herself, riding that high for a few moments. She teased with the index finger, getting it slick, easing partway into herself then backing off. She turned her head, burying the side of her face in her pillow, and drew a deep shuddery breath before sinking two fingers in and taking up a slow, steady fuck.

It was good. But not enough.

Lachlan's fingers would be thicker. Longer. And that would be better. But what she really wanted, what she really *needed*, was his cock. God, she wanted to relearn what the long, slow slide and stretch of a man filling her felt like.

And she wanted to feel that same moment, that same heady, weightless thrill, when he pushed into her ass. What would that be like? The careful push. The clench and drag.

She shuddered, her spine arching as she teased a finger over her anus, spreading her own slick before wriggling inside.

She froze, holding her breath, her eyes clenched tight, and pushed back the electric shocks pulsing low in her body. She didn't want to come yet. Didn't want this to end.

Sometimes she could go more than once. Sometimes she could do this for hours, and tease countless orgasms from her own body, until she was limp and sated. Tonight, sadly, she had homework to do and way, way, way too much pent-up need to want anything but to take herself too high, just once, then crash back to earth.

She looked forward to the post-orgasmic lethargy almost as much as the peak.

With a sigh, she pulled her hand from her body and rolled onto her chest, curling her legs up against her ribs to lift her ass in the air and leave her face smashed to the bed. She thrust her arms under the pillows and clutched her toys before sliding both hands down between her wide-spread knees.

She didn't know why she liked this position so much, but she adored how it made her feel open. Ready. She was unspeakably grateful she hadn't figured this out by the time Blake took up cinematography. At the same time, it was infuriating that there were so many things that she would never have a chance to try with someone else—and that she couldn't even get through one goddamn masturbatory session without thinking about that asshole.

She closed her eyes and took a deep breath, clearing her mind of thoughts of the past and settling back on a future she couldn't have, and probably shouldn't touch herself thinking about, but that featured Lachlan anyway.

What would he think of this?

She smiled, imagining him kneeling between her feet, his mouth hanging open as she offered herself up. His big hands on her ass, opening her up to his view.

She was still shuddering from that image when she switched

on her favorite vibrator and pressed it to her clit. She gasped at the sharp jolt of sensation, her brain wiping clean for a moment as she took deep breaths and tried to settle into it.

She knew her body so well it took only a matter of seconds. Lachlan, or any man, would be at a distinct disadvantage this way. He'd have to read her outward reactions and make sense of them. Would he notice how her mouth was open, pressed to the sheets as her breathing sped up? The arch of her back and neck, the spread of her legs. She didn't have to manage these things when she was by herself. Would she act differently if Lachlan were with her?

She supposed one of the advantages of autosexuality would be that you never had to be self-conscious. Too damn bad that even after all these years, she knew she *wasn't* autosexual. She'd learned to take care of herself out of necessity, but it still wasn't her preference.

She wished someone—*Lachlan*—was here. Doing this to her. With her. Maybe she would still be the one holding the vibe, but it would be the warm, blunt head of Lachlan's cock, rubbing over her, wetting himself so that he could ease into her.

Her neck arched at how the walls of her pussy stretched to make room as Mr. Big slid in, opening her and forcing a groan up out of her chest. The first thrust was always good, and she hung there for a moment, so close, but not quite where she needed to be. What she wanted, what she *needed*, was a good fucking. One that wouldn't leave her wrist sore and didn't require her to keep at least one part of her brain grounded in reality and logistics.

But then, Mr. Big had something no man would ever be able to offer her: a vibrate function.

She shouted into the covers as shocks zoomed over her body, her spine snapping tight, her arm arching as she pumped the heavy dildo into herself.

She pictured Lachlan there, doing *this,* holding the toys and working her over, his cock hanging heavy and untouched between his legs. He'd turn all his considerable focus to pleasing her. He would *want* to do that. He was so thoughtful. So careful.

57

She shook as the tension coiled in her belly, her clit screaming from endless stimulation, her imagination firing off flashing images of Lachlan stroking the hair from her face, steadying her with a hand on her hip, brushing his warm skin and soft lips against her.

A sob tore from her when she finally tipped over the edge. She rode the swells of pleasure for as long as she could stand it, until she trembled and ached with overstimulation. Her clumsy fingers frantically fumbled for the off switches, the vibrator dropping to the bed with a dull thud.

She bit her lip and dragged Mr. Big out of her body, then collapsed onto the bed and sucked in a few good, long breaths, wallowing in the release of tension. In the twitching aftershocks of pleasure deep in her core.

Her eyes slid closed, heavy, and she almost fell to sleep before jerking herself awake and jumping from the bed. She staggered before catching herself up against the mattress.

God, she wanted to get back into bed, but she had at least a couple of hours of work she had to do tonight.

She took a moment to let her legs steady beneath her before cleaning up, putting on the warm, soft clothes she'd promised herself earlier, and stumbling out to the living room. Fang jumped up on the couch, ready to snuggle up the moment she landed on one of the cushions, and she was tempted again to lie down and close her eyes.

Her phone lit up with a text message.

Walk tomorrow? 8am with breakfast?

When did having breakfast start to feel like a huge breakthrough? She hastily typed out a reply. *Yes! Meet in my lobby?*

Ok.

Michaela was still grinning a few minutes later when she checked her email and saw the message from her brother, titled "Lachlan Morrison? Anything you want to tell us about?" with a link to some blog.

Her hands shook as she clicked on the link to the *Crimson Gossip*.

Chapter Six

Lachlan strode down Mass Ave, feeling good about the day ahead. He had his graduate-level course and office hours this afternoon, both of which had proven to be interesting and lively over the past couple weeks. He'd taught several of these students before, but there were a host of new and fascinating minds in the mix now, too. He liked how the two groups were coming together, and seeing how much the students he already knew had grown, how their thinking had expanded and changed. It was enormously satisfying.

He stopped in front of Michaela's building, hovering for a moment.

Mike, of course, appeared before Lachlan could get it together. "Good morning, Professor," he called before holding the door open for him—an invitation that Lachlan had always refused in the past.

He didn't intend to today, but then Mike let the door swing shut, leaving them standing together on the sidewalk. Lachlan frowned and looked through the window to where Michaela sat on a padded bench in the lobby, studying her phone.

"It's not my place," Mike began as he took a couple quick steps closer.

Lachlan braced, as if for impact.

"But do you know what's bothering her? She's been like that since she came down fifteen minutes ago. Hardly said good morning."

Lachlan shrugged. "Maybe she's just not a morning person?" he ventured.

Mike shook his head. "I see her at this hour all the time. She's always up early. Any other day she'd ask after me, or about my niece, my mother, or if anything weird has happened."

Lachlan's gaze narrowed on Mike. "Anything weird?"

"You know, like those creepy guys who try to take pictures

through her windows from the roof across the street," Mike explained, pointing casually to the office building in question. They both frowned when they saw someone was, indeed, on that roof, looking out over the street toward Michaela's building.

"God damn it," Mike muttered, glaring. He tipped his head toward the lobby. "You go see if you can cheer her up, and I'll make sure those idiot security guards stop letting assholes onto their roof for a twenty."

Lachlan nodded dumbly, because Mike was already taking off through the traffic on Mass Ave, and what the fuck was going on in the world when creepy guys with cameras were perched on the roof across from Michaela's windows?

He looked over his shoulder to where Michaela still sat hunched over her phone. She was too smart to let them see into her apartment. Too aware and diligent. But, boy, did the idea of her having to keep her curtains constantly drawn piss him off.

He took a deep breath and let that go for now. Mike thought something was wrong, something more than the man being shooed from the roof across the street as Lachlan watched. He prayed for strength and the ability to actually speak the necessary words, and went through the door. He even tried to smile.

Michaela's head snapped up and she studied his face closely. His smile faded the longer she looked at him.

"You ready to go?" he asked, uncertain what he could do to help other than take her on a walk and hope she'd tell him if something was wrong. Maybe he'd even ask? It wasn't like he was good at drawing people out, for Christ's sake. He couldn't even draw *himself* out.

"Yeah. Um...can you come here for a minute?" she asked, pointing at the bench beside her. He couldn't remember her ever sounding so serious. Or uncertain. As uncertain as he constantly felt around her.

Lachlan fought a spurt of panic, with limited success.

He walked toward her stiffly, telling himself to relax, but not able to pull it together completely. He realized he hadn't been nearly as uptight with her of late. Not nearly as bad as he'd been when they'd first started this, at least.

Now he was so wound up, it felt like their very first walk all over again.

He perched on the cushion and tried to give her his attention, which mostly involved looking at her cheekbone or over her shoulder. Eye contact was outside his abilities at the moment.

"I'm sorry," she began, "I'm not sure how to tell you this, but it seems someone has decided to jump to some conclusions."

"I—what?" He swallowed around the lump in his throat, hoping that it was enough to prompt her to say more, since it was all she was getting out him, apparently.

Michaela sighed and held out her phone. He only had to glance down for a second to recognize what she was talking about.

A metric ton of pressure eased from Lachlan's shoulders. "Oh. I've seen that."

Michaela's had snapped up. "What?"

"Anna showed it to me. She thought I'd like to know." Lachlan actually managed to shrug, proud of himself for recovering in record time.

Michaela searched his face. "And this isn't freaking you out?"

"Uh…" He wasn't sure how honest to be here. He decided *not* to mention that he'd dodged his boss yesterday. This clearly was freaking *her* out, which for some damn reason made him want to be all sensible about it. "No? I mean, I'm not thrilled about the Dr. Snorrison thing. But these kids are full of shit anyway. No one believes what they write."

Michaela let out a humorless laugh. "You'd be surprised."

"Well, there's nothing we can do about it, right?"

She studied him with a puzzled expression. "No."

"Right, so let's go get breakfast. I'm starved." He jumped to his feet.

Michaela stood more slowly, looking at him like he was a complete stranger, or possibly crazy. It was, sadly, a familiar look.

"You still want to go to breakfast with me?" she asked, as if she didn't understand.

It was a fairly straightforward proposition, he thought. "Of course. What did you think, that I'd just ditch you?" he asked, half joking.

Her brows drew together. "Well, *yes*."

"Geez." Lachlan's shoulders slumped. "I know I have shitty social skills, but give me *some* credit."

"No! That's not what I meant," she said with a whap against his arm, which he guessed meant he was being funny? She still looked serious, though. "I just figured you must hate to be in the spotlight. And this is my fault. I'm a terrible person for you to be friends with, Lachlan. The worst. I would totally understand if you'd rather I just stayed away from you."

"You're *not* a terrible friend, and I don't want you to stay away from me," Lachlan said, more forcefully than maybe he'd intended.

Michaela stared at him, eyes wide. "Okay."

"Okay," he said with a decisive nod, willing himself not to blush—which had never worked before and didn't this time, either.

He put a hand on her back in an attempt to nudge her gently toward the door, but she didn't move. He wondered what else he could say and if there was any way he could do it without looking directly at her.

He snuck a peak at her face then froze, his heart jumping stupidly as panic and something else he didn't want to examine too closely burst to life in his chest. She was smiling at up at him, the kind of smile that always fucked him up, but this time it was *worse*. This time she had tears in her eyes.

Lachlan barely resisted the urge to throw his hands in the

air, because *what the fuck was that?* And what was he supposed to do now? Was she happy or was she crying? How was he supposed to figure this shit out?

Completely flummoxed, he did the only thing that had ever worked when his sister was being equally confusing.

He hugged her.

Michaela's eyes widened comically, and she made an almost wounded sound as he wrapped his arms around her and tugged her close. Their chests bumped together, her chin glancing off his shoulder, while she remained absolutely rigid in his arms.

So, once again, he'd probably done the wrong thing here. And, to top it all off, Michaela Price was definitely *not* his sister. In so many ways, she was nothing like his *sister*.

Shit.

He tried to step back, but her hands suddenly jerked up and curled into the back of his shirt, holding him close. Then the confounding woman went utterly limp against him. He held on tighter by instinct alone. It seemed like a better idea than letting her slither to the floor.

"Thank you," she said, her voice even smokier than usual.

What the hell was she thanking him for? "For breakfast?" he guessed wildly.

She shook in his arms, her face pressed to his shoulder. He had a moment of sheer, unadulterated terror when he thought she was crying for real, then he realized she was laughing.

"What?" he asked, utterly exasperated. He was pretty sure he'd just broken his own record for most awkwardness in a five minute period.

She shook her head, rolling her face against his shoulder, but didn't let go. He was trying very hard to ignore his increasing awareness of the press of her body, the strength and tone of her torso and in her arms, her long, long, fucking *long* legs tangled with his.

"No one has touched me in almost six weeks."

The confession was muffled against his shirt, but he heard it.

His first instinct was to tell her he hadn't gotten laid in months, either, but figured maybe that wasn't what she was talking about. He silently congratulated himself on keeping that thought in.

But she couldn't mean she hadn't been touched at all, could she?

He tightened his hold and she snuggled in closer, which he hadn't thought was possible until her hip bone tucked up against his groin, way too close to his dick. He shifted, but that really didn't help at all.

Think about something else!

Six weeks. He often went six weeks without touching people, didn't he? He thought back and remembered his sister hugging him, and Rhian's leg pressed to his in a booth while they had a beer. Even Anna, pulling a chair up to the desk so they could go over student's work with their shoulders pressed together.

What if he didn't have any of that for six weeks? With no real hope that it would change?

He shuddered. That was...that was actually a really long time.

"I'm sorry," he said. "I didn't realize. I can touch you more. I like touching you," he added helpfully, about two seconds before it occurred to him *what he'd just said.*

Michaela started shaking again, her hands clenched in his shirt as a delicate snort vibrated against his shoulder.

"Oh! No. I just said, but I didn't—I mean..." he trailed off.

Jesus fucking Christ.

He dropped his arms in utter defeat. He could only imagine what his face was doing, since it felt like it was on fire and when she stepped back, her expression became concerned, if still highly amused.

"You okay?"

He opened his mouth. Twice. She waited patiently, her eyes bright, her smile poorly contained. Finally, he just shook his head.

She looked sympathetic, and on anyone else it might have been patronizing, but her smile was genuine and her hand on his arm was gentle. "No words, huh?"

He grimaced, his cheeks still ablaze.

"How about that breakfast, then?" she said breezily, as if the last ten minutes hadn't been a little bit of a fucking disaster. As if *he* weren't a complete fucking disaster.

Michaela strolled along the street with Lachlan utterly silent at her side. His color had returned to normal, at least, but he didn't seem ready to speak yet.

She could wait.

He directed them to Stella's, a little restaurant on a side street, packed with people both inside and under umbrella tables on the patio out front. Michaela hesitated before going through the door, wary of such close quarters. This could be bad.

Lachlan's hand on her back gently urged her forward and she went, if for no other reason than after terrorizing the poor man this morning, the least she could do was try to suck it up for one meal.

The hostess recognized her instantly, if her slow, stunned blink was any indication. But she also recognized Lachlan.

"The library, Dr. Morrison?"

"Yes, please," he said.

The hostess led them through the restaurant, countless heads swiveling as they passed. The muscles in Michaela's back were so tight by the time they'd made it to the hallway, it was a wonder she could walk at all. It was pure relief to escape into the enclosed stairway to the second floor, and she gasped with unexpected pleasure when it led them to another, quieter dining room—this one lined with built-in shelves, laden with old books.

"Wow," Michaela breathed, looking around. There were only ten tables up here, well-spaced and separated by tall plants and more free-standing shelves. Theirs was by the fireplace, the mantle lined with books, antique clocks, and a couple of stuffed pheasants.

She eyed the birds frozen mid-strut glaring down at her. "You got a thing for taxidermy?" she asked wryly once they were alone.

Lachlan looked up sharply. "No?"

He speaks!

"The Natural History Museum, and now these sad souls," she said, waving at the pair of fowl.

Lachlan's lips quirked and he shook his head. "Coincidence."

"Uh huh," she drawled, like that was utter bullshit.

"I thought it would be sufficiently private up here for you to be able to relax and speak freely."

"Oh," she said, touched by his thoughtfulness. "Thanks. This is great."

He nodded once as he carefully studied the menu she could guess he'd seen plenty of times, given his greeting downstairs.

"So, does this mean you're able to talk again now? Or am I to speak freely to myself?"

He didn't look up. "You know, everyone else ignores it."

"What's that?"

"My...issue."

"Yeah, not my style, I guess."

"No shit," he said with a smirk, still directed more at the menu than at her.

Michaela laughed, but stifled her humor when the waiter approached to fill their coffee cups and deliver a plate of sinful-looking cinnamon buns. She beamed up at the young man, and he smiled back.

"I hope you don't mind me saying so, Ms. Price," he began, and Michaela could feel the muscles in her face going tight, years of training holding her smile in place. "But thank you for all the work you do. The Price Foundation helped start a shelter and community center in my hometown that made a big difference for me and some of my friends. It meant a lot to us."

The tension in her chest left in a rush and a genuine smile returned. "Where are you from?"

The waiter ducked his head. "Asheville, ma'am."

And now she could hear the hint of the south in his voice. She also knew that the shelter they'd helped start was for LGBTQ youth who weren't getting the support they needed from their families and community.

"What's your name?"

"Craig."

"I'm glad we could help you and your friends, Craig. Thank you for saying something. The Albemarle House means a lot to me, too."

His smile made her heart hurt, and when it seemed like they might both get a little overcome by it, Craig quickly got down to the business of taking their order.

She watched him walk away with their menus tucked under his arm and hoped he was still getting the support he needed.

"You care. A lot," Lachlan observed quietly.

"I love what I do," she agreed with a shrug. "It was never about redeeming my reputation."

"I never once thought that it was."

She sighed at his frown. "Most people do. I understand why, too. I've traded on my notoriety to draw attention to my causes and the charity work I do."

"Why?" He seemed only curious. No judgement. No questioning of hers.

So she told him the truth. "It was the only good thing I could make out of the fallout from that stupid tape."

"You were very young. That must have been extraordinarily difficult. You were—*are* very brave."

She waved that off. "Not really."

"As we've previously discussed, you could have become a shut-in. Or at least gone into hiding."

68

"That's not me."

"No, it's not. You're brave."

"You say that like you're not. Like you wouldn't have done the same."

"I can say with absolute certainly that I would not have done the same. Don't tell me you're going to join the rest of the world in pretending I'm not a total failure at social stuff."

"You're not a failure," she said sharply, annoyed that he would say that.

He cast her a dubious look. "I liked it better when you were yanking my chain about it."

"I don't see what you do and what I do as all that different, actually."

That made him laugh. "Really? Because it looks like black and white to me."

"We both deal with intense social situations in a way that gets us what we want—which, ultimately, is distance. I do it by manipulating people and situations, and the press especially, as much as possible. I count on them to make assumptions about me and use that. You do it by withdrawing. The net result, though, is the same."

Lachlan appeared to think about that while Craig delivered their food and refilled their coffee.

"Why do you want distance?" he asked when they were alone again.

"So no one can hurt me," she said simply, painfully aware that she'd never spoken with anyone about this.

"Does it work?" he asked skeptically.

"Mostly. They can insult the person they think they know—the one they've created out of mountains of speculation and only a few grains of truth. But I'm not that person on the cover of those magazines. I don't scare off men, and I certainly didn't make your brother gay."

Lachlan chuckled at that, but his smile didn't last. "It's not really working, though, is it?"

"What?"

"The not-getting-hurt thing."

Michaela looked at him in silence for a long time. "Not really. You?"

His smile was wry. And a little sad. "Loneliness is its own kind of pain, isn't it?"

"Yes, it is."

Chapter Seven

Michaela Price: Celebutante to the Stars, Friend to No One.

Michaela Price has been on campus for a month now, and while her professors stoutly refuse to offer up any insights into her academic performance so far, her fellow Crimsonites are more than happy to talk about what it's like to have her in class.

"She's not really friendly," one fellow law student reports. "She keeps to herself and doesn't talk to the people around her. The one time I saw her talking to some of the other students in her Business Law class, she looked suspicious and one of them was rolling his eyes when they walked away."

Another student complained, "You can tell she's all the professors' darling. One guy calls on her all the time. Seriously, almost half of the class, he's getting her to show off how she's keeping up with the work when the rest of us are struggling."

Which begs the question, does she pay people to help her?

"I haven't seen her with anyone, so I'm not sure who would help. Maybe someone in the class above us?" suggests one of her classmates. "But who knows? With that kind of money, I wouldn't be surprised if she sent someone to class to take notes for her, let alone do the readings."

Not everyone is convinced she's trying to cut corners, though. "Maybe she just works hard," said another woman who claims to sit near Michaela in several of her classes. "She looks focused when I see her, and I don't think you can fake knowing the answers to these questions, you know?"

Maybe not. Or maybe there is a sucker born every day.

--- **Crimson Gossip**, Blog Entry 1737.

Michaela closed the browser on her phone with a sigh.

The headline didn't even make sense, for Pete's sake. The only consolation was that she didn't think a lot people off campus read this shit. So far, the mainstream media was still pondering whether or not she'd driven Callum to be gay, or if he'd been sleeping with men all along behind her back. God forbid any of them try to find out the truth. Of course, she and Callum hadn't been entirely forthcoming with that, either, so what did she expect?

Regardless, being the favorite target of the *Crimson Gossip* was better than having this crap all over the newsstand, but it was still irritating. The site was determined to insinuate as much bullshit as they—she? he?—could possibly squeeze out of a few of Michaela's classmates and a lot of no-doubt out-of-context quotes. She liked that one of the women in her classes had defended her, though, and wondered if it had been Sadie.

She would have preferred it if everyone had simply refused to say a word. At least it seemed she could count on the faculty to be discreet. She'd been at this game long enough that she hadn't expected as much.

She smiled and waved as Lachlan crossed the street toward her. It took her a moment to figure out why he looked so strange to her before she realized he was wearing actual, honest-to-god blue jeans. And a nicely snug t-shirt that showed off his flat belly and muscled arms. And, well, Professor Morrison was looking *damn hot.*

"Hello!" she said with a big smile.

"Hi," he said, then shocked the shit out of her by drawing her into a tight hug.

She held on, one hand pressed between his broad shoulders, the other low on his back, her fingertips dipping into the trench of his spine. The heat of his body sinking into hers felt like heaven.

She forced herself let go and looked up at him with a mix of wonder and delight.

"What are you grinning about?" he asked suspiciously.

"Nothing," she said, biting her cheek. She could tell him, of course, but then she wouldn't have anyone to talk to for the next ten minutes. "You ready for our walk?"

"You bet."

They started out on their usual meandering route through the Square, bypassing the coffee when Michaela said it was too late in the afternoon for caffeine for her, and Lachlan just shrugged rather than go inside and get himself anything. They were back out into another quiet neighborhood when she noticed that his silence seemed different than usual. His frown less consternated and more constipated.

"Everything okay?" she asked gently.

"What? Oh, yeah." He laughed, and she got the impression it was at himself. "I'm just frustrated about a class I taught today."

"Didn't go well?"

"No," he said succinctly. "It was a disaster."

"Trouble with some of the kids?"

"Yes, but not the way you mean. The ones that bothered to show up at all were fine, I guess. Just..."

"What?"

"Bored. They were really, really *bored*."

Michaela bit back the urge to laugh. "Not the great philosophical thinkers of tomorrow?"

"Uh, *no*. But that's the thing. They don't have to be. I don't expect them to be. But I'm still not getting through to them, and I should be. Just because they don't want to be philosophers or major in philosophy doesn't mean this isn't interesting stuff, and there's no reason they can't enjoy learning about it. Except, apparently, that I can't *make* it interesting."

"You can't make it interesting as in it's impossible for anyone to do so, or as in that *you*, specifically, can't?"

"The latter, I'm afraid."

"So change it up."

Lachlan frowned, putting his hand on the small of her back to steer her around a muddy puddle on the sidewalk. "I don't know how."

"Can you ask for help?"

He smiled a little, looking down at the sidewalk. "I think I am."

"Oh," she said, pleased and thrilled that he would trust her with this. He was just full of surprises tonight. "Well, I don't know a blessed thing about philosophy, but I'll do whatever I can. And, you know, there are other people you can ask for help."

"Like who?"

"Anna?" she suggested gently.

He seemed to think that over for a while before saying, "Good point."

"And I'm sure you're not the only one to have this issue. What about your colleagues?"

"Ah, well. There is only one Dr. Snorrison."

She threaded her arm through his, pulling him close. "Come on, now. If I'm not going to let the *Crimson Gossip* freak me out, you're not allowed to either."

"That sounds good in theory, but harder in practice."

"Welcome to my world," she said with a wry smile, pleased when he smiled in sympathy rather than cringing with distaste. She thought most people would have run screaming by now, and she wouldn't have blamed them. Hell, most people didn't bother to even try to approach.

Which, actually, reminded her she'd wanted to talk to Lachlan about something.

"Speaking of asking for help, I was hoping I could pick your brain," she said, waiting for him to nod before continuing. She smiled at how serious he looked as he leaned in, his attention absolute as they walked on. "I was thinking about what we spoke about at breakfast the other day. About being alone. Do you think I can get through school without any help?"

"I do. You work very hard. But what makes you ask?"

"I was approached by some people who are in a bunch of my classes, asking if I wanted to join their study group."

74

"I can tell from your voice that you doubt their sincerity."

She looked up at him. "Wouldn't you?"

"No?" he answered, bemused.

Michaela sighed. "Look, this is going to sound...weird, okay? But people don't want to be my friend. They just...*don't*. Trust me."

"I'm your friend," he pointed out gently, and it had to be a testament to how far they'd come that he didn't even blush or stammer when he said it.

She smiled at him. "You are. But let's be honest, that's only because I didn't really give you a choice."

He opened his mouth, and she could tell he was going to argue, but then he smiled ruefully. "That's actually true," he conceded grudgingly, and she laughed. "But that was because of my issues, not because of who you are. As a person."

"But that's just it, Lachlan. No one knows who I am as a person. They just see the recognizable face. The reputation. *That's* who they're approaching. Or avoiding, as is often the case."

"But you said these people were in your classes, right?"

"Yes?"

"So, they know you share at least *some* things in common with them, even if it's just your coursework."

"I guess," she allowed slowly.

"I don't know these people, but it's entirely possible that they just need another person in their group to round things out. It's pretty common for a few students who are on the same course track to pull together to split the workload and share study materials."

"But why me?"

Lachlan frowned. "Why not you? If you take away the weird shit that is your life, you're just another student."

Michaela laughed. "But that shit *is* my life."

"Maybe they don't care? And even if they do, a little, you'd

75

still get to have some help in your classes.

"I like the idea," she admitted. "The readings alone are killing me."

"That's not unusual, especially in law school. This study group would certainly help, and you might end up friends with them. And if you don't, you still get the benefit for your classes."

"Maybe," she said, turning the idea over in her head as they walked in companionable silence. She *would* love to have some help, but she couldn't shake the fear things would go sour, as they always had in the past.

They were almost back to the Square when Lachlan stopped on a corner, his eyes staring off to the distance. He looked to be deep in thought, contemplating the universe and all its philosophical nuances. Then she realized his gaze was fixed on a bar down the street.

"Wanna get a beer?" she asked with a slow smile.

He looked at her, brows raised. "You don't mind?"

"Hell, no. I could use a drink. It's been a long-ass week."

He laughed and pulled her across the street, his hand over hers on his arm as he led her towards the bar's front door.

Lachlan was a bit nervous about dragging Michaela to his favorite pub, but he thought it would be okay. It was insane how little privacy she was allowed when out in public, but he'd successfully figured out the library room at Stella's would work for breakfast. So maybe McGinty's would work almost as well for a drink.

Students rarely set foot in McGinty's, and when they did they didn't last long. The owner, Finn, was famously cantankerous and had zero interest in catering to the wild weekend parties that overtook most bars in the area, let alone the underage drinkers that often went along with those. Lachlan had seen him card students Lachlan knew to be over twenty-one, then declare their licenses were bogus and toss them out.

Lachlan and Michaela pushed through the heavy wooden door to the tavern and stopped, blinking against the change in light. The afternoon sun outside was utterly lost inside the dark wood-paneled walls—the only thing allowed to shine in this room was the impressive row of taps above the bar. The sounds of traffic and pedestrians were muffled the moment the door thumped closed, the noise was replaced by the up-tempo beat of a traditional Irish folksong. Finn ruled the sound system with an iron fist, and at any given moment the music was as likely to be bagpipes as it was to be Led Zeppelin.

"This looks...nice," Michaela said, and he smiled at her hesitation to find the right word.

"It is," he promised, then raised his voice. "Don't let the asshole behind the bar convince you otherwise."

Finn looked up from his conversation with another regular and smiled. "Hello, Lach!"

Lachlan smiled back, then turned to Michaela. "Go ahead over that way," he said, pointing to the mostly walled-in table in the back corner. "I'll get the first round."

She chose a beer from the impressive selection, thanked him, and walked away, hopefully unaware of Finn's long and totally unsubtle look.

He turned to Lachlan with both brows disappearing under his shaggy bangs. "Well, well, Dr. Morrison, you've managed to surprise even me. Congratulations."

"She's just a friend," he said mildly.

"Well, then, I'm sorry for you instead," Finn replied with a smirk, already pouring Lachlan's drink.

"Me, too, actually," Lachlan admitted, surprising even himself.

"What are you waiting for, then?"

"Hell to freeze over?" he quipped dryly.

Finn glanced over his shoulder toward their table and back at Lachlan. "I don't think *snow*balls are the kind you're lacking, my friend."

Lachlan snorted. "Thanks."

"I'm a bartender. It's my sworn duty to give out the very best advice there is to be given."

Lachlan rolled his eyes and ordered Michaela's drink, beating a hasty retreat to the corner as soon as he could, ignoring Finn's chuckle as he went.

Finn meant well, and it was nice to have friends who thought he could just be with any woman he wanted to be with, but Lachlan was more realistic than that. No matter how much he liked her, or how much his attraction to her grew with every walk and each conversation, Michaela Price wasn't for him.

He was a quiet college professor. And she was...out of his league.

Though, honestly, he hadn't had much luck with the college professor set either. He'd dated his fair share, and enjoyed their company just fine, but ultimately, it had always seemed a little dry. A little *boring*.

A lot like his Introduction to Philosophy class, apparently.

Maybe he should ask Michaela's help in fixing both these problems. The idea was sort of hilarious and promptly dismissed.

A couple hours later, they were still talking over their empty dinner plates when Lachlan offered to get them another round. He was surprised when she agreed, but pleased, too. It felt like they'd both happily hunker down in their corner, ignored by the other occupants in the increasingly well-trafficked bar, for the rest of the night.

He shot the shit with Finn while he poured them two more pints. When Lachlan felt a hand on his arm, he turned, expecting to find Michaela.

"Oh, uh, hi. Can I help you?" he asked the tall blonde woman pressed up against his side.

The bar was crowded, but not *that* crowded.

She wore a big, friendly smile. "I didn't see you here earlier. Did you just come in?"

"Uh, I—you. No?"

"I'm Gabrielle. My friends call my Gabby."

Lachlan stood frozen to the spot, staring down at the woman, and despaired as his brain flailed from one thought to the next, blitzed by this unforeseen attack. Not that she'd attacked him. She seemed nice? And was attractive, but in an obvious way. Not at all like Michaela. He wondered if maybe she'd lost a button on her blouse. Or if that was on purpose. It seemed like a *lot* to be looking at when he was just some stranger in a bar.

She cocked her head. "Aren't you going to tell me your name?"

Right. *Right.* She'd told him her name. He should tell her his. Only he really didn't want to. He wanted to go back to his table. To Michaela.

"This here is Lachlan," Finn offered helpfully as he plunked down the two drinks Lachlan had ordered and walked away. The dick.

"Lachlan is a nice name," she said, her smile still in place, though he could tell she was reaching for it now. He felt bad that he couldn't even find the words to excuse himself politely, let alone make decent conversation. He told himself to blink, but even that seemed overwhelming.

He needed to get *away*.

He looked over his shoulder, desperate for an escape. Maybe seeing Michaela would be the inspiration he needed to unglue his tongue from the roof of his mouth long enough to explain that he was there with someone and that he hoped Gabby would have a nice night but he really had to go. Away. *Now.* Because he knew the right words, even what order they should go in, but he just couldn't get his fucking mouth to work.

Instead of inspiration, he found Michaela looking back, watching him with a little frown creasing the smooth skin between her brows. He snapped his head back around so fast his neck hurt.

Gabby's eyed him with undisguised alarm.

"I have to go," he blurted, far too loudly. Horribly rude.

Finn looked up from his conversation half way down the bar and excused himself the minute he saw Lachlan's face. Lachlan's heart skipped in its gallop, because that was bad. Finn having to come save him was terrible, but nothing he hadn't done before. But in front of *Michaela,* it felt a thousand times worse.

Lachlan briefly considered just walking out the door without another word for anyone. But then he'd never be able to look himself in the mirror again, let alone face Michaela.

And he really *liked* Michaela. She was his friend, damn it. He liked being the one who gave her hugs and made her smile.

Gabby eased back, putting some space between them, her smile gone. This was how it always went. The only question was whether she would treat him like he was a serial killer or just an asshole.

"What's your problem, dude?"

Asshole it was, then.

Lachlan opened his mouth, because he really wanted to apologize, but before he could get a word out, a body pressed to his back.

Michaela hooked her chin over his shoulder. "Lachlan, honey, what's taking you so long? Are you holding my beer hostage?"

Gabby eyes widened comically. "Holy shit, you're—"

"Hi, I'm Michaela," she said, and Lachlan could *hear* the smile in her voice. Could see how it utterly disarmed Gabby. Michaela stepped to his side and held out her hand. "Are you a friend of Lachlan's?"

Gabby smiled uncertainly. "Oh, no, I—we just met?"

"That's nice," Michaela said, smoothly dropping her hand when Gabby didn't move to take it. Michaela turned to Lachlan, and all he could do was stare into her warm brown eyes as relief swamped him.

The spell was broken when Michaela glanced at the bar. "Oh, our drinks are ready!" she announced cheerfully, as if she hadn't been able to see them from the booth, sitting there neglected for the last five minutes. She picked them up. "Well, if I'm not interrupting..."

"Oh, no," Gabby said, immediately. "It was, uh, it was nice to meet you both. I have to get going."

She turned and fled—not just the conversation, but the *building*.

Lachlan's shoulders slumped the moment the door closed behind her.

"You okay?" Michaela asked gently.

He could only nod, tearing his gaze from the door to stare down at the drinks in Michaela's hands.

"Come on," she said, turning toward the back of the bar. "Let's go sit down."

He thought about arguing. He should probably just go home. Instead he found himself following her silently to their table.

Michaela sipped her beer, watching Lachlan regroup. He'd chugged half his beer the moment they sat down, but now was playing with his pint glass more than actually drinking from it.

Once his color had returned to normal and his long, strong fingers were steady as they drew in the condensation on his glass, she broke the silence.

"Are you being quiet now because of me, or because you're embarrassed by what just happened?"

"Sort of both."

"Explain?"

"I'm embarrassed you witnessed what just happened."

Michaela frowned, her chest aching at how miserable he sounded. She hated how he kept his eyes trained on the table, never so much as glancing at her when he spoke.

He jumped when she hooked her ankle around his under the table. "Hey, don't worry about me. I've seen it before," she reminded him with a wry smile.

Lachlan's cheeks went pink again, but a smile hovered, too. "Yeah, you have."

"And now you're over it."

"Mostly," he agreed. "But I want it on record that you still scare the shit out of me on a fairly regular basis."

She grinned, oddly flattered by the admission. "So noted. And, I have an idea."

"Do I even want to know?" He was finally looking at her again. And the smile no longer just hovered, but curled his lips and lit up his eyes.

It was little wonder that people hit on him all the time.

"I think you need to practice."

"Practice what?" he asked suspiciously. No one ever said Lachlan was a fool.

"The ins and outs of social bullshit."

"The what now?"

"The game. The art of small talk and social niceties. You've already got good manners down pat, which you should thank you mother for, since without those you'd be up shit creek. But we need to get you used to playing the game, and then you'll see it's not that difficult."

"I'm one hundred percent certain it *is* that difficult."

"It's not. We'll determine what freaks you out in what circumstances" —and she'd already started to formulate some theories about that— "and then we'll figure out how to make you comfortable enough to get through it, so that you don't feel trapped."

Lachlan grimaced. "That is exactly how I feel when I freeze up like that. How did you know?"

"Everyone feels that way sometimes. We just don't all react the way you do."

"You mean like a complete idiot?"

"Yeah. Like that."

Lachlan laughed. "You're not very good for my ego."

"Lachlan Morrison, you're handsome, you're brilliant, you can be funny and kind and generous, and you know how to laugh at yourself. Being a total dork sometimes doesn't outweigh all the rest."

"Uh."

"Your ego feel better now?"

He nodded, unsurprisingly speechless. Michaela grinned. "Don't worry. A couple lessons from *Michaela's Rules for Managing the Public* and you'll be the life of the party."

"Well, let's not get ahead of ourselves. Though I do appreciate the offer."

An offer she had no intention of allowing him to refuse. "I have a thing next weekend. A charity event. Would you be my escort?"

"Oh, uh, what? You mean, like a party?"

More like work than a party, though she was almost looking forward to it now, the idea of having Lachlan along taking root. "A fundraiser dinner. Food, drinks, maybe some dancing, though we don't have to. Do you have a tux?"

"I can get one, I guess, but—"

"Great."

"*But* you don't want to take me to something like this. I'll embarrass you."

"You will not."

"I will. I can't—"

"Will you come if I promise you don't have to speak to anyone, and no one will be the wiser?"

Lachlan's brows went up. "How will you pull that off?"

"Just you wait."

Chapter Eight

Michaela was feeling decidedly less confident about her own abilities to manage difficult social interactions as she strode across campus the next morning. She was on her way to her Business Law class, and she was on a mission.

It had been a long, long time, but she could do this. She could take a chance. She could ask to join the study group, if they'd still have her. She was a good student. She was doing well in all her classes. She was brave.

She was totally going to chicken out.

"Hi, Michaela," a cheerful voice said from her elbow.

Michaela nearly jumped out of her skin, then laughed at herself as she looked to find Sadie walking at her side, smiling at her hesitantly.

"You're stealthy. I didn't even see you there."

Sadie grinned. "Sorry. I was coming down the other path and I figured since we're headed in the same direction..." She shrugged.

"Yeah. Okay, great. I'm going to Business Law, which I guess you are, too. Thanks." Michaela sealed her mouth shut, wondering how she suddenly sounded exactly like the Lachlan she first met.

This was a sign. If Lachlan could get over his fear of speaking to her, if he could agree to face down a ballroom full of strangers because she swore she could help him, then she could absolutely do this.

"So, actually, I was going to try to talk to you before class today," she began.

"What about?" Sadie asked.

"Is the offer still open? To be in the study group with you guys?"

Sadie's eyes widened. "Yeah, sure. I kind of thought you weren't interested, though."

"No. I am. I am interested. It's just...uh...you see..." She ran out of words, her brain struggling to find something to say that wasn't the ugly truth, or inappropriate, or just plain idiotic.

God, she *was* turning into Lachlan. Was *this* how he felt when that woman hit on him? Nerves feeding into themselves until he was stuck, wishing he could just walk away and be left alone for the rest of his life? She suddenly felt guilty for pushing Lachlan so hard, and a wave of admiration for how far he'd let her push him. How well he'd done. And he'd been right all along. She totally *should* have become a recluse. Because sometime between acing preschool and today, she'd apparently lost the ability to make friends.

"Let me guess," Sadie said. "You had to figure out if we wanted to study with you or if we wanted to bask in your limelight or some such shit." She didn't sound pissed so much as cynical, and maybe a little amused. Though that last part may have been wishful thinking on Michaela's part.

She frowned. "That's...that sounds even more awful out loud than what was in my head. I'm sorry. I wish I could say you're not at least partially right."

Sadie shrugged philosophically. "Tanner *does* read as pretty shady. I would have had him checked out, too, if I were you."

Michaela blinked, shocked, then saw the smirk on Sadie's face and laughed. "I'm going to tell him you said that."

"Go ahead. He could stand to be knocked down a peg or two," Sadie replied easily, completely unconcerned.

"Well, for what it's worth, I didn't have you *checked out* or whatever. I wouldn't. I just had to think about it for a while," Michaela said, looking down at the bricks on the walkway as they passed beneath her feet. She glanced to the side and found Sadie studying her face.

"I get it. Shit's complicated for you," Sadie said.

If there'd been even a whiff of pity or scorn, Michaela wouldn't have answered honestly. "Yeah, that's one way of putting it. But, you know, a beast of my own making, so it's not like I can complain."

Sadie's brows knit together. She looked like she wanted to say something but she just pursed her lips and stayed silent. The third time someone took their picture, Sadie stuck her tongue out.

Michaela tried not to cringe. Maybe this was a really bad idea after all.

"Sorry," Sadie said. "I probably shouldn't have done that."

"It's okay. I totally understand that urge. But, it's just—I don't want you to get crap because of me."

"I'm the one that stuck my tongue out."

"Yeah, but." Michaela gestured at herself helplessly. "I'm the gossip magnet."

"Your life is fucked up," Sadie observed with breathtaking honesty.

Michaela grinned, oddly pleased that Sadie was willing to point right to the elephant in the room. Or on the quad, as it were. It was exactly what she'd done to Lachlan when he'd persisted in freaking out around her.

Needless to say, she liked Sadie's style.

When they arrived at their classroom, Tanner and Eric were already in their seats at the back of the class.

Sadie slipped into the seat next to Tanner and looked at Michaela expectantly. Michaela hesitated for a second, then slid into the last seat in the row next to Sadie.

"Guys, Michaela's on board." Sadie turned to Michaela. "We'd already made a plan to meet in the library this afternoon to go through the syllabi and divide up the readings. Will that work for you?"

"Oh, yes, but I don't want to intrude if you guys are already all set."

"Eh, don't worry about it," Tanner said. Michaela was beginning to wonder if that smirk was a permanent fixture on his face. "It means less work for us in the long run, right?"

"Yeah, right," she said. She smiled at Eric when he glanced her way, encouraged when he smiled back.

Their professor then kicked off his lecture with a stern look for the four of them, and dove into his usual rambling monotone while glaring at Michaela.

She wasn't surprised when his first question was for her.

Lachlan stared in horror at the note taped to his door.

Please come see me when you have a moment. —Dick.

What the fuck year did his boss think this was? 1985? Why on earth wouldn't he have just sent an email, or left a voicemail, instead of posting this where his colleagues and students could see it?

"Oh boy," Anna muttered from his side.

Lachlan refused to hang his head like the naughty student called before the principal—even though that was *exactly* how he felt.

"Do you think he saw the new article?" she asked quietly.

Lachlan looked over at his TA. "There's another one?"

"Not about you," she said reassuringly. "Just one questioning Michaela's academic and ethical integrity."

"Oh, is that all?" he asked sarcastically.

Anna shrugged apologetically, and Lachlan frowned at himself. It wasn't Anna's fault that any of this was happening. He apologized and patted her shoulder awkwardly in an attempted show of gratitude for her patience.

When it became clear she found his lame social skills more alarming than comforting, he yanked his hand away and plucked the note from his door. He turned toward Dick's office, grimly determined.

"He's not there," Anna said.

"He's not?"

"No, I just walked by, and his light is off."

Lachlan's shoulders slumped. "Oh, thank Christ." He dodged into his office and smiled when Anna closed the door quickly behind them.

"So, what did you need?" she asked, reminding him that he'd asked her to meet with him this morning.

This conversation seemed almost as daunting as the one looming with Dick. He indicated she should sit in one of his guest chairs, then sat behind his desk, trying to find the right way to broach the subject.

He finally accepted he was just going to have to rip the Band-Aid off all at once.

"I want you to help me be more interesting."

Anna blinked at him owlishly. "What?"

"I mean, my lectures. I want my lectures to be more interesting. To the freshman, particularly. I'm tired of getting paid to be a university professor when, in fact, all I'm doing is acting as a sleep aid."

Anna grinned. "It's not that bad."

He arched an eyebrow high and waited.

"Okay," she conceded, still smiling. "It can be that bad. But I have an idea."

"You do?"

"Yes," she said enthusiastically, pulling out a notebook and a pen. "We need to figure out how to tie what we're teaching them to what they're experiencing in their lives. We need to figure out what's important to them."

"I'm pretty sure I don't have a lecture that will help freshman find the cheapest pitcher of beer in a bar that doesn't require ID."

Anna laughed. "And that's your problem. You need to think outside the box."

Lachlan resisted the urge to point out that he'd taken this job because he *liked* the box. This place was all about the box.

Hell, this place might actually *be* the goddamn box.

Based on the look his TA was sending him across his desk, he didn't need to say it anyway.

Michaela would readily admit that she was often wrong. It was just that she wasn't often *this* wrong.

Joining a study group had clearly been a terrible fucking idea.

She winced as Sadie grabbed Tanner by the arm and dragged him away down the library's main aisle, her fingers digging in hard enough that Tanner's skin went white around them.

Michaela and Eric hovered uneasily outside the study room their group had apparently reserved. He looked desperate to dive through the door and hide, but they both held their ground. She thought about nudging Eric into motion, but he was an adult. He had as much right to watch the spectacle unfold as she did.

No one acknowledged the two random assholes who were taking pictures of Michaela and grinning at each other as Tanner was hauled away, protesting mightily. Michaela could guess they were friends of Tanner's. Their impudent smirks were certainly familiar, and they wore the same hungover-preppy-frat-boy clothes. Michaela wondered if they all shared a closet.

"What the fuck did you do?" Sadie snapped in a harsh whisper that carried across the deathly quiet library as loudly as a shout would.

"Nothing," Tanner whined defensively, rubbing his arm when she let him go with a shove.

Sadie came right back with a biting, "Really? Then who are those two douche-bros with the cameras?"

"They're my roommates," Tanner admitted, quailing in the face of Sadie's fury, his shoulders curling inward.

"We are here to *work*. Not to take pictures, or stalk Michaela, or whatever the hell they're doing. Make. Them. Go."

Tanner nodded quickly and stomped toward the two men failing to hide in the stacks near Michaela. His furious whisper was as useless as Sadie's. "Get the fuck out of here, guys. I told you this wasn't cool."

"Duuude, that's *Michaela Price.*"

Tanner's eyes cut to the side to peek at her, his cheeks going red. She turned her head and looked at nothing, wishing she'd had the good sense to not come here at all. What the hell had she been thinking? She'd *known* this was how it was going to turn out.

Michaela shifted her bag higher on her shoulder, trying to ignore the skirmish breaking out between Tanner and his friends a few rows away. She smiled wanly at Sadie when she returned.

"So, hey, that was awkward," Sadie said in an artificially bright voice.

No one laughed. Eric winced when a loud yelp issued from the stacks.

Sadie's left eyelid twitched. She looked for a moment like she was considering turning around and joining Tanner's fight. Instead she took a deep breath and gestured toward the door. "Why don't we go in and get settled. I'm sure Tanner will be along shortly."

Michaela thought it would be better if she just left. "I—"

"*Now.*"

Turned out, Sadie at the end of her patience was actually pretty scary. Eric and Michaela bolted through the door. The three of them had barely settled into their chairs with their syllabi and calendars out when a red-faced Tanner stumbled into the room and shut the door firmly behind him.

He wouldn't look at Michaela. Sadie closed the blinds with a loud snap. Eric still hadn't spoken a word.

Michaela really, really wanted to leave.

"Right," Sadie said, glaring at Tanner. "Let's just agree that we're never, ever going to do that again, shall we?"

Tanner nodded quickly and without lifting his gaze from the papers in front of him.

"Okay, then." Sadie looked around at all three of them. "Any objections to starting with Business Law?"

The men agreed, and when Michaela didn't answer, Sadie pinned her with a look.

"Uh...okay?"

From there, at least, it got marginally less painful. Which wasn't saying much, since Eric remained completely mute unless spoken to directly, and Tanner didn't stop blushing for the first twenty minutes.

It was, in a word, agony.

She'd been an idiot to even think about trying this. Her instinct had been to say no. She should have listened to that. Instead, she'd listened to Lachlan, and the minute they were done here, she was going to march over to his office and tell him just what she thought of his pie-in-the-sky ideas about making friends and having help with her schoolwork.

Then she'd email Sadie and quit.

Lachlan walked briskly down the hallway toward his office, having just returned from giving his afternoon lecture. He refused to run. Running would be ridiculous. Anna *was* jogging, though, just to keep pace. Even pulling ahead a little as they tried to dash into his office.

"Dr. Morrison! Can I have a word with you, please?"

Damn it.

Lachlan acknowledged Anna's deeply sympathetic look as they pulled up just shy of his door, then turned to greet his boss.

"Sure. Yes, of course. What's up?"

Dick walked up to him sedately, and Lachlan wondered if he was trying to make a point. "Let's speak in your office."

Lachlan's stomach went heavy with dread. He led the way

into his office and turned to close the door, surprised to find Anna still hovering in the hallway. He couldn't imagine what she thought she could do to help, but he smiled gratefully before closing the door and facing Dick.

"How are you, Lachlan?"

"I'm well, thank you," he said automatically, distracted by thoughts of how to get out of this meeting. Then he remembered his manners. "How are you?"

"Fine. Just fine, thank you."

Lachlan gestured Dick toward one of his guest chairs, somewhat alarmed when Dick chose to remain standing. Lachlan hovered, uncertain, then took a seat behind his desk. "What can I help you with, Dick?"

His boss looked as uncomfortable as Lachlan felt. Which might have been reassuring, in some circumstances, but was mostly alarming at this point. Maybe Dick was here to talk about something other than Lachlan's social life and a certain student blogger's observations. He sincerely hoped so.

"It's come to my attention," Dick began, "that you've been spending time in the company of Michaela Price."

So much for that hope. Lachlan tried to keep his expression neutral and meet Dick's gaze steadily. "Yes?"

Dick shifted on his feet. "She's garnered quite a bit of attention since her arrival."

"Yes?" Lachlan said again. Where the hell was Dick going to go with this? "Through no fault of her own," Lachlan added, because while he was trying to give his boss the benefit of the doubt, he definitely did not like the sour look on Dick's face.

"How do you mean?"

"I mean, she's here to learn, just as any other student is. She doesn't seek out the attention she receives. It just seems to...follow her," he finished lamely. He had plenty more specific things to say on the subject, but he didn't think Dick wanted to hear it.

With every passing second of this conversation, Lachlan was

more convinced that what Dick *needed* to hear was that he should mind his own fucking business.

"The Philosophy Department prides itself on being one of the least controversial or politic departments in the entire university," Dick announced.

Lachlan frowned in confusion. "Yes. I like it that way, too."

"So, I'm concerned about what this will mean. Ms. Price, should she manage to complete her degree, will be here for three years, possibly longer."

Lachlan ground his teeth together, his discomfort rapidly losing ground to anger. Dick never questioned whether any other students would make it to graduation. "I assure you, she *will* graduate. I would not be surprised if it were with honors."

"Oh," Dick said, surprised. Lachlan was insulted on Michaela's behalf. "Then she's a good student?"

Lachlan had no idea, actually, but he knew Michaela. "She works hard and is very serious about her studies. She feels her degree will help her protect the Price Foundation, and allow her to expand its reach and the number of people it can help."

"Yes, well, that is admirable," Dick said, though Lachlan got the distinct impression Dick wasn't entirely convinced.

"Isn't it," Lachlan said firmly, rising to his feet. "I intend to do whatever I can to help in that effort, of course. When my brother asked if I would show Michaela around and help her get settled, I jumped at the opportunity."

Which, okay, was pretty much the opposite of the truth, but Lachlan didn't feel even a little bit guilty.

"That was very kind of you," Dick said awkwardly, perhaps having realized he was losing control of the conversation.

"Yes," Lachlan agreed. "It's been rewarding. Michaela is a bright and driven student. I believe you'd enjoy speaking with her as well, Dick. Perhaps if she comes by to see me here sometime, you might pop in and introduce yourself. I'm sure you'll see her now and then going forward."

He wondered what Michaela would think if he invited her to

have lunch in his office. With the door open, so his boss would be sure to see her.

"That would be...lovely."

And Lachlan had thought *he* had a shitty poker face?

"I'll be sure to mention it to Michaela when I see her."

Dick opened his mouth to say god only knew what, but was interrupted by a sharp rap on the door.

"Yes?" Lachlan called, grateful to whoever was saving him from this fiasco of a conversation.

The door opened to reveal Michaela and Anna.

Chapter Nine

Lachlan smiled grimly and watched all the color drain from Dick's face. Served him fucking right. Lachlan then turned to his visitors.

"Splendid timing! Come in, come in," he said cheerfully, coming around his desk and waving them into the room. "Michaela, allow me to introduce you to Dean Richard Chomelsky. Dick was just saying how much he admires the work you do with the Price Foundation. Dick, this is, as I'm sure you've surmised, my *dear friend,* Michaela Price."

Michaela's smile was warm and completely genuine looking. She shook Dick's limp hand firmly. "It's a pleasure to meet you, Dr. Chomelsky. Lachlan speaks highly of the work you do here."

Lachlan's smile grew. He was pretty sure he'd never mentioned Dick once.

"Yes, well, thank you. It's nice to meet you, too," Dick practically stammered. For all that he liked to emphasize his desire to avoid the politics on campus, Dick was generally far more adept at handling these sorts of situations.

Michaela's smile widened, which shouldn't have been possible. She looked at Lachlan, and he swore her eyes were full of laughter. No one else would be able to guess, though.

A sudden and wholly alien feeling grew in Lachlan's chest as they held each other's gazes. For a moment, it was nothing but wonderful. Then he realized what was happening, what he was feeling, and froze up. *Shit. Shitshitshitshit.* What should he say? What should he *do?*

Michaela's eyes narrowed on his face, as if she could see his panic before he could even react to it, and turned her attention back to Dick. "I was just stopping by to see if Lachlan had a free moment to talk about something he's been helping me with. I hope I'm not interrupting anything."

"No, no, not at all," Dick said quickly, "I was just on my way out."

Thank god, Lachlan thought silently, still trying to recover from whatever that moment had been with Michaela. Anna saved him from actually having to speak by opening the door wider and stepping out of the way.

Which was...not subtle.

Dick either didn't notice or didn't care as he fled Lachlan's office, wishing everyone a good evening.

The moment he was out of sight, Anna shut the door firmly and grinned. "So, how did that meeting go?"

Lachlan rolled his eyes, a smile tugging at his lips. *"Delightful."*

Anna laughed. "Sorry I couldn't save you this time."

He cast a furtive glance at Michaela, hoping Anna would understand that he didn't want her aware of whatever Dick's issues were with their friendship. "I sincerely hope that's the last I'm going to hear anything about it," he said. "But thank you for your help. I would have been much worse off if I'd been blindsided."

Anna shrugged, but her smile said she was pleased by his gratitude. Michaela stood to the side, watching their conversation with what Lachlan thought was undue interest.

"Well, I should go," Anna said, waving at the door. "I'll see you tomorrow morning for office hours."

"See you then." He waited until the door was closed before turning to Michaela, worried he was going to start having grossly inappropriate feelings again, but was distracted by her expression.

She look amused, and possibly confused. "Can I ask you something?"

"Uh...sure?" he said, fairly certain he was going to regret it.

"Are you aware that your TA is drop-dead gorgeous?"

Lachlan felt his lip curl. *"Eeeww."*

Michaela burst into laughter.

"What?" he asked, exasperated. He hadn't been trying to be

funny.

She choked back more laughter, looking up at him like he was a very amusing puzzle to be worked out. "You have no idea that Anna is beautiful, do you?"

"No! She's a student. She's *my* student."

Michaela planted her hands on her hips. "And that makes her...unattractive?"

"Well, yes. Of a sort. I mean, I guess objectively all her features are arranged nicely and she's fit and—ugh, this conversation is starting to give me the creeps." He shot Michaela a dirty look. "I am *not* attracted to Anna. She's a student."

"So, you've never had a hard time speaking to her? Working with her?"

"Of course not."

Michaela nodded, as if storing a fascinating new data point. "And me?"

"What about you?"

"Why couldn't you speak to me? The first ten times we met, you barely said a word, and when you did say anything, I felt like I should apologize for making you do it."

Lachlan blinked, then blurted out the truth. "Because I *am* attracted to you."

Michaela stared at Lachlan, who stared back with an expression of such abject horror it should have been insulting, but for some damn reason, cracked her up again.

"Okay, wow," she gasped. "I didn't think you were going to say that."

Lachlan looked genuinely upset. "I apologize."

"What? No! Don't apologize. I'm flattered." And she was. More than she could remember being in a long time.

"I don't want to make things weird."

"They're not going to be weird. We'll just say we're not going to let it be weird and it won't be."

Lachlan gave a disbelieving snort. "Funny, because that's *never once* worked for me before."

"What hasn't?"

"Telling myself not to be weird. I'm always weird. I can't seem to figure out how to be with people, especially women I find attractive, and not be awkward and ridiculous."

"You are not ridiculous," she said sharply.

"But I *am* awkward?" he shot back.

And, well, she couldn't *lie*. "Yes, you are."

Lachlan's shoulders slumped. "Awesome."

"But hey, this is good. I get it better, now. People kept saying you were shy, and you *were* with me, but I couldn't figure out why you weren't with everyone else."

"I assure you, I'm plenty *shy*—as you're so generously calling it—around a lot of people, not just you."

"Right. But not men, as a rule."

"No," Lachlan frowned thoughtfully. "Not men. Unless they're really, blatantly, flirting with me. Then sometimes I do my weird thing again."

Michaela thought it would be *really* fun to see that someday. "Okay. So, flirting does it?"

"Yeah. I—It's even worse if someone is coming on strong. I totally shut down."

And that she had seen, and she hated it, if for no other reason than because it was obvious how much Lachlan despised that about himself. She put that aside for now.

Instead, she pointed out, "But I wasn't flirting with you, and you couldn't talk to me."

"You're, uh..." Lachlan swallowed audibly, his face going red. "You're remarkably beautiful."

Michaela smiled and ignored the zing that his comment sent down her spine. "Thank you."

"You're welcome," he croaked. Frankly, she was surprised he could speak at all.

She brought them back to her point. "So, it's people who flirt with you and people who you find attractive. I had begun to guess as much, but then there was Anna."

"Who I am *not* attracted to."

Michaela smiled. "Right. Because she's a student."

"Right," he said firmly.

"Do you ever get nervous around your coworkers? Some of them are quite beautiful, I'm sure."

Lachlan shrugged. "Not really. I meet them through work, so it's professional. I've never think about them as anything other than colleagues, with a few exceptions, and that always came about later."

Michaela arched an eyebrow. "Exceptions, huh?"

Lachlan's cheeks went red again. "Umm..."

"Oh, *really?* We are so going to talk about that at some point."

"Do we have to?" Lachlan almost whined.

Michaela laughed. "Yes. But not now, because I don't want you to stop speaking to me."

"It's tempting already," he muttered.

"Whatever, buddy. I'm no longer fooled. If you can talk to Anna without any issues, there is no reason why you can't speak to me."

"It's really not at all the same," he said grimly.

"But it *is* the same. Look, this social stuff—it's all a game. You just never needed to practice playing it."

Lachlan suddenly stood up straight, his eyes wide. "Shit. *A game.*"

"What?"

"I have a hockey game in an hour. I have to run home and get my stuff, then get to the rink."

"You play hockey?" she asked incredulously.

"*Of course* I play hockey," he said in the same voice someone else might say, "Of course I breathe oxygen."

Michaela laughed. He was, after all, a Morrison.

Lachlan dove behind his desk and started shoving papers into his bag. "Did you need me for something?" he asked Michaela. "You told Dick that you wanted to talk to me."

"Oh, right. Hey, about Dick—is everything okay? He looked kind of alarmed when I showed up."

Lachlan waved it off, hoping his face wasn't giving anything away. "It's nothing. Department politics."

She seemed to accept that, though she was studying him again. He threw the strap of his bag over his shoulder and ushered her out of his office, locking the door behind them.

"I can come back another time," she offered.

"No, I really want to hear what's on your mind. Walk with me?" He tilted his head for her to follow him and started down the hallway.

Michaela fell into step beside him. When she didn't say anything right away, he continued out of the building and across campus toward his house, mentally ticking off what he'd need to grab once he got there. He was happy to give her time to collect her thoughts. God knew, he understood perfectly that sometimes it took a while to figure out what, exactly, to say.

Hell, half the time he never succeeded.

The silence stretched, and Lachlan appreciated how comfortable it was. He had Michaela to thank for that. She'd really stuck by him over the past couple weeks. And now she knew *why* he'd been freaking out and seemed okay with it.

Though, he couldn't help thinking that her reaction to him declaring that she was beautiful and he was attracted to her as...odd.

He wouldn't have been surprised if she'd waved off what he'd said, or demurred, disbelieving. And he certainly hadn't expected her to throw herself at his feet.

But it was almost as if she didn't think it was *real*. Not that she thought he was lying, but that somehow it didn't make a difference. She'd said he was handsome and smart and he'd lost the ability to *speak*. But Michaela hadn't even blinked when he'd blurted out the truth. Of course, he should be grateful that he hadn't made things hideously awkward, but part of him kind of wanted to say, *You do realize that when I say you're beautiful and that I'm attracted to you, it means I harbor a strong desire for us to get naked and freaky, right?*

Fortunately, no part of him was actually able to say those words out loud. Ever.

"I met with my study group," she said, startling him out of his wandering thoughts.

"Hey, that's great," he said, genuinely pleased. Then he looked at her face, and thought perhaps his enthusiasm had been misplaced. "Umm...that's *not* great?"

She sighed. "No. Not great."

She fell silent when they stopped on a corner to wait for the light, and Lachlan wasn't sure if he should ask her more, but then he noticed the people staring at her and realized she couldn't continue even if she wanted to.

Seriously, her life was a pain in the ass.

As soon as they were on the far side of the road and away from other people, she told him what had happened at the library that day. She ended with, "It was a disaster. So incredibly awkward. I'm sure they agree now that it's just not worth it."

"What's not worth it?"

"Asking me to be part of their group. Sadie and Eric seem to have the best intentions, at least, but even then, I still don't understand why they asked me."

"Aren't you doing well in your classes?"

"Sure. I mean, I've done well on the first couple papers and I contribute to discussions. Professor Monroe seems to have a hard-on for trying to catch me off guard, but he hasn't succeeded yet. So, I'm doing okay."

Lachlan frowned, disturbed by the idea that one of his colleagues might be singling her out. He wondered if he should find Professor Monroe and speak to him.

"You look like my brothers when they wanted to beat up the boy who pulled my pigtails," she observed with a laugh.

Lachlan forcibly did not allow himself to picture Michaela in pigtails. That whole "naked and freaky" thing wasn't going to go away anytime soon, even without that charged image.

"Sorry," he said, shaking his head at himself. She was more than capable of taking care of herself. He'd bet good money Professor Monroe would only end up embarrassing himself if he insisted on continuing his stupid game.

He forced himself to focus on the issue at hand. "So, you have something more to contribute to the group than just work. You understand what you're all learning about."

"Mostly," she conceded wryly.

"And the meeting wasn't all bad, right?" he ventured carefully. "You at least managed to sit down together and sort out the division of work."

"I know. And I feel terrible about that."

Lachlan was confused. "Why do you feel bad?"

"Because I have to quit, obviously. And when I do, they're going to have to go through that entire exercise again. But that's still nicer than subjecting them to another debacle like what happened in the library today."

Lachlan sighed. He clearly still had a very hard time putting himself in Michaela's shoes. In this case, though, he suspected it wasn't so much a function of his social incompetence as it was that they were very strange, very difficult shoes to fill.

"You don't have to quit," he said carefully. "It was only the first meeting. I suspect Tanner—who was the one responsible, by the way, *not* you—has learned a lesson."

Michaela nodded, albeit grudgingly. Then she almost smiled. "I thought Sadie was going to kill him. I'm not sure what she'd do if those guys turned up again."

"There you go," Lachlan said encouragingly as he turned up his front walk. He'd jogged up his steps before realizing she hadn't followed him. He looked back at her. "This is my place. You can come in, if you want?"

"No, you go ahead," she said with a wave. "You have your game and I don't want to make you late."

"You could come," he said before he really thought about it.

"What?"

"To the game. Uh, you know, you could come with me. To watch. People do that—bring friends to watch. So you could, you know. Be my friend. Watching."

Jesus, he was so smooth.

Michaela smiled. "Okay."

Chapter Ten

Michaela sat in the stands at the rink and tried to be inconspicuous. It was not going well.

For one thing, she was shivering her ass off. She was dressed perfectly sensibly for a sunny New England fall day—which meant she was comfortable outside in the sixty-something degree weather, but not so much in the arena where the temperature had to be closer to fifty. Or less.

Lachlan had pointed her in the direction of the stands where his teammates' friends and family usually sat, and then disappeared down a long hallway toward the locker rooms. She'd smiled and said "hello" as she'd climbed up the stairs past the fifteen or so other spectators, feeling conspicuous in her dress and bare legs, and sat by herself a few rows back.

They'd obviously recognized her, given the storm of whispers her arrival had set off, but no one made any move to speak to her directly or ask her to come join them.

Which was fine. Except that they all looked so *warm*.

"Michaela?"

Michaela whipped her head around toward the entrance, then jumped to her feet.

"Savannah!" she called with a wave.

Lachlan's sister made a beeline for her, trailed by the two men she publicly referred to as her "roommates", but who Michaela knew were, in fact, a hell of a lot more than that. Michaela could still remember the horror on Callum's face when he'd explained that his sister had two lovers, and that the three of them were in love with each other. Not that he was judging, but Callum would have preferred to pretend Savannah would spend her entire life in blissful virginal innocence, just so he didn't have to accept that his sister had sex.

Michaela thought it was awesome that the three of them had found each other. She didn't know them that well, but was so happy to see them—and not just because Rhian was carrying a blanket under one arm.

Michaela hugged them all hello, grateful when the men sat on either side of her and Savannah, sharing their body heat and throwing the blanket over all of their laps. It was a stretch, but they managed to huddle in close enough.

Michaela grinned up at Garrick beside her. "Thank you so much. I don't think I would have made it through the game as it was."

"Wasn't expecting the rink to be so cold?" he asked with a smile.

"Wasn't expecting to watch a hockey game," she admitted.

Savannah asked, "Are you here to surprise Lachlan?"

Michaela laughed. "God, no. I would never do that to him. You know how he hates it when people sneak up on him."

Three sets of eyes blinked at her. Oh right, Lachlan said no one really talked about his issues.

Rhian, normally the quietest of the three, was the first to laugh. "You're right, he would freak."

"So, he knows you're here?" Savannah asked.

"Sure. He brought me. We were talking and we didn't get a chance to finish our conversation, so he suggested I come along. I guess we'll finish our discussion after the game."

Which, now that she thought about it, was kind of silly.

"Wait," Savannah said slowly, "you were *talking?*"

Michaela grinned, feeling oddly proud. "Yes, we were. We've actually been doing that a lot recently."

"You *have?*" Savannah asked with total disbelief.

"Oh, yeah," Michaela said. "He gets over it eventually."

Rhian really started laughing then. He winked at Michaela. "I think you must be good for him."

"I think I must be driving him crazy," Michaela countered, "but he puts up with it."

"I think he's lucky," Garrick said in a quiet voice.

105

Michaela bumped her shoulder to his. "Flatterer."

She actively ignored the way Savannah was looking at her like she was some kind of eighth wonder, delighted for the distraction of the teams coming out on the ice.

Somehow she wasn't the least bit surprised to see the C stitched on Lachlan's jersey. She smiled and waved when he looked up at the stands. Her companions also waved wildly, all with shit-eating grins on their faces.

Lachlan rolled his eyes and plunked his helmet on his head.

"So, is this a league for the university staff or something?" Michaela asked.

Savannah chuckled. "God, no. I'm not sure Lachlan would want to play with that crowd, even if he could find enough players to fill a roster. That would be a sight to see, though."

Michaela tried to picture Dick Chomelsky out on the ice. She just couldn't do it. "So who are these guys?"

"Just people from around the area. One or two are guys Lachlan played with in high school or college, but mostly they're just crazy old guys who still want to play hard hockey," Rhian explained.

"Who are you calling old?" Garrick grumped from her other side. "Most of those guys are my age."

"Yeah, old man, and you're *retired*," Rhian fired back with an affectionate smile. "And *you* were a professional hockey player. A trained athlete. Bob is an electrician. Finn owns a bar. And Mike teaches third grade, for crying out loud."

"Be real," Michaela said seriously. "Not one of us is tough enough to teach third grade."

"Good point," Rhian conceded with a dramatic shudder. "Children scare me witless."

Garrick reached across Michaela and Savannah, under the blanket, and grabbed hold of some part of Rhian—Michaela could only hope it was his hand—squishing her and Savannah in the middle.

"Come on now, Rhi," Garrick said softly. "You know you're

going to be an amazing dad."

"We," Rhian said firmly. "*We* are going to be amazing dads."

Michaela looked at Savannah and the blush rising on her cheeks. "Oh, yeah?"

"You can't tell Lachlan," she said quietly. "It's too early to be sure. We just started trying."

Michaela wrapped her arms around Savannah and hugged her. "Well, I hope it works out. Any child would be lucky to have the three of you."

Savannah held on. "Thanks," she whispered in Michaela's ear.

The sound of a whistle rent the quiet air around them and Michaela pulled away from Savannah's warmth, smiling when Savannah left her arm around Michaela's waist.

Lachlan was lined up at center ice, ready for the face-off.

"So, how long has Lachlan been playing in this league?" she asked when it became clear her companions were all going to stare at each other, moony-eyed, all night if she didn't distract them.

"He actually just started this league a few years ago when his old league fell apart. He managed to get this arena thanks to his connections with the university, and a bunch of those guys jumped on board."

"Lachlan *runs* the league?" Michaela asked incredulously.

Savannah laughed. "I know, right? He doesn't seem like he'd enjoy it, but he really does."

"Oh, I don't know. It's not like the league is co-ed. Then he'd be in real trouble. All those hot hockey-playing women?" Michaela laughed at the image, then cringed when the opposing defense slammed Lachlan into the boards. "Holy crap. I guess I see what you mean about hard hockey."

"Yeah, and why this isn't a co-ed league," Garrick agreed. At the dirty look from Savannah, he held up a placating hand. "Not that you couldn't kick all of those men's asses, honey."

107

Michaela had been to a lot of hockey games in her life, and more than she could count in the past five years while she'd been "dating" Callum, but this one stood out. She couldn't remember being more invested in a win, let alone a particular player. Maybe it was because Callum had been in the goal, and therefore far less likely to be plastered to the boards or knocked clean off his skates by the lunatics he was playing against. Michaela leapt to her feet alongside Savannah, Garrick, and Rhian, hollering for Lachlan's team. She also gasped, her hand clapped over her mouth, whenever Lachlan took another of what appeared to be an endless series of hits.

Savannah laughed at her. "You look so worried. You know he loves this, right?"

Michaela didn't know. Or she hadn't. But she could see the feral smile on Lachlan's face from all the way up in the stands. He looked not even one iota like the gentle, thoughtful college professor who'd driven her to the rink earlier.

He'd looked handsome, then. Sexy, in his quiet way. Now he looked *hot*. Not just sweaty-hot, though he was certainly that as he pulled off his helmet and shook the opposing team's hand at the end of the game. He exuded confidence, his smile genuine if perhaps just a shade smug while facing the men his team had just soundly defeated.

Michaela crossed her legs, telling herself it was ridiculous to feel *turned on* by a hockey game. By a man. By *Lachlan.*

Her body just wasn't listening. It wanted. *She* wanted. Too much.

Lachlan sat in the back corner booth at McGinty's and laughed at Rhian's imitation of the stern lecture Savannah had delivered to one of Rhian's teammates the other day. Funnier was the scowl on Savannah's face.

Lachlan was still feeling the high of a well-played game, his muscles and bruises all aching in the best way. He'd barely rinsed off at the rink, rushing to see everyone as quickly as possible. He needed another shower, and wished he had some fresher clothes, but he felt fucking fantastic. He'd chugged a ton of water when they'd arrived, but now he was enjoying his second beer, feeling loose and happy with life.

Michaela sat across from him, her back to the room where the rest of his teammates and their friends were harassing Finn at the bar. Rhian had generously sat with Lachlan, facing the room, and informed Michaela that any looks directed their way were for him—and he *was* a very popular player in Boston these days, so Lachlan thought he might be at least partly right.

Rhian seemed to guess what Michaela might need, what might make her more at ease, without being told, and Savannah and Garrick didn't question it. Michaela had said she didn't have friends here, except for Lachlan. After tonight, that was clearly no longer the case. He'd liked looking up in the stands and seeing her squished in between his family. He knew how much she needed that kind of contact, that kind of connection, in her life.

Michaela listened to the bickering breaking out beside them, smiling and laughing in a way that he rarely got to see. When Savannah threatened to withhold her favors if Rhian didn't knock it off, Michaela grinned, her tongue caught between her teeth, and warmth pooled low in Lachlan's belly. God, he loved that particular smile. He'd like to blame his body's potent reaction on the adrenaline from the game still working its way out of his system, but, of course, that would be total bullshit.

He wanted her. She'd been abstractly attractive as a stranger, but as his friend, as a woman for whom he felt an oddly protective and yet not-at-all familial affection, she was just so goddamn compelling.

He leaned over the table as his sister and her partners fell into a whispered debate about things that Lachlan, as her brother, didn't need or want to hear.

"I'm sorry we didn't get a chance to finish talking," he said to Michaela, just loudly enough to be heard over the din.

"That's okay. I was thinking about it some during the game,

and I think I might give the study group another try."

He smiled. "That's great. I'm glad."

She shrugged, her expression grim. "I can always back out if it goes badly again."

His smile fell. She looked away, but he put his hand over hers, drawing her attention back to him. "I get why you're worried," he said in a low voice. "But maybe go into it with the goal of trying to stick it out for a while? It might get weird. Hell, you know it will. Hanging out with you gets weird, frankly."

"Gee, thanks," she said dryly.

"Hey, you're the one who's always telling it like it is."

She chuckled. "I guess I deserve that."

"Seriously, though," he said, squeezing her hand. "They might act freaked out, or not think before telling someone they're meeting with you. And they're going to have a strange response when people do the awkward shit they do around you. But don't jump to conclusions. I can testify that it's hard to know how to act when that happens. Most of us don't have as much practice with it as you do."

Michaela pursed her lips thoughtfully. "That's true."

"Just think about it," he said, running his thumb encouragingly over the back of her hand.

She nodded. Lachlan became very aware of the silence from the rest of the table and Savannah's pointed stare at their joined hands.

He sat back and pulled his hand away, ignoring his sister in favor of asking Rhian how he was feeling with the first weeks of training camp under his belt.

It was late by the time they left the bar, and Lachlan was still feeling the effects of the beers he'd drunk. They said goodbye to Savannah, Garrick, and Rhian, and sent them on their way. Then he smiled sheepishly at Michaela.

"Do you mind if I walk you home? I can leave my car where it is for the night, and I don't think I should drive."

She grinned. "You feeling it, Dr. Snorrison?"

"Ugh. Don't call me that."

"Why not? I kind of like it, now that I've seen you play hockey," she said as she threaded her arm through his and turned them toward home.

"What does that mean?" he asked.

"It means you're the least boring professor I've ever met. I'm sure none of my other teachers ever started a fight with a defenseman twice their size."

Lachlan rolled his eyes. "Please. He wasn't *that* big."

"So you don't deny you were trying to get him to take a swing at you?"

"I admit to nothing, Attorney Price."

She laughed, her head thrown back, and Lachlan almost tripped over his own feet. For the first time that night his words abandoned him. He couldn't stop smiling, though, as they walked the short distance to her building.

He was surprised when she steered them around to the back of her complex.

"Where are we going?" he asked.

"Mike's not on duty at this hour," she said, which wasn't really an answer.

"So you don't go through the lobby?"

"Nope. I don't really know the night or weekend doormen. They've been hard to talk to. So," she said with a shrug.

Lachlan frowned, unconsciously pulling his arm and Michaela in closer.

The back door to her building was poorly lit on a quiet street, and led to a dim hallway by the elevators. Normally he would leave her at the door—the *front* door—but he didn't love the idea of leaving her here. It wasn't like she didn't come and go this way all the time, he was sure, but he said he'd get her safely home, and this didn't meet the standard.

"Can I walk you to your apartment?"

"You don't have to do that."

"I want to."

She shrugged, but was smiling, so he didn't think he'd overstepped. "Okay. Though if I'd known I'd have company, I wouldn't have dragged you back here."

"What," he said, grinning, "you don't sneak all your dates in through the back door?" Which—wait, shit—that made it sound like he thought this was a date.

"*What* dates?" she asked, hitting the elevator call button harder than was strictly necessary.

He frowned. "No luck with men here in Beantown, then?" he asked, wondering if was possible for him to sound more like a giant dork, or possibly his dad.

Michaela laughed, but it was tinged with bitterness. "No. No dates."

"I'm sorry," he said, though he wasn't sure what exactly he was apologizing for.

"No, it's okay. I'm just touchy about it."

"Dating?"

"Or rather the lack thereof," she said dryly, stepping into the elevator.

He had to be missing something, because seriously. "I can't imagine it's hard for you to find a date."

"Yeah, no. I'm sure I could find plenty of dates. But try dating anyone when everyone on the planet has seen you having sex. Or could, with one easy internet search."

"That doesn't mean they would. Or will. Or have." He made a face at himself.

"I guess," she conceded, then shook her head. "But I can never be sure of their motivations. Maybe they like me. Or maybe they like my face. Or fame. Or notoriety. I get lewd comments all the time from complete strangers. And even lewder offers. How do I know the guys who ask me out aren't just thinking the same things, but have enough control to keep them inside? One guy I went on a date with ended up admitting he'd only done it for the bragging rights. I think he thought I'd be *flattered*. And he wasn't even the worst. There are a whole lot of guys that seem to think it's okay to touch me, and not in the usual date kind of way. Like being the unwitting participant in a sex tape makes me, what? Public property or something?" She shuddered. "You can't believe what people think they know about me. The liberties they try to take and the things they're convinced I'll want to do. It's made dating, let alone having sex, too…"

"Hard?"

"Scary. Almost impossible, really."

"I'm sorry," he said again, feeling wholly inadequate, because what she'd described was a nightmare. An infuriating nightmare.

"Yeah, well, I guess it's just hard to figure out who's real and who isn't, you know?"

He didn't know. Not really. He couldn't imagine what it was like to live like that. But he could certainly respect her hesitation.

"I should warn you," Michaela said as they stepped off the elevator on her floor. "Fang is going to want to make sure you know who's boss."

"*Fang?*"

Her smile widened. "You'll see."

She put her key in the lock and immediately a barrage of high-pitched barks echoed from inside the apartment, followed by the door shuddering—very, very gently.

"He sounds ferocious," Lachlan said in a very serious voice, pleased that it made Michaela giggle. In truth, Fang sounded like he would fit in Lachlan's pocket.

Which, it turned out, was about right. The moment the door opened, a little ball of fluff and attitude flung itself at Michaela's legs, then spun on Lachlan.

"Oh my god, what *is* that?" he asked.

Michaela shushed her dog, who obeyed immediately and planted his butt on her toes. He looked up at her adoringly, then turned back to Lachlan and lifted his tiny little lip, revealing an even tinier little fang.

Lachlan was horrified to find it so adorable.

"This," Michaela said, "is my little protector. The best thing you can do is just ignore him for now."

Lachlan nodded, uncertain that would really work, given the way Fang was staring at him like he wanted to gnaw on Lachlan's Achilles tendon like a Milkbone wrapped in bacon. He stepped into Michaela's apartment carefully, worried he would crush the tiny creature circling his feet. Lachlan was pretty sure that would get him kicked back out again pretty quickly.

Michaela dropped her bag on a side table. "Can I get you anything?"

He hadn't come upstairs with any intention of staying, but now his brain was sort of stuck on what she'd said.

"You know *I'm* real, right?" he asked her, trying to gauge her expression in spite of his limited skills in that department.

She smiled. "Yeah. I know."

And that certainly looked like the truth, which was maybe how he found the courage to ask his next question.
"So, do you want to have sex?"

Chapter Eleven

Michaela let out a huff of incredulous laughter. "*What?*"

"Do you want to have sex?" he repeated, articulating each word as if the issue might possibly be her hearing instead of him asking her a fucking insane question out of left field.

"Like, again? Ever?"

He frowned and said, "Well, yes, that," but she got the sense that wasn't really what he'd meant.

Michaela bit her lip. He was probably just curious, right? This was how his gigantic and often-confusing mind operated. He was always trying to puzzle out how people worked, why they did what they did, and so often the answers were a mystery to him. She suspected that, at the root of it, this was why he got so flustered around women.

"I miss it," she admitted, trying to reconcile herself to having this conversation with Lachlan Morrison, of all people. "But not so much that I'm willing to change what I've been doing."

"Which is to not have sex at all," he stated baldly.

She tried not to cringe. "Lately? Yes." At least not with other people.

"But what if you could have sex?"

"How?" Because if he had some idea, some plan for vetting the creeps and users from the rest, she was all ears.

"With me."

Michaela's mind went completely blank. "Buuhh—I beg your pardon?"

"We could have sex."

"What *now?*" she asked, because he couldn't possibly mean—there was no way he was saying—he didn't mean *they could have sex*, did he?

"Yes, now, if you want. Though maybe just a little, since I'm still gross from hockey," he said, utterly sincerely, gesturing at himself apologetically.

"Maybe just a little…" Michaela repeated and laughed, all kind of breathless and only slightly hysterical. "Okay, Lachlan, I think you've had too much to drink."

He jerked back. "I would never have asked you to have sex if either of us were intoxicated."

And he just sounded so earnest. So *offended.* A giggle escaped her before she could force it back. "Oh my god, you would *never* ask me to have sex with you at all."

"I just did!" he said, exasperated.

"But you didn't *mean* it."

"I didn't *mean* it?"

"You're not even attracted to me."

"What are you talking about? Of course I'm attracted to you. I just told you so in my office a few hours ago. You're stunning and funny and until *this very moment*, you've been incredibly intelligent. How could I *not* be attracted to you?"

"But—" Michaela croaked, because this couldn't possibly make sense. "You can *talk* to me."

"I can talk to you," he repeated flatly. "What does that have to do with anything?"

"You talk to me, now. That means you're over it."

"I'm over it? You think that I—" Lachlan snapped his mouth shut and narrowed his eyes. "If you're not attracted to me, that's okay. You can just tell me."

She grabbed his arm to stop him from stepping away. "What? No, that's not it at all."

"Then what's the problem?" he asked, apparently bewildered.

And she had to hand it to him—this was the strangest proposition she'd ever received, and she'd had some real beauties come her way.

"There is no problem—" she began.

"Good."

She only had a moment to think *he's not really going to—*

116

before *Lachlan fucking Morrison* was kissing her. Michaela didn't move. Didn't respond at all. She was too stunned, trying to wrap her head around the fact that Lachlan, a man she regularly made mute just by teasing him, who used to freeze up and stammer when she smiled, was *making the first move.*

And he was doing a damn fine job of it, too.

His soft, warm lips teased hers gently. Just a taste. And she wondered at how one kiss, or maybe the brush of his nose along hers, of the trail of fingers down her arm, could set her heart racing like this.

He eased back and studied her face. "Okay?"

Okay? She blinked up at him and thought she probably ought to know the answer to that question. Some part of her brain sent up a tiny little flag, warning her that this had to be a bad idea, but damned if she could come up with a single reason why right now. And, actually, she wasn't sure she'd care much about those reasons later, either.

So, yeah, she supposed she was perfectly okay.

Lachlan's steady gaze never wavered. He wasn't nervous. Or concerned. He was just holding himself perfectly still. And waiting.

A shiver worked down her spine. His confidence in this, of all moments, was more alluring than even his ridiculously handsome face or broad shoulders. Though those held plenty of appeal, too, of course.

She cupped his cheeks in her hands, skimming her thumbs across his cheekbones and tugging him toward her. A smile lit his face, just a flash of teeth and a sparkle in his eyes, then he was kissing her again. The tease and drag of his lips was hypnotic and she swayed against him, leaning into him as he slowly, carefully, lit her up inside.

God, how she'd missed this. How she'd ached for the thrill of a simple kiss without wondering what the other person was really getting out of it. Without questioning *why* they wanted to kiss her.

Lachlan's almost clinical proposition was so refreshingly and horribly unromantic, so honest, that he had disarmed her. She had no defense against his earnest compliments, almost resentfully given because of how she affected him.

His tongue traced her lips and she opened to him, licking into his mouth, their tongues meeting and tangling with equal aggression. He tasted of beer and smelled faintly of the sweat still clinging to his skin after the game, and it was a hundred times more intoxicating than the rich colognes her previous lovers had favored. He smelled like a man, not the perfume counter at Macy's. He smelled *real.*

She tilted her head and delved deeper, her hands running up into his soft hair. She adored how he didn't give an inch, while his groan of approval pushed her on to take and touch and taste what she wanted.

He met and matched her, his hands running over her body, the fingers of one hand finally anchoring into her hip, pulling her closer even as she arched to be there anyway. Her breasts ached against the rough lace of her bra as their chests pressed together, so close now that the angle of the kiss was awkward until he wrapped her long hair around his fist, tilting her chin higher with a gentle tug that that made her knees so weak.

Shuddering, she slid her arms over the thick muscles of his shoulders and around his neck. She had to, just to hold herself up, because Dr. Snorrison was kissing her senseless.

And damn him, he *knew* it, too, based on the low, knowing chuckle shaking his chest and buzzing against her lips. Her knees wobbled again and he wrapped a strong arm around her waist to pull her weight against his chest.

She murmured against his mouth—a question or approval, even she didn't know—as he walked them backward, hips bumping and feet very nearly tangled. She wondered where the hell he was taking her, and if she even cared, until her shoulders hit the wall and their bodies plastered full-length together.

Their kiss died when she gasped and he let out a long, low groan.

This was everything she'd felt when he'd hugged her, times a thousand. Everything she'd missed, and needed so badly. The wash of relief was disorienting, a tension she'd carried for so long drained from her, finally appeased, even as her pulse sped and heat pooled in her belly and new longings and long-forgotten aches bloomed to life. She wanted to thank him. To wrap her legs around his waist and pull him closer still. To shove him away and make him promise to never offer her things she was no longer allowed to have.

But she *was* allowed. Here. Now. She could have this with him.

She laughed, breathless and happy, and felt the responding curl of his lips against the sensitive skin under her jaw. She tilted her head back, encouraging him to explore and further ruin any attempt to catch her breath.

She ached with the hope that she'd extinguished years ago, that she could be really and truly *touched* like this. By someone she trusted. This was not just some stranger, some man she barely knew, but someone she could be herself with.

Gripping his hair, she brought his mouth back to hers, kissing him once, briefly, before pressing their foreheads together.

"Thank you," she whispered, realizing only after it had left her mouth that he might not understand that she was thanking him for so much more than just a kiss.

Not that she wasn't *extremely* grateful for that, too.

He shifted, pinning her hips to the wall with his, and it seemed she wasn't the only one who was delighted to be here. She squirmed, temptation pressed right against her belly in the shape of a long, hard cock.

"You're welcome," he murmured, a slow, wicked smile on his face.

Her brain made a valiant effort to go offline as she stared at him, because Jesus fucking Christ, that was hot, but she forced the words from her lips, an attempt at an explanation. "No, but, not just for—"

He kissed her again, stopping her explanation. "*I know,*" he said against her lips, his voice little more than a rasp.

She arched against him and tugged his hair, still clenched in her fingers, until she could capture his mouth again. She reveled in the slow, heavy throb consuming her body. Every inch of her skin prickled with heat, her blood humming, rushing to nipples and clit and all the swelling parts that cried out for more. One of his legs slid between hers and she ground against it shamelessly, firing off shocks of pleasure that zipped up her spine with every twist of her hips and left her skirt rumpled around her hips.

She nudged her bare thigh against the rigid bulge beneath his soft jeans, and he ended their kiss with a gasp. She practically purred with satisfaction when sucked in a huge, shaky breath. She wanted to undo him as thoroughly as she'd been undone.

"God, you feel good," he murmured against her lips. He trailed his mouth across her cheek, her jaw, nibbling and sucking and licking as he went. She tilted her head back so he could do what he wanted, reach wherever he wanted to go. His hands curled around her hips, yanking her closer, so that she rode his thigh fully, her feet barely touching the floor.

He nosed along the shell of her ear and sucked her lobe into his mouth, making her gasp his name.

"That's it. I want to hear it. I want you to tell me what you want. How you want it."

She whimpered, unable to form words as he sucked the skin at the point where her neck met her shoulder. Had some self-preservation instinct made her forget how good this felt? She clutched at his shoulders, his hair, holding him against her while he sought out and conquered a dozen spots she hadn't known would drive her crazy. By the time he dipped his tongue into the dent between her clavicles, she was unable to stop the high, desperate whines escaping her throat.

"Shhh..." he murmured against her skin, pressing soothing kisses up her neck, then diving back in for another deep kiss.

God, how was he so good at this? She was hardly aware of the hand coasting up her side until he cupped her breast in his hand, his palm firm against her aching nipple. She pushed against that pressure, wanting more, wanting his mouth there, too. Needing relief.

His other hand rubbed her back, from waist to shoulder, until it came to rest against the nape of her neck. He sucked her lower lip into his mouth, releasing it with a pop. "Can I take your dress off?"

It should be too much. Too soon, too fast. But it wasn't, and she wanted it. She liked that he'd asked. She *loved* that he sounded wrecked.

"Yes," she said in a low whisper.

He kissed her again, his thumb stroking across the sensitive curve of her breast, then pinching her nipple against the side of his hand.

She jerked, tugging the aching tip free, which was so great and, yet, terrible because it had *stopped*. "God, please. Do that again."

His hand ran the length of her back again and again. "Okay, baby. I'll take care of you. I'll do anything you want. You just have to tell me—how the fuck do I get this dress off?"

Michaela groaned and laughed, her head falling back against the wall. Just her luck. "It's a side zipper. It's...fuck, it's really complicated." And an absolute pain in the ass to get out of. She silently swore she'd never wear it in Lachlan's presence again.

Lachlan stared down at her breasts, and, presumably, the offending dress, like it was a battle he was determined to win. Even a guy smart enough to get a PhD, though, wasn't going to conquer the dreaded side zipper.

It should have been funny, but mostly she wanted to find the nearest pair of scissors.

Before she could suggest such drastic action, Lachlan grabbed her hips and spun her away. She yelped and barely managed to keep her feet under her, slapping her hand on the wall to stabilize herself. Maybe he was trying to get another look at the damn dress, but she didn't get out a word of warning about how futile that would be before his mouth pressed to the nape of her neck, cutting off all thought.

"I can work with this," he promised in a low voice that tickled the fine hairs under his lips.

She had no idea what that meant, and she didn't much care as his hands slid over her belly, pulling her back until her ass was cradled by his hips. His cock pressed against her, making her burn for more. She arched her back, trying to get closer. To feel more.

"Is that good?" he asked and she nodded, though she doubted very much any answer was needed as she writhed against him and he thrust back, her head dropping to the side. He laved her neck with his tongue and brought one hand up to her breasts. He cupped and squeezed and petted, stroked and pressed, until he pinched her nipple and she cried out. Then it was one hard pinch after another, moving between her breasts, back and forth. She thrust her ass back harder, faster, grinding his erection against her ass, and arching her breasts into his hand.

She ached, empty and wanting, reaching back to pull his hip tighter against her. "Please, Lachlan. I need, I need..." She trailed off, distracted by a long, hard pull on her right nipple.

"You like that, huh?" he said, and she could hear his smile. She turned her head to see it and was mesmerized by his profile, cheek pink, eye dark, looking down over her shoulder at his hand on her breast, the gather of fabric between his fingers as he pinched her tight and pulled.

"I do," she whispered.

"Does it hurt?" he asked curiously.

"Yes."

His hovering smile flashed wider as his eyes slid closed. He hummed. "May I?" he asked, and she had no idea what he was asking for until his other hand, the one not torturing her nipples, coasted up her thigh and edged under the hem of her dress.

"Yes. Lachlan, yes, please, you can—" *do anything*, she thought, the words cut off by the shudder of pleasure he pulled from her as his hand dragged higher, lifting her skirt until his fingers teased at the top of her thigh, just below the panties she knew were soaking wet.

She dropped her head back on his shoulder and sighed. "Please."

He laughed, just a puff of air and the pleased curve of lips against her neck. A whimper of protest caught in her throat when he released her breast. She was even more confused when he tugged her hand from his hip and planted it on the wall.

He pressed his hand over hers and tucked his nose against her temple, his lips to her ear. "Hold on."

A shudder worked its way down her spine until she was quaking against him in anticipation, panting with desire. Jesus fucking Christ, how was he so *good* at this?

He hooked his hand around her thigh and hitched her ass higher, until she was standing with her knees locked, legs spread, and both hands against the wall. She would have felt vulnerable, oddly exposed considering she was still fully dressed, but his warmth draped over and wrapped around her, made her feel safe.

Brave.

Lachlan slid his hands up and down Michaela's long, strong thighs, his palms buzzing as silky skin quivered beneath his touch.

Goddamn, she was something else. All he wanted to do was touch her. Fuck her. But he had enough presence of mind left, barely, to recognize that perhaps they should have slept on his proposition before diving right in.

Not that he had any regrets about what they had done so far, or what they were doing right now. It was just that he intended to keep it that way, so he'd set some hard—god, they were so fucking *hard*—limits for himself.

He could only hold her like this, taste her and touch her and listen to the ridiculously sexy sounds spilling from her lips and caught in her throat, for so long before he lost his mind and did something outside the scope he was determined to stay within.

He traced her ear with his lips, enjoying how it made her shiver. "I'm going to touch you," he murmured as his hands slid up her legs again.

She nodded immediately and he squeezed his eyes shut, his fingers tracing through the evidence of her arousal slick on her thighs. She canted her hips, jamming his already aching cock against her spectacular and remarkably firm ass. He'd have to ask her—at some other point, *not now*—about her training regime, because she clearly worked her body hard.

In fact, he wanted to learn everything there was to know about her, about her body, so that he could work her hard, too.

His fingers brushed over the soft fabric between her thighs and she jolted, her breath catching before leaving her in a rush. The cotton was wet, thoroughly soaked as he gently peeled it away from her body, petting the soft hair beneath as he eased her panties down until the strings dug into her wide-spread thighs. It was far enough.

He cupped her in his hand, the soft pad over her pubic bone nestled in his palm, his fingers teasing over her slick folds.

"Ready?" he asked, his voice hoarse from the desire choking him.

She groaned, her frustration almost tangible. "Lachlan, please. Touch me. All I want is for you to touch me, to fuck me. *Please.*"

And that. That was exactly what he wanted, too. Goddamn, those limits sucked. But there was still so much they could do. So much he could give her.

He drew one finger over her swollen clit, and she jerked violently and cried out, more sensitive and responsive than he ever could have dreamed. She told him what she liked without words, demanded more with every twitch and thrust. He circled his fingers faster, pressing forward with his hips to steady her as the most amazing, desperate groans vibrated from her back into his chest.

He'd thought he could go on like this for hours, building her up higher and higher, but it wasn't long before *he* was so fucking lost his cock ached, leaking steadily as she dragged her ass over and against it time and again.

He changed directions suddenly, flicking a finger over her clit, hard and fast, setting a steady rhythm that drew new cries from her lips, the sounds sweet and then cutting off abruptly when he sank a finger deep unto her pussy.

"Oh god," she groaned, riding his hand, her head thrown back.

Jesus, she was so wet. So ready for him. His cock throbbed against her ass, strangled in his jeans and fucking begging to be freed. He clamped down on the urge to do exactly that and focused on her.

"That's it, baby. Take what you need."

"Need you. Need you to—"

He added a second finger and curled them both, setting a rhythm to match his other hand, still working her clit.

"God, I want to fuck you," he growled against her ear. "I'm so fucking hard, I can't imagine how good you would feel."

She whimpered. "Do it. Please, Lachlan."

He clamped down on the instinct to give her anything she wanted and thrust his hand harder, curving his wrist to go deeper and still drag his fingertips over her g-spot.

She bucked against him, her hips kicking in circles as desperate little whimpers exploded from her throat every time he thrust in. The muscles around his finger fluttered, his hand drenched, and he knew she was close. His balls were drawn tight, aching and full, and he wondered dizzily if he might come in his damn pants without a hand on him—something that had never come *close* to happening to him before.

He'd be perfectly happy if it went down that way, but not before she'd found her first orgasm. He released the delicate skin of her neck he hadn't even realized he'd pulled between his lips.

"Come on, Michaela. *Take* it."

She shuddered against him, her head shaking. Long strands of her hair fell over her face, but he could still see how her mouth hung open, and her eyes were tightly screwed shut. She was gorgeous, reaching for her pleasure. So fucking close. But it wasn't enough, she wasn't *there*.

This was totally unacceptable.

His third finger garnered a loud, sharp shout, followed by higher-pitched moans. Her cheeks flushed darker, her long back arching until her hips canted higher, locked against his. Her only movements now were the tremors that ran through her body, but it still wasn't enough.

He kept his fingers deep, making short, sharp furious thrusts against her g-spot, his pinky stretching out to tap the tight knot of her asshole.

Her high cries were cut off a low, needy moan. And *that* was the magic he'd been looking for, right where he hadn't even dreamed he could look.

"*Fuck*," he gasped. "Do you want me in there, too? Do you like to be fucked in the ass?"

She keened something that sounded satisfyingly like his name, her head dropping as she clamped down around his fingers. Her legs shook and she collapsed back into him, grinding her clenching pussy into his hand, riding out her climax for as long as she could.

When her knees wobbled dangerously, he pulled the hand away from her clit and pressed it low on her belly, holding her against him. Holding her up. She let out a whine of totally unabashed disappointment when he eased his other hand from her body.

Jesus Christ, she was really something else.

As soon as he felt reasonably sure she could support herself, he leaned back just far enough to gently turn her around, tug her dress back into place, and prop her against the wall.

God, she looked magnificent. Her hair was a mess, her lips swollen, her face and neck pink from his late-day stubble. She was still breathing hard, her eyelids at half-mast and gaze vague.

He kissed her, once, letting himself sink into it but not pushing too close. He thought if he touched her, felt her lax, sated body against his, there was no way he wouldn't demand to be shown the way to her bedroom so he could start all over again.

He ended the kiss with a sigh. "I should go."

Her eyes fluttered open. "Go?"

"Not because I want to. Because I should."

She stared up at him from where she remained slumped against the wall. "You don't have to. I want you to stay."

He smiled, pleased, and pressed a gentle kiss to the crest of one cheekbone. "Thank you. But tonight I think you should think about my offer."

Her slow smile was devastating. "I'm pretty sure I already gave you an answer."

"And I liked it," he assured her, leaning in so their cheeks pressed close but holding the rest of his body away. "But if I'm going to do all the things you want me to" —he ran a suggestive hand over her ass— "then I need you to be sure."

Her head hit the wall with a dull thunk, as if her neck could no longer support the weight. "I'm not going to let you go if you keep doing shit like that."

He was perfectly aware his smile was smug.

"You're nothing like I imagined you'd be," she said with a low chuckle.

He could spend days watching her face when she smiled like that. "So, you imagined this? Being with me?"

"Oh, yes. More than once."

"And what did you imagine?" he asked, almost afraid of her

answer. Afraid it would send all his good intentions straight to hell, with him not far behind.

Her big toothy grin made his heart beat funny in a way that couldn't be explained by arousal alone. "Well, for one thing, I figured you'd be dead silent."

Lachlan chuckled, pleased that he'd surprised her. He was already planning how he might do it again.

He kissed her once more, briefly, because she was fucking irresistible like this. "Goodnight."

"Goodnight."

He slipped out her door, leaving her propped against the wall, watching him with heavy-lidded eyes. It almost fucking killed him to walk away.

The quarter-mile walk home was the longest, most painful of his life. He prayed with every step that he wouldn't bump into anyone he knew, walking with his hands thrust in his pocket, the right curled protectively around his aching dick.

It took his shaking fingers a while to cooperate enough to get his goddamn front door open. The moment it slammed shut behind him, he was tearing at his jeans and shoving them and his boxers out of the way. He dropped to his knees, the cold hardwood floor barely registering as he wrapped his hand around his cock. Just a few brutal strokes later, he came so hard he had to catch himself with one hand against the door, his voice cracking mid-shout.

Chapter Twelve

Michaela skipped up the steps to the building where Lachlan was just about to finish teaching a class and reminded herself that she would *not* allow this to be awkward. So she'd come all over his hand while shouting his name. They were grown-ups, for Christ's sake. The only thing she was embarrassed about was that she'd let him walk away with that massive erection and not done anything about it.

Honestly, she hadn't had a lot of lovers, thanks to the douchebag, but she'd had enough to know that it was *not* okay to leave your partner hanging like that. She was determined to never be that selfish again, even if it had been Lachlan's own damn fault for scrambling her brains like that and walking away before she could recover.

She was sort of giddy to think that she would have a chance to make it up to him. It had been a long time since this sort of thing was even a possibility, let alone a reality. And it *would* be a reality. Lachlan had wanted her to think about it, and she had. All night. Through two more orgasms, she'd thought about it. And nothing that had come to mind or entered her fertile imagination had convinced her that this wasn't a terrific fucking idea.

So she stood sentry outside the Emerson building, ignoring the looks from the students flowing out the doors. She heard a deep voice and stepped forward a moment before Lachlan and Anna stepped outside.

"Hi!" she said, perhaps a shade too brightly.

Anna startled, then returned her smile. "Hello."

Michaela found she was too nervous to look directly at Lachlan, which was hilariously bad, since where the hell would it leave them if neither one of them could look at the other or speak?

"Good morning, Michaela," Lachlan said, his deep voice washing over her, and, damn him, she could *hear* the laughter in his voice.

She turned her biggest smile on him, the one that usually made him go silent. "Good morning, Dr. Morrison."

She had the satisfaction of watching his cheeks go pink, but he didn't look away. In fact, the devil arched one eyebrow.

Who was this man and how soon could she rip his clothes off?

"And to what do we owe the pleasure of this visit?" he asked.

Michaela shrugged and straightened the very fashionable scarf looped around her neck and over the hickey she intended to give him hell about. "I was hoping you had time for a walk. Or maybe lunch?"

"I'd like that." He turned to Anna, who appeared to be trying very hard not to laugh. "Would you mind if I took off from here?"

"Of course not! You two go have fun."

Lachlan tried to frown at his TA and her blinding grin, failing miserably at making a dent in either. Before he could say something—though Michaela couldn't imagine what—Anna turned and practically flounced down the stairs with a cheerful wave goodbye.

Michaela made sure no one else was standing nearby. "She totally thinks something is up."

Lachlan turned to her, frowning. "I'm sorry. I know you prize your privacy."

That was a massive understatement, but she waved away his concern. "I'm not worried about Anna. Unless you are. I'm sure you don't want your department gossiping about you."

He opened his mouth to say something before apparently reconsidering. Instead, he touched her elbow and they started down the stairs, away from the students still trickling out of the building.

"Anna would never gossip about me," he said at last.

He sounded certain, and Michaela had already suspected that was the case. Anna was obviously fond of her mentor, which, as far as Michaela was concerned, was totally understandable.

"So, where are we going?" Lachlan asked as they cut across the quad under the watchful gaze of everyone in the vicinity.

"Oh! Well, as tempting as it is to just invite you to up to my place," she began, thoroughly enjoying his reaction to that suggestion, his gaze hot and zeroed in on her, "I thought we should talk about your tux."

He blinked. "My what?"

"Your tuxedo. We have the Fall Ball on Saturday, if you remember?"

"Oh, shit."

She patted his shoulder and bit back any urge to let him out of it, because she was absolutely not going to do that. "You're going to do great," she said instead. "And the first tenet of *Michaela's Rules for Managing the Public* is that you have to dress for the role you want to play."

Lachlan smirked. "So, I can wear something that matches the wallpaper in the back corner of the ballroom?"

She laughed. "Very clever. And no. You probably couldn't carry off the floral chintz look anyway."

"What will you be wearing?"

"Well, that's an interesting question," she said as she turned off the main drag and onto a much quieter one. She ducked into a recessed doorway and towed him along with her. "I was going to wear a blue strapless dress I got a while back, but I've discovered a sudden taste for the halter top."

She turned her back to the street and tugged the scarf away from her neck.

Lachlan's eyes widened. "*Oops.*"

Michaela grinned at Lachlan's aghast expression. She'd been pissed for all of ten seconds last night as she'd stood in front of the mirror, gaping at the bruise that had only begun to settle into the glorious deep purples it was now. Then she'd recalled how good it had felt to receive it, and just thanked god the weather had turned cooler.

"Oh my god, Michaela, I am so sorry. That is...that is *not* discreet. I shouldn't have—"

"Stop." She put her hand on his chest to soften the interruption. "All I ask is next time, you restrict yourself to leaving marks lower down, where people can't see."

Lachlan swallowed heavily and stared into her eyes. "Next time, huh?" he said, his voice huskier.

She shivered. Jesus, maybe they *should* have gone back to her place, just so they could work off some of this tension before attempting to do anything so civilized as shopping or eating in public.

She had to clear her throat, twice, before she could speak. "Right, well, let's get back on topic, shall we?" She stepped back onto the sidewalk and he followed, walking by her side. "So, do you own anything in the way of formal wear?"

"Does my kilt count?"

She laughed, because honestly, that would be her preference, but the goal here was to make moving through social interaction easier, and that wasn't the way to start. "Maybe sometime later we can upgrade you to the full regalia," she suggested, "but perhaps this go round, we should stick to something simpler."

"I don't own a tux, but I can get one."

"You don't mind?" she asked. She didn't want to force him to spend a lot of money on something he wouldn't see as useful, and she was pretty sure she could guess his reaction to her offering to buy him one.

"I don't mind. I've rented enough of them that I probably would have been better off buying one years ago."

"Okay," she agreed. "There's a shop I've heard a lot of good things about that I'm certain will have something classic that won't ever go out of style." Because men were fucking lucky like that.

"How do I choose?"

Michaela smiled up at him. "Do you trust me?"

Lachlan stopped, his expression more serious than the

question warranted. "Absolutely."

Her heart beat a little harder against her ribs. "Then let's go."

Lachlan climbed out of the taxi downtown and turned to give Michaela a hand out. She smiled gratefully while they both ignored the gasp from someone on the sidewalk behind him.

Seriously, people were so fucking weird.

Michaela slipped ridiculously large sunglasses over her eyes, and sailed forward through the lunchtime crowd, a friendly smile on her face. Lachlan was impressed that she could manage to look so happy, so pleasant, while clearly giving off a "leave me alone" vibe. He hoped learning how to do that was one of the lessons she had in store for him.

In the meantime, he followed in her wake, like a big dorky shadow, as she went directly to the door of the Boylston Haberdasher.

Stepping into the shop was like stepping into a different world. Almost like entering McGinty's, the way the sound of the traffic and the crowd disappeared the moment the door closed behind them. Only, rather than being greeted by a cantankerous bartender-cum-defenseman, they were approached by an impeccably dressed middle-aged woman.

"Ms. Price, we're honored to have you visit our shop. Welcome."

Michaela smiled, but Lachlan noticed her shoulders still seemed tight, and there was no recognition in her expression. "Thank you," she murmured. "This is my friend, Dr. Lachlan Morrison," she said with an absent wave, biting her lower lip in an uncharacteristic display of nerves.

Dammit, why was she nervous? It was making *him* nervous.

The woman's smile brightened considerably as she gave Lachlan a blatant once-over. "It's a pleasure to meet you as well, Dr. Morrison."

Lachlan licked his lips. Twice. "Uh—"

133

Michaela cleared her throat delicately, drawing the shop clerk's attention. "Is Robert available today?"

The woman's smile froze. "Yes, I'll go get him for you." She gave a polite nod and walked away.

Michaela watched her go. At one point she lifted her hand, as if to call the woman back but let it drop by her side again.

Lachlan eyed Michaela warily. "You okay?"

"Yes, of course," she said, a little too firmly to be believable, then smiled at him. "I was going to ask you the same thing. You know she was just examining your inseam, right?"

"Is that a euphemism?"

Michaela laughed, the sound fading when a man about their age, in a trim dark suit, came through the curtain at the back of the room.

He stopped short, the curtain still swaying behind him. "Michaela?"

"Hello, Robby," she said softly.

The man just stood staring at Michaela for a long time. Then he shook himself and came forward quickly, taking her hands in his. "It's so good to see you. What are you *doing* here?"

"I'm going to school up here, now," she explained, though Lachlan got the impression that hadn't been what Robby was asking. "And my friend" —she waved at Lachlan— "needs a tuxedo. I knew you'd be the best."

Robby smiled and turned to Lachlan. His perfect eyebrow arched high. "He's a Morrison."

"How'd you know that?" Lachlan asked.

"I follow hockey. And the gossip." He shot Michaela a meaningful glance. "Also, I never forget eye color as pretty as that. If your brother Callum hadn't made a habit of breaking his nose, they'd be about the same, too."

"Wow," Lachlan said, starting to fidget under the close scrutiny, but telling himself Robby was probably just checking out his inseam, too. "I'm impressed."

134

The other eyebrow went up. "It's mutual, I assure you," he murmured, still staring at something below Lachlan's belt.

Lachlan kind of wished the floor would open up beneath him and swallow him whole.

Michaela grinned and cuffed Robby on the shoulder. "You haven't changed at all. He's strictly off-limits to you, you man-thieving bitch. I brought him, and I'm taking him home."

Lachlan's felt his mouth drop open.

Robby appeared to be delighted. "It was *one time*. We were *twelve*."

Michaela sniffed. "I'm still not over it."

"Apparently not, princess."

Michaela's expression went achingly soft and sad at the nickname, but Robby didn't see it. He was too busy casting a critical eye over every inch of Lachlan again.

"I suppose I can content myself to *dressing* him." He held out his hand. "I'm Robert Wigglesworth, proprietor of this shop, and old boarding school friend to the princess here." He tilted his head toward Michaela.

"And boyfriend thief?"

"Is that what you are, a boyfriend?" Robby drawled, his eyes narrowed.

"Oh, ah, I didn't mean—"

"Leaving him alone, Wiggles," Michaela said with a warm smile. "He's here to get a tux, not an interrogation."

Robby harrumphed, as if to say, *we'll see about that.*

Lachlan tried very hard not to look half as terrified as he felt. He had to admire the man's ability to say a whole lot more than the words he actually chose to speak. He and Michaela working together could conquer all of society and still have time for lunch.

"Well, come along," Robby said, turning toward the back of the shop. "I already know what we'll try first, unless you have ideas."

"I would never presume," Michaela said demurely, waiting for Lachlan before following Robby toward the curtain.

"I thought you said you didn't have any friends up here," Lachlan said quietly.

"Oh, well, I haven't really spent time with Robby in years," she hedged.

"And whose fault is that?" Robby sing-songed through the curtain. The man apparently had ears like a bat.

Michaela sighed and pushed through the curtain, towing Lachlan with her. The space beyond looked like an opulent living room, with ornate chairs and couches grouped in roughly a horseshoe around a coffee table laden with a silver tea and coffee service. The seating was angled toward a platform surrounded by mirrors. There was a door to one side of that, and two curtained cubicles on the other.

Michaela sat in the chair directly facing the platform and poured herself some tea. Even Lachlan could tell she was stalling in the face of Robby's arch stare. Lachlan hovered behind her, torn between feeling vaguely protective and being frankly curious.

"I didn't want to drag you into the middle of it," Michaela said at last. Lachlan had never seen her act this way, not even when he was freaking out. She seemed hesitant. Almost shy.

He hated it.

Robby, however, looked unimpressed. "What made you assume that would've happened?"

"You're best friends with Blake," she said to her tea cup.

"I am *not*," Robby snapped.

Michaela looked up at him. "But you were so close. What happened?"

Robby slammed his hands down on his hips, positively radiating righteous anger. "Would you believe my asshole *former* best friend took a video of himself having sex with this wonderful woman, who I love very much, and sold it to pornographers? I've not spoken a civil word to him since."

Michaela's cup rattled against the saucer before she managed to put both back down on the table. Lachlan took a step forward, alarmed when he saw tears gathering in her eyes.

Robby beat him to her, perching on the couch closest to her and taking her hands in his. "How could you think I would forgive him? I wrote you emails, tried to get your hideously stubborn brothers to tell you, but I never heard back."

"I didn't—" She swallowed, wiping at her eyes fruitlessly, the tears still spilling over. "I changed my email addresses. Told my family I didn't want to hear what anyone was saying. Everyone...they left me, Robby. They were supposed to be my friends, and they either laughed it off or jumped ship. How could I expect *his* friends to be any different?"

"Oh, princess. It's good you're so pretty, because you're really fucking stupid sometimes, you know that?"

A wet but happy laugh burbled out of Michaela. "And you were always such a bitch," she said with a wealth of affection.

"But you've missed me anyway."

"I really have," she confessed, falling against Robby's chest as he reached for her. He pulled her onto the couch with him for a long hug.

Lachlan edged back, giving them time and privacy as they spoke quietly to each other. He checked Michaela's face occasionally, just to be sure she still had that small, happy smile, but kept his distance. When it didn't seem like they would run out of things to say anytime soon, he decided maybe he'd go wander around the block a couple times and let them be alone.

"Stop right there, Mr. Thirty-Four-Inch-Inseam," Robby drawled the moment Lachlan's hand touched the curtain.

Lachlan froze. "Uh..."

"Where do you think you're going?" Michaela asked, her voice laced with amusement.

"I was just going to leave you two to—uh, bond, or whatever," he said, turning back to find them both grinning at him.

"Nice try," Michaela said, moving back to her chair with far more dignity than most people could manage, since it meant she practically had to crawl off Robby's lap. "Now go stand on that platform and let Wiggles do his thing."

Lachlan obeyed, since Robby was probably faster—and definitely craftier—than him, and wouldn't hesitate to tackle him to the ground if he tried to make a break for it.

As soon as he was on the dais, Robby smirked and flapped his hand up and down in front of Lachlan. "Take it all off."

"*Wut?*"

"Well, okay, you can leave the boxer briefs on. And the undershirt, if you must," he added with a long-suffering sigh.

"How do you know I'm wearing boxer briefs?"

Robby eyed his groin pointedly before smiling sweetly up at Lachlan. "I'm an expert at determining men's preferences."

Lachlan chuckled. Robby was a very difficult man not to like. Even his leers were oddly charming and, like the man himself, Lachlan suspected, completely harmless.

Michaela smiled and cocked her head, waiting to see what Lachlan would do next. She looked a little like someone had hit her over the head with a brick when he stripped down to his underwear, tossing his clothes—including the undershirt—onto the bench nearby.

It served her right.

Maybe he should have warned her that he rarely got flustered around a woman once he knew just how to give her an orgasm.

After yet another overly-familiar once-over, Robby approached with his tape measure out and a determined expression. Lachlan sent Michaela a long, bland stare as Robby took his measurements, including confirming his spot-on inseam estimate and taking extra care, Lachlan was sure, to give his junk an extra nudge here and there.

Michaela tried to hide her grin behind her tea cup.

"I have just the thing," Robby announced.

"We need it the day after tomorrow," Michaela said blithely, as if she assumed it would be no trouble.

Robby gave her a baleful look, then sailed from the room with his chin up, but without argument.

Michaela arched a brow at Lachlan as soon as they were alone. "I wouldn't have guessed you were an exhibitionist."

"Nothing you weren't going to see soon anyway," he murmured with a long, assessing once-over of his own.

Her cheeks went pink. "Why, Dr. Morrison, I do believe I'm discovering a whole new side to you."

"Well, *I* do believe that with those mirrors behind me, you can see all my sides pretty clearly already."

Michaela snorted into her tea cup, her eyes dancing.

Robby returned with a suit over one arm, pausing to take in the scene before him. He marched over to Lachlan and passed him the hanger. "I have to make a phone call," he announced. "No one will disturb you for at least ten minutes, at which time you should have this suit on."

He sent Michaela a long look Lachlan couldn't interpret, then made another dramatic exit.

Michaela stood and came to Lachlan. He looked down at her curiously, wondering what she was up to, but didn't hesitate to follow her when she wrapped her hand around his wrist and pulled him off the dais and into one of the curtained cubicles.

She hung the suit from a hook on the wall.

"If I'm willing to strip down out there, why would I care about having privacy to put clothes back on?" he asked, confused.

She put her hand on his cheek and he happily let her pull him closer. "That's not why we need privacy," she whispered in his ear, resting her hand low on his belly.

He shifted in a futile effort to stop the flow of blood to his cock. Goddamn, what was she up to? Did she *want* Robby to get an eyeful? Because there wasn't any way Lachlan was going to be able to hide what was going on his shorts right now. He could already hear Robby complaining about how his dick was ruining the line of the suit.

He shifted again, but that only served to drag her fingertips across his skin like five perfect, hot brands, catching on the line of hair below his navel.

He sucked in a deep, desperate breath. "We can't here. You shouldn't risk—"

"It's safe, I promise. And what I should never do is let you give me three magnificent orgasms and not at least give you one in return."

Lachlan's brain stuttered. *Three*? He'd only given her one, unless... "You. After I left, you..."

"I haven't come that hard in *years*," she told him, her voice husky, her lips brushing against his ear.

And Jesus fucking Christ, what else could he do but to kiss her?

It was frantic from the moment their lips touched, his cock smashed to her belly as he hauled her up against him. This was insane. And possibly stupid. But she'd said it was safe and he was beyond giving it more thought than that.

He grappled to keep her close when she put her hands to his chest, but she succeeding in prying herself loose.

"I haven't done this in a long time," she announced, then dropped to her knees at his feet.

Lachlan slapped his palms against the walls on either side of him and cursed viciously under his breath. She smiled up at him while tucking her fingertips into his boxers and tugged them down.

"Okay?" she asked.

And really, was she fucking kidding? He nodded maniacally, jerking to a stop the moment his aching dick popped free. She hummed in apparent appreciation, the muscles in his back and ass clenching tight when she wrapped her hand around the base of his shaft.

Then she just stared at him for a moment.

"You don't have to—"

"Shut up."

"Okay," he said meekly, wondering if he could actually die from blow-job anticipation alone.

She licked her lips, once, then opened her mouth and leaned forward.

His first and last thought as his cock was enveloped in soft, warm suction was, *Well, this isn't going to take long.* Robby had given them ten minutes and they'd already used one, maybe two. Lachlan would only need three more. Tops.

Michaela's chuckle vibrated around him, and he realized, dimly, that he'd done at least some of that math out loud. He groaned as she sucked him further into her mouth, hot sparks running up his spine. Her tongue wriggled miracles along the underside of his shaft as he watched it disappear between her lips. When her lips met her hand she hovered there, taking him apart with gentle undulations that he could feel all the way down to his toes.

Her cheeks hollowed as she pulled back, until she drew off with an obscene pop and gasped. She contemplated his dick almost curiously, watching the bead of pre-come form on the head before she licked it off.

He wanted to tell her how much he liked it, how good it felt, all the things he wanted her to do and wanted to do to her. He bit his lip, hard, holding back everything but the little, uncontrollable grunts each lap of her tongue tore from him.

She slid her hand down his shaft gently and he bit his lip harder, watching how she studied him while she rubbed the sensitive divot underneath the head with her thumb, mind-numbing little circles that teased out another drop. She promptly licked it away before poking the tip of her tongue into the slit, as if chasing more.

He legs shook with the effort to keep hips still, his lips sore from keeping the jumble of filthy words from falling out of his mouth.

"I want to hear you," she said, as if reading his mind.

"Nghgh," he offered helpfully with a burst of air.

She smiled, obviously pleased, and slid back down. When she drew back, she followed with a twist of her hand.

"Fuck," he gasped, finding control of his tongue after all. "You look so hot sucking my cock. Your mouth is fucking unbelievable. It's..." He trailed off when she sucked harder, his eyes almost crossing. Her hand cupped his balls, her thumb rubbing across, then tucking between them, separating them gently. The pressure was tremendous, almost too much, but perfect for it.

Two fingers pressed up behind his sac and his hips jerked forward, his cock sinking deeper into her mouth.

"Jesus, sorry. Sorry," he babbled, forcing himself to ease back and hold still. "But god, keep...just like that. I'm not...I'm not going to last," he warned.

She followed the movement of his hips, keeping him deep, her tongue and the suction relentless. His balls drew tighter against her palm and thumb, and she hummed happily, his groan a counterpoint in bass.

He fought not to thrust, his fingers digging into the cubicle walls as he gasped for breath and stared down at her. "God, I want to fuck your mouth," he blurted, the truth spilling out of him. "I want to wrap your hair around my hands and hold you still and fuck until I can't take it anymore and come on your face."

Michaela's eyelids fluttered and she whimpered around his cock, and—*fuck*—she wanted that. He could see it in her dark eyes and flushed cheeks, and the red swollen lips wrapped around his dick, still working him to the edge of reason. It would be so fucking good, but it wasn't for today. At least, not now.

He imagined taking her home after this and doing this again, with explicit permission to—

"Oh, shit, I'm gonna—" he said hoarsely, trying to warn her, but she only sucked harder. He dropped one hand, desperately threading his fingers through her hair and tugging back, but she just let go of his balls, and sank her fingers into the meat of his ass, tugging him closer.

Then the little vixen sucked *harder.*

He groaned, low and anguished, and let himself fall.

Michaela held on as Lachlan shook above her, his cock throbbing against her tongue as she swallowed the results of her hard work. When he gasped and gave a last, great shudder, she carefully drew back, licking him clean as best she could before releasing him with a final, soft kiss.

She looked up, ensnared by his wild-eyed stare.

"You're fucking amazing," he whispered, his voice raw, like he'd been the one giving head.

She smiled and rose to her feet as gracefully as she could manage. Her body felt hot, her head light. She wanted him so much she could taste it. She licked her lips, checking for any evidence he'd left behind. Boy, could she ever *taste* it.

"I'll be just a minute more," Robby called distantly, his voice muffled by the exterior curtains.

Lachlan jumped, his eyes widening in horror.

"Relax," she whispered, leaning up to kiss him gently. Quickly. "Next time you can come anywhere you want on me, but this time I thought it would be better if we kept things tidy."

He stood there, staring at her like she'd just punched him in the face. She grinned and tugged his boxers back into place, then threw the curtain open and sauntered back to her seat and her tepid tea. By the time she'd finished it, Lachlan had donned the tuxedo pants and was pulling the shirt over his shoulders and grabbing the jacket.

He'd just settled back onto the center of the dais when Robby breezed into the room. He took one look at Lachlan and turned for Michaela, rolling his eyes as he took a seat next to her.

"You're looking flushed with good...health, princess."

She grinned.

Lachlan muffled his chuckle with a cough as he pulled on the jacket.

They turned to look at Lachlan, and Robby's hand shot out and curled around her wrist. For a moment, all either of them could do was stare. Lachlan stood under the bright lights, his partially buttoned shirt gaping to reveal just a tantalizing hint of his muscled chest, one nipple peeking out when he twisted to look at the cut of the trousers, which was exquisite. They sat perfectly on his hips and across his flat belly, his firm, round ass framed beautifully without being too obvious. It was all the more sexy for his bare feet and hands, his strong wrists exposed by the open sleeves, his face still flushed, his hair in disarray.

Honestly, he was sexy as fuck.

"Do you have any studs I can borrow?" he asked Robby absently, his voice a thick rasp and completely different than it had been before Robby had left the room. Lachlan's eyes widened in horror.

Michaela barely suppressed a giggle and Robby gave her a long, proud look. He leaned closer and whispered, "I was just about to ask you the same thing."

The giggle escaped. God, she really had missed him.

He was on his feet and over to help Lachlan, pulling studs and cuff links from his pocket, before Michaela could explain that Lachlan wasn't really her stud. Or her anything else. He was just sort of...on loan until the disaster that was her life finally got too wearisome for him.

It wasn't a pleasant thought, so she focused instead on pouring herself more tea and settling back to watch Robby harass Lachlan through deciding on the right shirt, pant cuff, and cut through the waist of his jacket.

She didn't intercede until it came to price, at which point Robby named a sum that made Lachlan blanch. Michaela rolled her eyes and talked Robby down to almost half of what he'd first proposed.

They were still haggling over the details while Lachlan dressed in his own clothes and as they walked to the front door. "You're a shrew," Robby declared after accepting her final counteroffer.

"Well, you didn't think I'd changed, did you?"

Robby smiled. "I'd hoped not, anyway."

Michaela hugged him. Fiercely. And he held her just as tight. It felt as though she'd found a piece of herself she'd long ago convinced herself she wasn't missing. Now that piece had slotted home, and she was overwhelmingly comforted to have it back.

"I'm so glad you came," he said into her shoulder.

"I am, too."

Chapter Thirteen

Lachlan hooked his finger into the heavily starched collar of his brand-new tuxedo, trying to loosen the noose around his neck without dislodging his tie. Michaela watched him, amused, from where she sat beside him in the back of the town car.

"You'll be fine," she said, for at least the fifteenth time that night.

Easy for her to say. When he'd knocked on her door a few minutes ago, he'd been rendered speechless, though at least this time it was just the normal reaction any man would have to feeling like he'd been punched in the face by her beauty.

She wore a long, dark pink gown, the neckline somehow accentuating her full breasts and slim shoulders while still managing to hide the hickey he'd left behind a few days ago. Which was good for a lot of reasons, but particularly since she had her hair piled on her head in an intricate twist with a few soft curls left loose to brush her shoulders, drawing the eye to the length of her neck and perfect, bitable curve of her jaw.

Lachlan expected she'd be the center of attention the entire night. He was starting to give serious consideration to how bad it would be if he threw up on his own shoes in the middle of the party.

"Shouldn't we have practiced or something?" he said weakly.

"I already told you, the most important thing to do is to keep your eyes open and a smile on your face. There will be a lot of photographers there, and you don't want to look like you've suffered a significant head injury in the pictures."

"Right. Head up, smile on, don't blink," he repeated.

"If it doesn't seem like it's the time to smile, then try to look serene."

"Serene?" he asked incredulously, panic rising. "I have no idea what that means."

"Okay. How about interested? Intrigued. When people are

talking, look at them and nod like they're saying the most interesting thing you've ever heard. I'm sure you've been to a few work functions where someone was going on about something and you had to pretend you weren't bored out of your skull. Just like in those cases, in all likelihood, you won't have to say anything. I promise I'll be close by, so if you feel freaked out, or can't speak when you think you should, touch my arm."

He was going to spend the whole night clinging to her like a limpet.

Michaela smiled, an encouraging hand on his arm. "A lot of these people aren't going to hit your hot buttons, I promise."

Lachlan frowned. "I don't have hot buttons, whatever that means."

"You really do. But there's going to be lots of older people, in couples. You focus on them and I'll field the rest if you don't feel up to it."

"But what if I—"

"Look at me," she said sternly. He did. "Now smile—*ack*, okay, take it easy there. You don't want to look like a super happy serial killer."

Lachlan's smile dimmed considerably. "I'm screwed."

"No, like that, that's better. But maybe try to be less worried around the eyebrows and forehead."

"We definitely should have practiced."

Michaela just laughed. "You're going to be fine."

The car pulled up in front of the hotel and Lachlan stared out the window in horror at the sheer number of cameras pointed in their direction.

A doorman approached.

"Smile," Michaela ordered a moment before the door opened.

Lachlan plastered a smile on his face. It was the same one he used for the eternal hell that was Parent's Weekend on campus. He climbed from the car, catching himself before he blinked against the flashbulbs exploding in his face.

Jesus Christ, this was crazy.

He turned to offer Michaela his hand, grateful to have a moment to stare into the dim interior of the car. She held on reassuringly tightly and rose gracefully to stand beside him.

He'd thought the flashes were bad before? Lachlan wasn't sure if this was the red carpet or the apocalypse. His retinas were screaming for relief.

Michaela released his hand and he held out his elbow for her to thread her arm through. Her smile was wide, for all the world appearing as if she was absolutely thrilled to be there. Hopefully, no one would notice she was practically dragging him into the party.

The forty feet to the front door were the longest of his life.

The lobby was opulent—and blessedly devoid of cameras—but nothing compared to the ballroom. He was relieved to see other people standing just inside the door, gawping at the scene before them. Clearly, he wasn't the only newbie to this shit. And, unlike some people, he really didn't give a crap about the sheer wealth oozing from every corner.

"Now what?" he asked, putting his hand low on her bare back. The feel of her soft, warm skin grounded him.

"Now we mingle."

He looked down at Michaela with a wide smile. "I hate you."

"I know you do, honey," she said, patting his arm. "But you'll thank me later."

"I'm pretty sure I won't," he said in a low voice. He glanced up over her shoulder, almost equal in height to his own in the high heels she wore under her long gown. He found several pairs of eyes staring at them, at *her*, and he didn't like the looks on their faces at all.

How did these people not see that she was the most beautiful woman in the room? And that it had nothing to do with how she looked or what she wore? She was kind. Generous. Vulnerable, like everyone else here with a good heart. And they would condemn her for some thoughtless bastard's cruel revenge. All she'd done was have sex, which he felt confident everyone currently casting looks in their directions had done as well at least once.

A particularly gaunt and angry-looking older woman caught his gaze and frowned, honest-to-god tipping her nose in the air before pointedly turning away.

Okay, he wouldn't be surprised if *that* lady had never had sex.

He could feel his anger rising and decided the best course of action would be to spend the rest of the night looking at Michaela and ignoring everyone else. It wasn't like it would be a hardship.

"Do we start with people you know?" he asked.

"Oh, I don't know anyone here, I don't think," she said blithely.

"You *what*? Why are we even here if you don't know anyone? Who invited you?"

Michaela laughed, like he'd said something funny. It wasn't funny. The room suddenly felt even more like enemy territory. He wanted to grab her hand and run, to drag her out of there and go somewhere safe, where she'd be appreciated.

A man's voice boomed from halfway across the ballroom. "Lachlan!"

Lachlan jumped, his eyes widening in shock.

"Apparently, you'll be in charge of introductions tonight," Michaela said with a twinkle in her eyes.

Lachlan must have looked as terrified by the idea as he felt.

"Smile," whispered Michaela as they turned toward the silver-haired gentleman threading his way through the tables toward them.

A wave of relief crashed over Lachlan. "Seamus!"

Lachlan put his hand out, and let out an *oomph* of surprise when Seamus ignored it and yanked him into a hard hug instead.

He was still trying to smile and keep his eyes open, mindful of the discreet photographers circulating the room, but it was hard when all he could focus on was the sea of faces watching them. Everyone in the room seemed to have turned to look at Seamus's shout. Lachlan glanced at Michaela to see what she thought of all this, and found her staring at him with a crooked grin and something like wonder.

"Is that Seamus Lynch?" she mouthed silently.

Lachlan nodded, and stepped back when Seamus deigned to release him.

"Son, I can't lie. I'm surprised to see you here," Seamus said with a wide smile.

"You and me both," Lachlan said under his breath, which made Seamus chuckle and gave Lachlan a moment to remember his manners. "Seamus, allow me to present Michaela Price. She is a friend of the family. Michaela, this is Seamus Lynch. He is...quite dear to my sister and her meehh...Garrick and Rhian."

Michaela smiled at Lachlan's stumble, but kept her eyes on Seamus.

He studied her right back. "Ms. Price, it's a pleasure. You are even lovelier in person."

Lachlan's smile went tight. Did Seamus read those trashy magazines? God, had *he* seen the video? Lachlan had no doubt all the people staring at them were wondering the same thing. Honestly, some of these people were being blatantly fucking rude. How did she put up with this shit?

"Thank you, Mr. Lynch. It's an honor to meet you," Michaela replied smoothly. "You've done tremendous work here."

"Here?" Lachlan asked, distracted from their audience.

Seamus waved a hand at the room. "I host this every year to raise money for the Children's Hospital," he explained before turning back to Michaela. "You must call me Seamus, dear. If you're a friend of the Morrisons, then you're a friend to me."

Seamus kept a firm hold of her hand when she tried to pull it back, his expression determined. For a moment he and Michaela just stared at one another.

Lachlan didn't understand what was happening, or why Michaela looked surprised.

She cleared her throat. "That's very kind of you," she said, and for the life of him, Lachlan couldn't figure out why she looked so puzzled.

Seamus leaned in, tugging Michaela closer and tilting his head to indicate Lachlan should, too. "Bunch of judgmental old biddies here tonight," he whispered. "Frightful, the lot of them. As if their reputations are so sterling. I don't even dare invite Rhian, Savannah, and Garrick."

Michaela smiled gamely. "Next time you must. Just sit them with me—I adore their company, and no reputation can fail to shine next to my tarnish."

Lachlan jerked upright, scowling, but fuck it if he could hold on to a smile when she said shit like that. Michaela's voluminous skirts twitched a nanosecond before a pointy toe made contact with his shin.

Lachlan dutifully slapped on a smile and continued to dream of murdering every single person in the room giving them side-eyes.

"Michaela," Seamus said sternly, "I don't tolerate that kind of talk about or from my grandchildren, and I won't hear from you either." He held her gaze until her chin dipped in acknowledgment. Then he continued in a louder voice. "If anyone here doesn't like who I choose to spend my time with, then they won't get an invitation next year."

Everyone within a twenty foot radius shifted, and suddenly, miraculously, their faces were wreathed in smiles.

Seamus nodded in satisfaction. Lachlan looked at him with awe—damn, he was a wily old goat.

"Now, come," Seamus said, tucking Michaela's hand around his elbow and anchoring her to his side. "I will have things rearranged so that you can sit at my table with me. I apologize that I hadn't realized you were coming when the Price Foundation reserved their seats."

151

They sailed across the room, Lachlan trailing in their wake, watching in fascination as the crowd parted like the Red Sea.

Michaela was confused. She smiled and nodded and spoke to all the people she'd come here to meet and speak with on behalf of the Foundation, certain that no one, except possibly Lachlan, had any idea something was off.

The whole time, a single thought ran through her head on repeat: *What the fuck?*

She was distracted enough that she almost lost Lachlan to panic twice, but managed to drag him back from the edge both times. She would probably have bruises on her arm from how hard he grabbed her when an octogenarian widow groped his ass, but otherwise, he was doing great.

She, on the other hand, was twitching with the need to get answers. To do that, though, she had to get Lachlan alone.

The dinner and speeches took another hour, followed by Seamus plunging the entire ballroom into a stunned hush by leading her out onto the spot-lit parquet floor for the first dance. Even *she* couldn't believe he was doing it, and he'd warned her first—and completely ignored her protests that it wasn't necessary.

Then finally, *finally*, the dancing was in full-swing and she managed to get Lachlan and herself tucked into a quiet corner of the ballroom.

"You're friends with *Seamus Lynch?*"

Lachlan chuckled. "Yeah, I guess I am. He's a great guy."

"A great guy," she repeated numbly. "Lachlan, have you not noticed that almost everyone in this room is either in awe or scared witless of him?"

"Really?" he said, looking around the room as if he might find someone cowering under a table. "But he's so sweet."

"*Sweet?*"

"Well, yeah."

"How do you even know him? Is he friends with your parents?" she asked.

"No," Lachlan said, then drew her closer, too close. His lips brushed her cheek as he spoke. Michaela was acutely aware of a flash going off nearby, but was too interested to hear whatever Lachlan wanted to tell her to move back to a more respectable distance. "You can't tell anyone, but I have permission to tell you. He's Rhian's grandfather."

Michaela cocked her head to look at him, but kept her voice well below the sound of the orchestra. "Seamus Lynch is Rhian Savage's grandfather?" She racked her brain for anything she could remember about the Lynch family, and that just didn't make sense.

"It's a long story. One I'll tell you another time, but suffice it to say, he considers Garrick and Savannah, and, apparently, *me*, to be family."

"Wow," she said softly. "Well, that explains it, I guess."

"Explains what?" Lachlan said impatiently. "You've been acting like this entire night has been a surprise. I thought that was my role."

She grinned up at him. "Speaking of, you've been doing very well."

He grimaced. "I've hardly said a word."

"Which was the plan, if you'll remember. Most people just want other people to listen. Next time you can work on your small talk, but for now, all these nice people think you're charming, and you've survived the evening unscathed."

"Tell that to my ass, which may have actual claw marks on it now."

She waggled her eyebrows. "I can't wait to see it for myself."

"How about we leave now and you can do a thorough inspection as soon as we get home?" Lachlan said, trying for sexy but only managing to sound incredibly *hopeful*.

Michaela threw her head back and laughed. Heads turned,

but she didn't even care. She was bullet-proof tonight.

"Sorry, buddy, but you're not that lucky," she said apologetically. "And we can't leave until almost the very end, now."

Lachlan looked close to pouting. "Why not?"

"Because your friend Seamus has just staked our reputations quite firmly to his, and if nothing else, we owe him the courtesy of being flawless guests."

"He did?"

"Lachlan, I'm sure you've noticed the looks I get. Particularly when my back is turned."

He frowned down at her. "You know about those?"

She sighed, patting his arm soothingly. "Of course I do. It's much better than it was a decade ago, when they would give me those looks right to my face, and tell me what they thought besides."

"And now, what? People have begun to forget? Or just gotten over themselves?" he asked.

"No, my parents made me Chairwoman of the Price Foundation."

"Huh," he said slowly. "Clever strategy."

She smiled. "You understand people better than you think."

"I really don't. More like I know my Machiavelli—it's better to be feared than loved if you cannot be both."

Michaela rolled her eyes affectionately. "No wonder you're friends with Seamus. That's probably his motto. But I think my parents were thinking more along the lines of Sun Tzu."

Lachlan eyed her thoughtfully. "The supreme art of war is to subdue the enemy without fighting?"

"More like, in the midst of great chaos, there is also opportunity."

"Opportunity? I don't get it."

"For a long time, a lot of invitations that would usually have come, didn't. My parents, my brothers, they were all impacted, but they'd still get asked to things even when my invitations were often mysteriously lost in the mail. The only time I was asked to go anywhere was when someone wanted more press, or to give their guests a show. Someone to talk about."

"I'm really starting to hate these people," he muttered darkly.

"Not everyone was that bad, but it was a common enough occurrence, and it was making my parents crazy. They'd been ignoring the whole thing in public, of course, but in private they seethed that people they'd thought of as their friends would use me that way."

"I'm sorry."

She waved that away. "It was my own fault."

"No, it was not," he snapped.

She sighed. She really didn't want to get into all that now, so she plowed on. "The interesting thing was, I was good for attendance. Not just at these things," she nodded at the ballroom beyond his back, "but at smaller events. Maybe the press was only there to take my picture, but they had to mention the clinic, or the shelter, or wherever I was. Within days, donations would be up. I was accidentally generating awareness."

"Huh."

"Right? So, I figured if I couldn't repair my reputation, the least I could do was put it to good use. My parents helped by making me Chairwoman long before they had intended to name any of us to the position, and between the weight of the Foundation behind me and my reputation proceeding me, I've generated a lot of charitable donations."

"But at what expense?" he asked, too clever by half.

"The rewards have outstripped the costs by far," she assured him.

He didn't look convinced. For the first time in more years than she could remember, it mattered to her that someone understood. Unfortunately, now wasn't the time or the place.

"In any case, my original point was that in spite of my

parents' masterful politicking, the looks don't go away. Ever. And no matter how much money and power I bring to the table, there will always be those who can't forget my misspent youth."

Lachlan opened his mouth, but she went on before he could voice his protest.

"Seamus, though, has changed the game. If these people think of themselves as Boston's aristocracy, then he is their king."

"And you?"

"Have just been upgraded from entertaining pawn to untouchable."

Lachlan seemed to mull this over for a moment, his lips curling up slowly. "What would *Michaela's Rules for Managing the Public* say if I ran over and hugged Seamus right now?"

She laughed, and clamped a hand around his arm just in case. "Don't you dare. The last thing this court needs is another jester."

Chapter Fourteen

Lachlan slumped in the back seat of the town car on the way home, staring out the window at absolutely nothing while exhaustion set in. For a while there, at the end of the longest night of this life, he hadn't been sure if he was going to make it. If Seamus hadn't been there to talk to, Lachlan would have given in to the urge to toss Michaela over his shoulder and make a run for the lobby.

"So, what are you doing next Saturday?"

Lachlan turned his head, not even bothering to lift it from the seat, and stared at Michaela. She was peering down at her phone, somehow still sitting up straight, not lulled into the deep leather seats that Lachlan wanted to wallow in forever.

She looked, in fact, exactly the same as when he'd arrived at her apartment five hours ago. He would admire her for her fortitude, but he strongly suspected he should instead be admiring her ability to mask what she was really feeling.

"Would hiding under a rock be an acceptable answer?" he asked.

Michaela smiled. "Now, why would you want to do that when you could come to the aquarium with me?"

That…didn't sound bad. "The aquarium? Well, okay, I do love the aquarium."

"Excellent. Maybe I'll see if there is a fundraising event for it. Next Saturday, though, we'll be attending a fundraiser for Rosie's Place. Have you heard of it?"

"Everyone in Boston has heard of Rosie's Place."

"Good. Then let's see if we can help drive up donations. I'm hoping to chat with some of their leadership, to see if they'd be interested in program support from the Price Foundation above and beyond what will come with our two seats."

"Does anyone ever say no to that?"

"You'd be surprised."

After watching how people had behaved that night, he really wouldn't.

He watched Michaela pecking away at her phone, the first frown on her face since they'd arrived at the hotel earlier. It struck him that while he'd been working on his social skills all night, she'd just been *working*.

"Is that why you went to this thing tonight? To learn more about the Children's Hospital?"

She waved her hand. "Oh, no. That's not where we focus our attention, though it's a very worthy cause. I was there to meet a whole bunch of potential partners who might be interested in working with the Price Foundation on future projects."

Lachlan frowned. "So sick kids don't do it for you?"

Michaela dropped the hand holding her phone into her lap and glared at Lachlan. He barely suppressed the urge to sink further into his seat.

"Don't be a jerk, Lachlan. Of course I'm concerned with children's health and medicine. But we can't give to everything, even if we want to. The Price Foundation has a set mission, and that mission is focused on homeless and LGBT children, particularly where those two groups overlap. And we have learned, over the course of decades of giving, that we can make a greater impact with larger, focused donations. That's how we can create real change, real *safety* for these kids. If we spread ourselves out too much, we end up helping a lot of people a little, and having to cover a ton of administrative overhead instead of creating new centers and adding beds and services to the ones that are already working but struggling to meet the needs of their community. So do not, for one second, presume to tell me there is more I can or should be doing. I'm going to *fucking law school* because I want to be doing more, because I want to ensure the Foundation can persist long after I'm gone, and I won't be made to feel shitty because *you* don't think it's enough."

She snatched her phone from the folds of her skirt and held it in front of her face, her knuckles white around it. The death grip wasn't enough to hide the shake of her hand.

"I'm sorry," he said, painfully aware that he was stupid, not just for saying it, but for not recognizing that she, too, had had a long night. He was also acutely aware of the driver, who could hear them easily from the front seat. "That was uncalled for. I never thought you didn't give enough."

More and more, he thought the opposite—and he didn't mean the money.

She nodded stiffly.

"And despite what I said, I never thought you didn't care. Please, forgive me."

Her shoulders came down from around her ears, but she remained silent and focused on her phone. Now, thanks to him, she *did* look exhausted. The silence between them was nothing like comfortable.

He dug his phone out of his pocket, trying to act like nothing was wrong—for the benefit of the driver, if no one else.

He opened the text messaging application.

I'm an asshole.

He could just barely make out the hum of her phone vibrating over the sound of the tires on the pavement and the purr of the engine.

Her mouth twitched. Once. But she kept doing whatever it was that she was so focused on.

If I promise to never again complain about these stupid parties, will you forgive me?

Another hum. And a blink, lips pursed briefly. There was a slight movement beneath her gown and a stocking-clad toe peeked out. She had apparently slipped off her shoes. He could guess why. His feet were fucking killing him and he wasn't wearing high heels.

He focused back on his phone.

Will you consider forgiving me if I rub your feet?

He waited, watching to see what she would do. He carefully did not smile as she turned toward him, her eyes never leaving

159

her phone, and planted both her feet in his lap, her gown billowing on the seat between them and over his legs.

Slipping a hand beneath her skirt, he skated his palm down her calf and over her heel, then dug his thumb directly into the arch of her foot. Her eyes closed, briefly, then returned to her phone. The pressure around his ribs eased when she smiled, just a little.

He switched feet and juggled his phone with his other hand, typing with his thumb.

Groveling via text while giving a foot massage is really hard work.

The smile transformed, one side lifting to turn it into something closer to a smirk. She shifted one foot a little higher, brushing along the top of his thigh until it was tucked against his hip, her heel an inch from his dick.

He had no idea whether to interpret this as a reward or a threat. He kept rubbing her other foot—it seemed like a safe bet either way.

His phone buzzed.

Poor baby.

Her heel rolled in a long, slow circle, every muscle in his stomach clenching when it brushed over his dick, his erection rising to meet the press of her foot even while he silently prayed they didn't hit a goddamn pothole.

He slid his hand up her other leg, careful to keep his shoulder still and her voluminous skirts piled on his lap. Her knee jerked, just a little, when he traced his fingertips over the sensitive skin behind it.

You're very distracting, she sent.

He'd never know it to look at her, still tapping away at the screen. He stroked back down to the foot perched on his knee.

I'm sorry. Should I stop?

The foot he wasn't holding wriggled until it was pressed the length of his cock, her heel nestled between his legs and against his balls.

160

He was just going to take that as a "no". He massaged his way up and down her leg as best he could, sorely wishing this car hadn't come equipped with a rearview mirror. Her feet flexed when he dug into the tight muscles of her calf, and he kept at it until he could feel them loosen. Then the leg he held slid off his lap, her foot coming to rest on his shoes.

My other foot is sore too.

Lachlan sucked a deep breath as he stared down at his phone, wondering if she really intended to—she rubbed her foot in a long, sinuous glide along his dick—oh hell, that's exactly what she intended to do. He wrapped his hand around her foot and dug his thumb right into the arch, jamming it up against his thickening shaft, the little bone beneath her pinky toe catching up against the crown. It took everything he had not to hunch his shoulders, to curl into the pressure. His hips twitched, his thighs sliding silently over the leather seat as his knees spread.

It was impossible to tell who was working harder to make him crazy. He rubbed and soothed her foot, pressing it against himself, all while she rolled her ankle, slowly, over and over, until he was so hard it hurt. She twisted her leg, just a little, and curled her toes around his dick.

Goddamn, he didn't have a foot fetish, but he was willing to be flexible right now. There was only one thing holding him back.

His hand was shaking hard enough that typing out his message one handed was almost impossible.

If we don't stop, you're going to be the one to explain to Robby why I need another tux.

She grinned down at her phone, the tip of her tongue caught in her teeth as she typed out a response.

Lucky for you, we're home.

He looked up just as the car pulled over and came to a stop in front of Michaela's building. Her foot slid away, and she slipped her shoes back on as her doorman approached.

Lachlan made a point of buttoning his jacket before climbing

161

from the car, turning back quickly to give Michaela his hand while he took long, deep breaths of the cool night air and tried to will his dick into submission.

It didn't work.

He'd been planning to walk home after dropping her off, but didn't hesitate when she kept hold of his hand and towed him through the lobby. The wait for the elevator was interminable, the ride up just as long. He leaned a shoulder against the back wall, facing her, her arm pressed to his chest, their hands still linked. She focused on the floor number display as if her life depended on it, and a flush worked its way across her cheeks and down her neck.

He traced the band of fabric hiding the hickey beneath and strategized where else he might leave his mark.

Her grip on his hand tightened when they slid to a stop, and she was already moving before the doors had opened, practically dragging him out of the elevator and down the hallway to her door.

Not that he was resisting. He had his coat unbuttoned before she had her key out. They practically fell into her apartment it when the door finally swung open.

He caught himself before he stepped on Fang. Barely.

She kicked the door shut and shoved him up against it. "You are a fucking tease."

Which seemed unfair, really, but he didn't give a shit when her mouth was on his, their tongues tangling as he dragged her closer, stroking up her bare back.

He tore his mouth away. "Am I going to need a degree in engineering to get you out of this dress, too?"

She laughed and stepped away, her eyes locked with his as she slid a hand behind her neck, the other low on her back. With two deft flicks of her wrists, her dress pooled on the floor around her ankles.

"Holy shit," he whispered reverently.

She smiled and bit her lip as he ran his gaze over her from

162

head to toe and back again, lingering on the tops of her thigh-high stockings and the corset-bra-thingy that covered her from her hips to chest, but left her back bare for the dress.

He licked his lips, trying to decide where to begin.

Movement at their feet distracted him, his eyes widening when her dress tried to shuffle away.

Michaela giggled and stepped out of her skirts, heels still on.

Lachlan's dick made an honest-to-god bid for freedom through the front of his slacks.

"I'm just going to let Fang out," she said casually, toeing the hem of her dress until the little dog could wriggle his way free. "So we won't be disturbed later."

Then she turned and walked away, leaving him to stare at her almost completely bare ass, the strategically placed strings framing it perfectly and disappearing in the cleft between.

And that. That was just *bold.*

He grinned at her blatant challenge and ripped his coat off, letting it drop to the pile on the floor, then kicked his shoes and socks to a corner before chasing after her into the kitchen. She stood at the glass door to what looked like a roof deck, her body limned in the lights coming in from the city outside. His heart jumped when she turned to look at him over her shoulder, watching as he pulled off his cufflinks and studs, scattering them on the kitchen island all at once, like a game of jacks.

Soft tapping sounds cut through the haze of arousal and they both looked to see Fang bouncing off the glass door in a plea to get inside. Cold air wafted through the kitchen when she opened the door, lifting goosebumps across her chest and over her shoulders.

He wrapped an arm around her waist and pulled her in close. She shivered.

"Cold?"

She kissed him instead of answering. Or maybe that was her answer.

Michaela felt Lachlan's smile as their lips met and their mouths immediately opened to each other. It was messy and hot and left her wondering, who was this man? She'd just spent the night with the professor. The man she had gone on countless walks with, and who seemed so unsure, so confused by some of the most elementary forms of social interaction.

But this man. The one whose broad palm slid up her back, who pressed her close so that she could feel his erection against her hip, he was the man she'd seen at the rink the other night. The man who'd walked her home afterwards and left her panting on the floor of her front hall.

He seemed to have an *excellent* grasp on these baser forms of communication.

She slid her hand into the gap of his shirt, running her fingers through the coarse hair beneath. His skin was warm, and when she pulled back for a second, she could see the flush on his cheeks working down his neck and across his chest. His normally bright green eyes were dark, the color barely discernable in the light coming in through the patio doors.

"Are you sure about this?" he asked, his hoarse voice quiet.

She laughed. "I don't drop my dress in the foyer for just anyone, you know."

"Good," he said, kissing her again, his hand low on her back pulling her in until she could grind against his erection.

She didn't know if he thought it was good that she was sure or because she didn't drop her dress for just anyone, but right now it didn't matter. Both got her what she wanted.

Except for the other night, it had been so long since she'd had this. What felt like eons, now that she'd been reminded of what she'd been missing. She wanted to linger, to taste and touch every part of him, to drive him wild, but she was too far gone, and he was just as primed. The low sounds he made as they writhed up against each other caught in his throat every time her hip pinned his cock back against him.

Her knees shook, her thighs trembling with the desire to wrap around him, but she had other things in mind, too. She shoved her hands between them, tearing at his pants. He gasped, breaking their kiss and pressing his mouth to her shoulder.

"Fuck," he groaned, mouthing the word, and a few kisses besides, up her neck. "I was going to go slow this time. I was going to spread you out on a bed and take my fucking time. Take you apart."

"No. Yes." She whimpered nonsensically, arching her throat against his lips. "I want that. I want you to do that," she babbled. She finally managed to get his pants open without even looking at what she was doing and shoved them down.

They hit the kitchen floor with a thump, weighted down by whatever was in his pockets.

"But I can't wait that long," she admitted, ducking her head to seal her lips to his again, the last words muttered against his lips. "I need you to fuck me. Now."

He gasped into her mouth, his hands scrambling at her waist. Eventually he dug his fingers into her strapless, backless bra and growled.

"Why are you always wearing such complicated clothing?"

She half laughed, half groaned. Next time she was alone with him, she'd be tempted to wear a t-shirt and her rattiest old yoga pants. Clothes she hadn't dared wear outside the house in years. But Lachlan didn't care what she wore. What she looked like. That wasn't why they were friends.

He gave up on her clothes and pressed his hands along her jaw, tilting her head to deepen his kiss. She sank into it, giving herself up to the pulse pounding in her chest and her ears and her clit. Wallowing in the complete absence of *nerves*. Not since...well, the douchebag—who she refused to think about tonight—had it been like this. So *easy*.

The open edges of his shirt brushed against her breasts, teasing sensitive skin and catching on the lace, and she wanted the damn body armor off as much as he did. She arched her back, crushing her breasts against his chest as she thrust her hands behind her. He drew his lips down, licking and sucking down her neck and to the tops of her breasts, his big hands spanning her waist. She managed to get the first hook undone and from there it was easy.

The moment her bra hit the floor, he drew one nipple into the wet heat of his mouth. She cried out, carding her fingers into his hair and cupping the back of his head, holding him close. He wasn't gentle, sucking hard on one nipple, then kissing a path to the other. The sensations combined with the rush of cool relief racing over her skin from being freed from the stays that had been digging into her all night, allowing her to take a desperately needed deep, deep breath. Her head spun.

He bit down and she wavered dangerously on her heels, the spike of pleasure running right down her belly to her clit. God, she ached. She wanted something in her. She wanted *him* in her.

Now.

She curled her hand around his cock, but couldn't get a good grip with the way he was bent over lavishing attention on her breasts, even with how it was pushing hard against the front of his briefs.

Goddamn, sometime they were *really* going to have to do this when they could lie down and take their time.

She ran her fingers along his shaft, already intimately familiar with the length and breadth of it from their adventure in Robby's dressing room, and the car earlier tonight. He was thick, enough to be heavy on her tongue. Thicker than Mr. Big in the box beneath her bed. And almost as long.

And while he didn't vibrate, he pushed into her hand and groaned and grabbed her hips so hard he might leave bruises. And that was better.

He also kissed. And goddamn, she'd forgotten how much she loved to kiss and be kissed. How could she have forgotten that?

In answer, the tiny part of her brain not currently completely focused on shouting "fuck him now!" gave a meek cry of "self-preservation".

Mr. Big may have been lacking in many departments, but she trusted him. And that was another thing he and Lachlan had in common. She trusted him. Completely. And who knew when she would have that again?

She staggered back, forcing Lachlan to release her nipple with an obscene and almost painful pop. Her body throbbed in response.

"Come here," she said in a low voice, tugging the hand he held out for her to draw him across the kitchen. He hesitated only long enough to dig something from the pocket of his slacks on the floor, then followed.

She was fascinated by the remarkably tight and tiny briefs clinging to his hips and doing battle with his cock. Robby had scolded him not to wear boxers or even boxer briefs and risk ruining the line of his beautifully tailored tuxedo. Lachlan had apparently listened. She'd always thought she wasn't that into tight little underwear on men. For the life of her, she couldn't imagine why she'd ever been that stupid.

She was startled when her ass bumped into her table. She leaned there, panting.

"We're not going to make it to a bed this time either, are we?" he asked, almost regretfully. His eyes were fixed on the junction of her thighs.

She shook her head. "I don't think I can make it that far," she admitted.

He met her eyes and smiled. "Shame," he murmured, only his expression said something else entirely. He looked downright predatory, and she shivered in response.

Seriously, *who was this guy?* How could her slightly preppy, completely nerdy professor be so fucking hot?

She watched, mesmerized, as he reached out and tucked whatever he was holding on the table behind her, then hooked his fingers into her G-string at both hips. She'd had little choice in what gown to wear that evening, needing to cover the evidence of their first encounter, but the underwear she'd shamelessly selected with just this in mind.

He slowly peeled her panties down and helped her step out of them. He didn't stand then, as she'd expected, but dropped his knees to the floor and smiled up at her.

"Up," he said, his hands rubbing back up over her stockings to curl around her thighs.

"Up?" she asked, her brain shorting out as he licked his lips.

His fingers dug into her skin, just enough to nudge her back, her ass tilting from leaning-against to perching-on the table. The moment her weight shifted, he drew one of her legs up and draped it over his shoulder, his breath hot on her inner thigh. Then his lips were there. His tongue, swirling over the sensitive skin before sucking it between his teeth.

"Oh," she breathed, planting her hands on the table behind her, unable to look away from his gaze as he released her freshly-bruised skin and edged closer. She spread her legs until the other foot left the floor and she hung, suspended, above him. He clamped a hand around her thigh and pushed it farther up and out.

A helpless thrill raced up her spine at being so exposed. She'd never felt more helpless and *eager* in her life. Maybe she should have been embarrassed. Some part of her wanted to put a hand over her pussy, laid bare before him. She could see how her clit poked out, swollen and begging for attention. How her thighs glistened in the low light, her arousal slicking her skin even before she'd spread herself open for him.

But there was nothing embarrassing about the way he studied her, his eyelids heavy, lips a little swollen from their kisses. He glanced up, checking her face once more for who knew what, then slid his tongue right over her clit and sucked it in. Hard.

She almost fell off the table, her fingernails skittering over the cold wood behind her, searching for purchase as her back bowed into the pressure.

"Oh, Jesus," she gasped, shoving herself against his face. Some part of her made a bid for shame, the same part that had held her head high and refused to be cowed in public for the past decade screeching that this wasn't safe, this wasn't good form, but she squashed it ruthlessly.

There was no place for that with him. She didn't have to worry what he thought. Not because it didn't matter. Because she was sure, from the look on his face and the clutch of his fingers and the intimate hum he pressed directly to her clitoris, making it buzz and her gasp, that he wasn't judging her. Certainly not poorly, in any case.

As if reading her mind, his eyes flicked up to her face, and she could read his smile in his eyes almost as well as she could feel it against her clit.

It was the hottest thing she'd ever fucking seen.

He released her with a final, shockingly hard suck that made her hips buck hard enough that she would have fallen right off the table if it weren't for his long fingers clamped around her thighs. Then he thrust the point of his tongue under the hood of her clit, flicking it quickly, fiercely, over and over.

Her eyes fell closed and she groaned, not bothering to even attempt to hold still. "Yes, like that," she panted. "Fuck, I'm going to come."

He hummed again, and she took that as encouragement as he drove her higher, relentless. She couldn't stop the high, keening sounds from escaping her throat, her head falling back as the tension coiled tighter and hotter.

"Please, *please*," she pleaded, and maybe it was to god, since it wasn't like Lachlan needed any encouragement.

He listened, though, sinking two fingers into her pussy.

She fluttered around them, surprised by their penetration. The second thrust, though, was enough. She clamped down hard and came.

"Lachlan!" she shouted, her hips snapping forward to force herself onto his hand and against his tongue. He shoved back, holding her steady, riding out the uncontrollable movement of her hips, gasping against her when her foot struck his back and dug in.

He didn't let her fall, not off the table or down from her climax, his tongue keeping the powerful ripples going until she jerked away, taking one hand from the table to shove into his hair and force his mouth from her oversensitive clit.

He was panting as hard as she was, his lips shiny, his cheeks flushed a hectic red.

"Can you do that again?" he asked, wiping his mouth against his own shoulder and leaving behind the gleaming evidence of what they'd just done.

She had to take several deep breaths to get enough brain function to parse the words.

"What? Orgasm?"

His nod was little more than a quick jerk of his head. She looked down to see he had the heel of his hand pressed to his dick hard enough that it had to hurt.

"I...yes? Sometimes. I think. I mean. Yes. Now, yes." She gave up trying to make any sense and went for clarity. "*Hurry.*"

That seemed to work, given the way he slid her legs back to the floor, thoughtful enough to hesitate before letting go, making sure she could actually support her own weight. It was a near thing, god's truth.

Then he stood and shoved his briefs to the floor.

Yes, finally! She reached out to curl her hand around his cock, tugging him closer, tipping her chin up.

His hand slid around her neck and into her hair, his lips hot and possessive on hers as she ran her fist over his shaft, squeezing over the head before traveling down again. He stepped closer, until there wasn't room for her arm between them, his cock dragging up over her belly, leaving a sticky trail.

The kiss turned filthy, his tongue touching every corner of her mouth, her hair coming unpinned and tangling around his fingers. She licked her own taste from his mouth, his lips, and

170

wrapped her legs around his hips, whining with frustration when it became clear he was too tall for her to get what she wanted with her on the table like this.

He apparently agreed. He wrapped his hands around her ankles and pried himself loose. She reached for him, but he yanked over one of her chairs and collapsed into it before she could grab hold.

With a crooked smile, he watched her face as he reached behind her for the little foil packet he'd apparently been keeping close at hand, tore it open, and rolled it on. His cock stood tall and proud when he was done.

He arched an eyebrow and she laughed. "Fucking Boy Scout," she murmured, climbing unsteadily to her feet between his spread knees, her lower lip caught between her teeth.

Well, she'd looked forward to being back in the saddle again, she just hadn't expected to be the one literally doing the riding when they got to this.

Not that she was complaining.

She put a hand on his shoulder to steady herself, but he stopped her. She frowned curiously as he slowly turned her around.

"Like this," he said, his lips pressed to the small of her back.

"I don't..." she began, the words caught in her throat as he brought his knees together and encouraged her to straddle them. "Trust me," he said, his voice dark, his lips coasting up her spine.

She let him guide her, pressing a hand to the table for support as he helped her to sit in his lap, his cock running between her legs and along her folds.

She rolled her hips and hummed happily.

"Christ," he gasped. "You keep doing that and this will be over quickly."

"No," she said. She didn't want that. She wanted all that heat and girth and *promise* to be *in her*.

She reached between her legs, lifting a little and wrapping her hands around his shaft. His hands clenched her waist, holding her up, then holding her steady as she sank down again, this time taking him into her body.

She groaned at the long, slow stretch, how he filled her up, split her open. Her legs trembled, torn between making this last forever or letting herself fall and feeling him lodged deep inside her. His low, desperate moan vibrated through her, the sound cut off when her weight finally, *finally* rested fully on his thighs and she ground against him.

"Fuck. Fuck, god. Look at you." His hands ran over her hips and ass, then up her ribs and around, pulling her back against his chest.

Her head fell back onto his shoulder and she rolled her hips continuously. He thrust up against her and matched her gyrations, keeping himself deep while his cock did unspeakable things inside her.

"Does that feel good?" he asked over her shoulder, like the proverbial devil. Fortunately, there was no angel to balance it.

"God, yes," she gasped, shuddering at how his cock rubbed her just right inside, sending bright jolts of pleasure deep into her core.

She cried out when his fingers strummed over her clit, her hips losing their steady circles in favor of jerking helplessly. His other hand cupped her breast.

"Hold on," he murmured and she did, reaching down and back to cling to his hips, anticipation making her dizzy.

She moaned, low and shameless, as he slid lower in the chair and spread his knees, hers hooked over top, spreading with them wide. She tipped forward, her hair in her face, forced to release her hold on him to wrap her fingers around the edge of the table. She squeezed her eyes shut and whined low in her throat as his cock nudged deeper, as far as he could go, jolting against something that maybe hurt, but maybe felt fucking amazing.

She had no idea how long she hung like that, gasping and writhing on his lap, before she realized her feet were still able to touch the floor. She wondered, vaguely, if he'd known all along that her heels would give her control.

"*Yes,*" he groaned when she lifted up, and she heard the absolute relief in his voice, the sound cut short when she dropped back down again. The shock of their bodies striking fired an explosion of pleasure through her entire body, electrified jolts that reached her fingers and toes.

His hands slid over her ribs, damp with sweat now, trying to help and find purchase. She could feel how they shook. She shifted her weight forward, using the table as leverage as he pushed her down onto his cock, his hips twitching up rhythmically, each thud of skin on skin like a low bass drum of desire.

Her thighs screamed at the workout they were getting—in heels, no less—but that was nothing compared to the litany of swears and praise streaming from Lachlan's mouth. He told her she was beautiful, that he'd wanted to fuck her the moment he'd seen her, that he loved her quick mind and remarkably firm ass.

She laughed, joyous, and took her pleasure as he encouraged her to do exactly that. He'd given up on helping her move, focusing instead on getting her off. One arm curled around her hip, his hand dipping low and attacking her clit.

A noise tore from her throat, inarticulate for all that it was clearly begging.

"God, you like that," he grunted, satisfaction clear even through his labored breathing. "I want you to come," he told her. Demanded. "I want to feel you squeezing around my cock."

She moaned, shivers running down her spine at his words.

"I wish I could get my fingers in there, too," he growled and she whimpered, because she wanted that. She wanted him to stuff her full and take her apart like that.

His other hand slid between their bodies, tracing through her folds and around his cock. Then it was gone.

She whimpered when his slick fingers ran along the valley of her ass.

"I bet I could feel it here," he muttered hoarsely, tapping a finger against the thin skin and nerve endings bunched around the entrance to her ass. "I bet you'd squeeze my fingers so tight in here."

She nodded, not even sure what she was trying to say, but knowing that she wanted it. His words lit her up, making the hair on the back of her neck stand on end, her skin tingling as she ground against him.

He wedged the tip of one finger into her ass and she keened.

"Come on, baby," he urged, his voice ragged. "I need you to come. I'm going to fucking die if you don't come soon," he groaned, shoving his hips up harder to meet her, pushing his finger in farther in the process.

She sat back and ground down on his finger, the angle stretching her tight hole open while his cock thrust and rubbed and his other finger flicked over her clit. She rode it, rode all the sensations storming her body, letting them swell up, fill her limbs and her head, until they washed over her in a mighty rush.

Her climax poured through her, tearing a scream from her lips as his hips jabbed up against her, bouncing her on his cock and his fingers, drawing out the waves of pleasure until he jerked against her, his hips arched, and roared.

He was still twitching, the desperate clasp of his hands on her hips—she hadn't even noticed him pulling them from her body—holding her steady as she came back to her senses, her mouth open wide to suck as much air into her lungs as possible.

Wow.

She collapsed forward, her head hanging between her arms. She stared at the pins caught in the tangled hair hanging about her face and huffed out a laugh. She was a wreck.

He carefully eased her up and off of his cock, pulling his legs together so she could perch on his thighs while he addressed the condom behind her. She was still far too blissed out to move, let alone offer any kind of help.

Easing her to the side, he curled an arm around her ribs and another beneath her knees. She smiled and put her head on his shoulder when he stood with her in his arms.

There couldn't be that many philosophy professors in the world who could do this, she thought vaguely, pressing her face into his flushed, damp neck and savoring the smell of sweat and skin. Still no cologne, even for a night out on the town.

She smiled and decided she would never like those artificial scents again.

"Bedroom?" he asked.

"Little late for that, isn't it?" she murmured and pointed down the hallway.

He laughed softly into the disaster that was her hair.

"How are you even standing right now?" she asked in awe.

He put her down on her bed gently. "Sheer stubborn will," he assured her, pressing his lips to her forehead, then to the tip of her nose. Finally, her lips.

The kiss was slow. Languorous. And far too short.

Still, she didn't protest when he pushed her back onto the bed, then pulled off her shoes and stockings. She maybe even helped a little when he pulled down the covers and urged her to crawl beneath.

He kissed her again. "You okay?" he asked softly.

She smiled. "I'm *great.*"

She fell asleep to the sound of his quiet laughter and the press of his lips to her cheek.

Chapter Fifteen

Michaela crept into the library, looking up each row of stacks as she slowly made her way to the back corner study room Sadie had reserved for their group.

She didn't see any sign of Tanner's idiot friends. In fact, she didn't see much of anyone. She wondered if Sadie had known this place would be deserted at this hour on a Monday morning, and that was why she'd chosen it.

It was a nice thought, somehow.

She saw Eric go into the study room and slipped in behind him.

"Good morning," she said, and he jumped a foot in the air.

"Holy crap, we should put a bell on you."

"God, can you imagine what would happen *then*?" she shot back sarcastically before realizing that maybe he wouldn't find it funny. It wasn't like a quiet guy like him was ever going to appreciate all the extra attention hanging around someone like her would bring.

He surprised her, though, when he smiled shyly. "Guess that's not a great idea for you, huh?"

"Ah, no. But I'd take an invisibility cloak any day."

Eric gave her a funny look, then turned to set out his stuff on the table. Michaela sighed. *Way to make it awkward again, Michaela,* she chided herself, then swore silently that she'd just shut up for the rest of this meeting and see how it went.

She'd promised Lachlan she'd go into it expecting to stick it out, but it was hard not to think about how much easier, how much more painless, it would be if she just walked.

Tanner came in next and tried to smile. It looked painful. Michaela just nodded and returned to organizing the abstracts she'd prepared for her assigned readings.

"Look, I'm sorry about the other day."

Her head snapped up and she stared at Tanner. Jesus Christ,

were they going to *talk about this?* A glance at Eric told her he'd rather they didn't either.

"It's fine," she said woodenly, when it became apparent Tanner was waiting for some response.

"No, it wasn't cool. I didn't think when I told them that they'd do that. It was total asshole behavior. I can make them apologize if you want."

Michaela's eyes widened in alarm. "No! Please, no, that's not necessary."

And maybe she'd been too forceful, because Tanner winced and now looked even more pained. "Okay. Sorry. I didn't mean—"

"No, it's okay. I just don't want...that."

"Right," Tanner said crossly.

Michaela looked at Eric desperately for help, but he was sunken into his chair, silent and miserable looking.

She looked back at Tanner, who was also slumped in his chair, not looking at her. "I appreciate the offer," she said, sincerely. Because she did. People rarely saw the need for anyone to apologize for the shit they did around her.

"I won't tell them when we're meeting anymore," Tanner said.

Which was a probably a good idea, but Michaela still felt guilty. "I don't want to put you in a position where you feel like you have to lie."

Sadie came into the room then and paused. "Who's lying?"

"No one," Tanner muttered. "We're just establishing some ground rules, I guess."

Michaela's heart sank. "If you'd rather, I can go," she said softly. It really would be easier for all of them, except that there were *so many goddamn readings*.

"No," Tanner said firmly. "It was my fault, anyway." He turned to Sadie. "You ready? I think we should just get to work."

Sadie nodded slowly and sat at the table, taking the time to look at each of them before pulling out her laptop and papers.

From there it got a little easier, though Tanner was still stiff, Sadie still studied them all curiously, and Eric remained mostly silent. They exchanged the abstracts they'd each been assigned, and reviewed them together, the atmosphere gradually easing as it became clear that while their lives might be very different, when it came to their coursework they were all pretty much in the same boat.

Even better, where one of them had a question, usually at least one or two of the others could fill in the blanks. It was such a huge fucking relief that Michaela found herself smiling and then arguing right along with the others. When Eric admitted he could imitate Professor Monroe, they badgered him into giving a performance that left them all breathless with laughter.

She didn't think of bowing out when they made plans to meet a couple times over the next week. They all agreed that it would benefit everyone if they went back and did the abstracts for the readings that had been assigned before they'd formed this group, which meant more work in the short-term, but hopefully less when it came time to study for their exams later in the semester.

It wasn't until they'd packed up and opened the door to leave their room that Michaela remembered all the reasons this was still not a good idea. A half dozen students were waiting for the room, and as Michaela and the others filed out, everyone went silent, elbows nudging neighbors' ribs and mouths dropping open as they passed.

Based on the looks on her study group's faces, they hadn't enjoyed the reminder of what it meant to have Michaela in their midst any more than she had.

Lachlan *hated* talking on the phone. As a rule he ignored his cell phone, often leaving it on silent and then listening to the voicemails later. Though he also hated voicemail, so it wasn't like people expected that to get him to call them back either.

He was still tempted to let it ring through when he saw his phone vibrating on his desk. The only reason he answered was because it was Callum, and he'd already left two messages in the past three days alone.

He immediately regretted not *listening* to those messages when his brother's voice boomed over the phone.

"So, what's this I hear about you dating my best friend?" Callum said, trying to sound stern. He was undermined, somewhat, by Rupert laughing in the background and telling his husband to be nice.

"What?" Lachlan said, his brain jumping to an image of Michaela draped over his lap, destroying him with her uninhibited enthusiasm.

"I hear you and Michaela are getting *awfully* close."

Callum had *no* idea.

Lachlan worried, suddenly, if he should have been keeping better track of the gossip blogs. "Who the hell did you hear that from?"

"Mom."

"*Mom?*"

"Who heard it from Savannah."

"Ugh." Lachlan dropped his forehead onto his desk.

"Who assured me, when I called her, that it was all true. Something about Michaela watching your hockey games and dragging you out to fancy-schmancy parties?"

"*Fancy-schmancy*—really? Weren't you the one who used to go to all those parties with her?"

"Yes, I was. And we were *dating.*"

"No, you were not. You were *pretending* to date." Which, actually, wasn't the point. "And we're not," he clarified.

"Pretending to date?"

"Right."

"So, you're dating for real?"

179

Lachlan was more than a little alarmed by how hopeful Callum sounded. Lachlan knew he was the last person on earth who Michaela should date. Or who should date Michaela. His brother was clearly deluded.

"No," Lachlan said firmly.

"So, let me get this straight. You're not pretending to date, and you're not dating for real, but you are going on dates. How does that work, exactly?"

We hang out and have a lot of fantastic sex.

Yeah, no, he'd just keep that to himself. Unless he *wanted* Callum to drive down to Boston and punch him in the face.

"We're friends," he said instead.

"Well, that's good. God knows she could use a few more of those," Callum said, sounding a little sad.

"She's doing okay here, Cal."

"Is she?"

"Yes. She's even connected with an old friend from school. I think they're planning to have lunch next week."

"Yeah? That's good. She doesn't have a lot of friends from before."

"Well, in this case, she hadn't realized he was someone who would have stood by her all along."

"*He?*" Lachlan grinned at the suspicion in his brother's voice.

"Down, boy. Robby was way more into flirting with me than hitting on Michaela."

"Oh, ha. That's okay then."

"And it wouldn't have been okay if it was a man who might be interested in dating her?"

Callum sighed. "I don't know. I worry. She didn't fake-date me just for fun, you know?"

"So, why did she?" Lachlan asked, wondering if Callum would answer. Lachlan knew that Callum had been content to pretend to date his best friend in order to stay firmly in the closet. But he'd never understood Michaela's motivations. And

180

Callum had refused to explain it to anyone in the family when they'd asked.

"The press likes to talk about how she can't keep a man. It's ridiculous. And infuriating," Callum said, voice dark.

Lachlan agreed, but it didn't really answer the question. "And so she thought she could keep you?"

"What? No. Nothing like that. It was just to get the press off her ass for a while. She'd dated a few men since, you know, the whole sex-tape thing, and just like for most people dating at that age, it didn't work out for various reasons. Only, instead of getting to be a normal person who can walk away and be done with it, she'd get hit with articles about how *sources close to him* had told reporters every little thing she'd done and a bunch of shit she hadn't."

"Jesus Christ."

"Right. She's under a lot of pressure. A lot of eyes are on her. So, when it comes to the men in her life, I worry. A lot."

"I don't blame you. I have no idea how you went to all those functions with her and didn't end up punching someone in the face. If it wasn't for Seamus, I'm not sure I would have made it through even one night. I'm probably screwed next week."

"You're going out on *another* non-date next week?"

"No. Yes. Stop," he said with a sigh. "It's not a date. It's more like...a class."

"A class," Callum repeated flatly.

"Right. She's trying to help me get over my issues. You know, with talking to women and stuff," he mumbled.

"Of course she is," Callum said.

"What does that mean?"

"Nothing. It's not important. What matters is that you two are having fun. I'm glad you've become *friends.*"

Lachlan felt like there was another whole conversation happening that he wasn't getting, but he let it be. "Thanks. I think."

Callum laughed. "If it helps, now I'm going to worry less. I'm glad you're there for her."

"Yeah. I mean, I'll try."

Lachlan really didn't know what else to say. Or what else Callum might want him to do, other than be Michaela's friend. He was reasonably certain, though, that Callum wouldn't appreciate *all* Lachlan was doing for—and to—Michaela these days.

He closed his eyes and saw, for the thousandth time at least, her dress dropping to the floor and her gorgeous ass as she walked away, bold as you please.

Lachlan was getting another erection, sitting at his desk at work while speaking to his brother on the phone. And that was just *wrong.* It was definitely time to change the subject. And while Lachlan might not be the most adept conversationalist, he knew how to derail his brother.

"So, how are the boys?"

It turned out Michaela's trick of just listening and making appropriate noises of interest worked as well on his brother as it did on the doyens of society. Then he'd only had to mention that he was due to meet Michaela and take her with him to his hockey game for his brother to cut him loose.

Lachlan had to run to get home to grab his gear, and found Michaela was waiting on his front porch. One of his neighbors was standing on her own porch, two doors down, gawping.

He waved and she didn't even blink, like he was invisible. Honestly, what was *wrong* with people?

"I'm sorry I'm late," he said to Michaela as he leapt up the stairs two at a time.

Michaela got out of the way of the door, waiting until he was working at the lock before whispering, "And here I was hoping we'd have time to warm you up before heading over to the rink."

He promptly dropped his keys, letting out a hoarse chuckle as he bent to retrieve them. "You're making me want to miss my game," he grumbled.

"You wouldn't."

182

He smiled. "You're right. I wouldn't. But you make me wish I would."

Her smile was more than ample reward for his honesty. He opened his door and reached for the bag just inside. They were in his car and on the way to the rink before he finally got up the courage to ask her what he'd been wondering about since she'd more or less propositioned him in his porch.

"Would you be okay having sex at my house?"

Michaela looked over at him curiously. "That's a strange question. And I think we both know the answer."

"Well, yes. Now, I mean. But I just figured, with what happened..." He shrugged. "I'd understand if you wanted to restrict our more intimate meetings to places where you could be sure you weren't being filmed."

Michaela's smile turned softer. It made Lachlan's stomach do funny things. "I don't get why you think you're not good with people. You're one of the most perceptive people I've ever met."

Lachlan focused on the road. "That doesn't say much about the people you've met."

"Maybe," Michaela agreed with a laugh. "But you're right. I don't, usually, take any risks."

"But with me you would?"

"I don't see it as a risk. I trust you."

Lachlan had thought his stomach was doing funny things *before*, now it practically flipped over.

"Thanks," he said. "I mean, it's mutual, for what it's worth. But I get that it's a bigger deal for you. So, thanks."

Michaela didn't say anything, but she slid her hand over his knee and left it there. They were lucky he didn't drive right off a bridge and into the Charles River. He put his hand over hers, if for no other reason than because if she moved a few inches higher, stripping down in the locker room would be awkward, to say the least, and putting on his jock impossible.

Also, it was kind of nice. He'd never really done this sort of thing with a friend before.

He took off to get changed as soon as they arrived, mindful that he needed to check in with the refs about some administrative stuff beforehand. He felt bad leaving her in the stands, sitting alone, knowing his sister and Rhian were in Anaheim. It wasn't until he was lining up for the first face-off that he saw Garrick sitting next to her, both of them laughing over something on Garrick's phone.

Lachlan turned to face his opponent and forgot about anything but the game.

Two hours later he was a sweaty mess, in desperate need of a shower and glowing with the satisfaction of another victory. He hung around on the ice with their latest recruit for a while, talking to him about his backcheck until the new guy's girlfriend was shouting that they had to go and how he didn't have time to shower and would stink up her car.

Lachlan chuckled and made his way to the locker room. Everyone else was heading out, saying goodnight as they went. He took a quick shower and threw on his clothes. He'd almost made it back out to the stands to find Michaela when a delicate, familiar hand reached out of the almost-closed trainer's room door and yanked him inside.

He was kissing Michaela before he knew what had hit him, which was his only excuse for taking a few seconds to get with the program and drop his gear bag onto the floor. He pulled her close then walked her backwards until her shoulders hit the door and he could reach the knob to lock it. Once secured, he relaxed into the kiss, not coming up for air until his lungs screamed at him that there was no other choice.

"What was that for?" he asked, breathing like he'd just come off the ice after a hard shift.

"Watching you play hockey makes me hot."

He let out an embarrassingly breathless laugh. "Remind me to email you the rest of the schedule for this season."

"You do that," she said in a low voice before kissing him again.

184

The adrenaline of the game was still pumping through his veins, making him lightheaded *before* all the blood in his head raced south, filling his cock so fast it ached with every brush of her body. He ran his hands down her sides and cupped them around her ass. He barely had to lift before she was hitching her legs up around his waist.

The first slow roll of his erection against the apex of her thighs made them both moan.

"Are we *ever* going to make it to a bed?" he gasped, dragging his lips over her cheek and down her arched neck.

She chuckled, as breathless as he. "God, we can't here, though."

"But you want to," he said, because he was beginning to figure out a few things about Michaela.

She moaned and didn't deny it.

"Just like you liked sucking me off in Robby's changing room," he said, lifting his head to study her face.

She nodded, her eyes closed as if concentrating on the continuous grind of their hips.

"And rubbing my dick in the back of the car," he added.

Her little smile slipped a little, her expression serious when she opened her eyes to look at him. "I'm not an exhibitionist."

"No, you're not," he agreed. "But you do like having sex in public places—just not *in public.*"

"How did you—"

He rocked against her, wedging the hard seam of his fly against them both until they were panting.

"There are no cameras in here," he promised.

She licked her lips, her eyes dilating. "Are you sure?"

"Absolutely certain. This is considered a medical space. No windows. No cameras ever."

Her fingers curled in his hair, tugging it as she wriggled against him. He had to kiss her again, his tongue darting into her mouth as she writhed, her back sliding along the door.

185

She needed to decide, and soon. As it was, he wouldn't be able to walk out of this room for a good five minutes if they stopped right now.

He had another thought and pulled back. "How complicated is your clothing today?"

She laughed. "I've learned my lesson. What are the chances you have a condom?"

"I *was* a Boy Scout," he assured her seriously.

She dropped her feet to the floor and he caught her hips, steadying her while he tried to figure out what her next play would be. He grinned when she kicked her shoes off, his eyes going wide as she stripped the tight black things he thought his sister called leggings down and off, a scrap of bright scarlet satin gone with them. Her long shirt brushed her thighs.

"Holy shit, did you just..."

She grinned, clearly quite pleased with herself. And goddamn, he was pretty fucking pleased with her, too, laughing as she attacked the front of his khakis. He scrambled to get his wallet out of his back pocket before his pants, and his underwear, were shoved down around his thighs. The cold air on his hot skin and hard cock made him shudder, but he managed to extract the condom without dropping it.

His wallet, on the other hand, fell from nerveless fingers when she wrapped her cool hand around his shaft and tugged. She plucked the condom from him and tore it open with her perfectly straight, white teeth.

No one would ever know how he whimpered when she rolled it down onto his cock. No one but Michaela and she still looked delighted.

"Ready?" she asked.

He blinked, his heart pounding against his ribs, which were still sore from the game. He was almost dizzy from the rush of endorphins mixing with lingering adrenaline, and for once, he had no words. And he really didn't need them.

Their mouths crashed together and he dug his fingers into

the meat of her thighs, barely lifting as she jumped to wrap her legs around his waist again. She yanked his shirt up before hooking that arm around his neck. Her other hand stayed clenched around his cock, wedged between their bodies as her shoulders, then her hips, hit the door.

He felt it the moment they were lined up, felt how wet she was already, and pushed forward. She pulled her arm out of the way and clung to his shoulder while he sank into her tight, wet heat.

She tore her mouth away and tipped her head back, moaning, "Oh, fuck. *Lachlan.*"

He grunted, his face pressed against her neck, shocks of electricity racing over his body as she twitched and rippled around him, adjusting to his girth.

His hips were moving before she'd taken her next breath. *He* wasn't breathing at all. Every ounce of his attention was honed down to his cock shuttling in and out of her body, the grip of his hands on her firm ass. He tilted her, jabbing forward and the new angle made her cry out with every sharp thrust.

"Fuck, harder," she cried.

Their bodies thumped together, hers pinned to the door as his hips worked frantically. A ball of fire was growing at the base of his spine, tightening all his muscles until the need for release clawed at him. He wanted to come so badly it *hurt.*

His options for getting her there, though, were seriously limited by the fact that his hands were decidedly full. But there was something she seemed to like. As much or more than sex in public places, or having her ass played with.

He couldn't reach her nipples. Or her clit. But maybe...

He thrust forward and stayed there, grinding against her clit with his pelvic bone. Then he pinched her ass, *hard.*

She bucked against him, almost managing to force him back a step before he slammed them back into the door and pinched her again.

She sobbed and yanked his hair. "Fuck, yes. That's. That

hurts."

And that was most certainly *not* a complaint.

His knees very nearly gave out as what little blood remaining rushed from his head. He fucked her again, and again, and pinched her ass as best he could, anywhere he could reach. When he was sure he would die—or worse, *come*—before she reached her climax, she curled her arms around his neck and pressed her face against her arm, muffling her increasingly loud cries.

On his next thrust, she clamped down around him, her legs like a vise around his hips, holding him there as she sobbed out his name.

He didn't have to think. Or move. Or do *anything* but hold on for dear life as his orgasm crashed over him. His hands slipped across her damp skin as they shook against one another. He pinned her as hard as he could against the door, locked his knees, and pressed his forehead against the door, gasping against her shoulder as his cock pulsed inside her, the heat of his own come filling the condom another shock to his overwrought system.

Way too much adrenaline.

As the last waves ebbed, they wobbled precariously. Michaela dug her fingers into his shoulders and tried to uncurl her legs. The issue was, of course, she was still impaled and couldn't go anywhere without his cooperation.

With a deep, shuddering breath, he eased back and she dropped her feet to the floor far more gracefully than anything he could have pulled off at that point. She wrapped her arms around his waist and he clung to her, trying to catch his breath.

"You okay?" she asked with concern.

"I think you broke me," he moaned with a hoarse chuckle. All joking aside, though, his heart was going *way* too fast.

She laughed and pushed him back. He was surprised his legs would hold him, but submitted to the indignity of letting her dispose of the condom—he only groaned a little, so that was an accomplishment—and pull his clothes back into place.

He didn't snap out of it until she'd pressed his wallet back into his palm and bent to pull her clothes back on. Thirty seconds later they were almost presentable for the public, except Lachlan still felt lightheaded, the edges of his vision alarmingly grey.

He leaned his back to the wall and took a deep breath.

"Are you sure you're okay?"

He grimaced. "Maybe you better get me a Gatorade from my bag."

She did. Quickly. He drank the entire thing in one go as she watched, nervously biting her lip.

He sighed when it was gone, hooking an arm around her waist and pulling her closer. She leaned into him, her head on his chest, and for a few minutes they just stood there while he slowly regained his equilibrium.

It was the closest they'd ever come to post-coital cuddling, which was just sad, since they were *standing up*. It felt good, though. Maybe better than it should, he thought with a frown, since really, they were just friends. Cuddling probably wasn't supposed to be part of the deal.

"This is nice," she murmured.

He smiled against her silky hair, glad, at least, that he wasn't the only one feeling it. And hey, there was no reason they couldn't make their own rules about how they did this, right?

To prove the point, he tugged her closer and pressed a kiss to the top of her head. He hoped she understood that as his answer.

Chapter Sixteen

The New England Aquarium was not nearly as opulent as the ballrooms and homes in which fundraisers often took place, and it was a hell of a lot dimmer, most of the light coming from the tanks and the low-glowing fixtures that wouldn't shine too brightly for the animals. This restriction also meant that no flash photography would be allowed, which was a welcome relief, since it was too dim for photographs to capture anything without the added light.

For these reasons alone, Michaela thought this event was pretty fantastic. She smiled down at the penguins splashing in their pools below the walkways, charmed by their antics as they slipped and slid around and over the rocks. When she looked up, she watched in awe as a shark swam by in the huge central tank, the main attraction of the cleverly designed space.

The very best part of the night so far, though, was that Lachlan clearly *loved* this place.

"Did you see the electric eel, yet?" he asked, tugging her hand to pull her to another tank.

She jumped when there was a loud zap, then laughed as Lachlan explained the meter beside the tank and how it worked.

He was like a kid in a candy factory. It was kind of fucking adorable.

He looked as dark and handsome in his tuxedo as he had the previous weekend, but somehow even better. To her, anyway. But maybe that was because every time she closed her eyes, she could still see him propped against the wall in the trainer's office at the rink, holding her close while his still-drying hair stood on end and his long, hard body cushioned hers.

Tonight, they'd not only survived their arrival and a round of introductions without incident, but it had been something of a success. She'd made him practice saying his own name, much to his chagrin, over and over on the car ride here. Then she'd had him repeat, "It's a pleasure to meet you," a few dozen times, ignoring how he rolled his eyes at her the entire time.

He wasn't rolling his eyes when he'd deployed his new skills on the way in. He'd made it all the way through several dozen couples without a single hiccough, even when one of the wives took the liberty of drawing her hand down his chest the moment her husband looked away.

Though, his scowl hadn't exactly been subtle. Safe to say that woman wouldn't try hitting on him again tonight. Not where anyone could see his reaction, anyway. Then again, she probably hadn't missed Michaela's fierce frown either.

Seriously, people were shameless.

She cast her eye around the gathering, trying to find the people she needed to speak with while still paying attention to her private tour guide. She jumped when a hard body slammed into her and Lachlan, hugging them both.

Speaking of shameless...

"Princess, aren't you a sight for sore eyes tonight," Robby cried gleefully, drawing a lot of attention, as was his wont. He stepped back and grinned at them both. "And Dr. Morrison. It's lovely to see you again."

Lachlan steadied Michaela with a hand on her back. "Mr. Wigglesworth," he said formally, his attempt at dignity belied by the twinkle in his eye. "I do believe that was *your* hand on my ass just now?"

Michaela grinned. "Honestly, Robby." She couldn't help but notice Lachlan hadn't stuttered or stumbled once.

Robby attempted to look innocent. "I have no idea what you're talking about."

"Of course you don't," Lachlan said dryly.

"I just wanted you to know how happy I was to see you both," Robby said.

"You just wanted everyone here to know exactly whose camp you're standing with," Lachlan clarified.

Robby smiled at him like he was a prized pupil.

Michaela frowned. "Robby, I saw your parents just a few minutes ago. Are you sure you want to do this?"

"I'm going to forgive you for asking me that, princess, because I know you're still getting used to the idea that I would have stood by you this entire time. My parents are aware of it, and their feelings on the matter are moot. Unless," he said, studying Michaela's face, "they were rude to you. In which case, I will address it."

"They weren't rude," she assured him.

"They were *cool*," Lachlan added, extremely unhelpfully.

Michaela sent him a baleful look. "Whose side are you on, anyway?"

"Yours."

She sighed, recognizing a losing battle. "Honestly, you two are like a pair of bulls in a china shop."

Robby waggled his eyebrows at her. "A bull, huh?" He cast a pointed look at Lachlan.

Lachlan turned an adorable shade of pink and cleared his throat. "*Anyway*," he said sternly, "While chatting with your parents, I learned I work near a building named after you."

As deflections went, it was a good one. Now Michaela was smiling at Lachlan like he was a prized pupil. Look at him, navigating difficult social situations.

"Oh no, not me," Robby said. "No one would ever dream of naming a building after me. I believe that Wigglesworth was all about divinity, and while I like to think of myself as divine, religion really isn't my jam."

Lachlan leaned closer to Robby. "Oh, come now, I'm sure you've been known to make a man call out to god now and then."

Michaela's mouth dropped open. She'd never in her life seen Robby *blush*. She covered her mouth to muffle her helpless giggles.

This was not at all how these sorts of events usually went for her. God, when was the last time she'd had so much fun surrounded by so many stuffy people?

"*Dr. Morrison*," Robby drawled, "you are *full* of surprises."

"He really is," she agreed, tucking her hand in his elbow. "Now, let us find our table."

"Oh, goody," Lachlan muttered. "I hope there is an hour of speeches to look forward to."

Robby took Michaela's other arm. "I don't care who I have to blow, I'm getting my plate moved to wherever you two are."

The speeches weren't quite as boring as the last go round, so Lachlan found himself listening more carefully. Seamus's event had been very nice, but it had felt much more like a bunch of wealthy people congratulating themselves for being so generous, just for the bragging rights. The atmosphere tonight felt much more like it was about helping people.

When the meal and the speakers were done, they remained at their table. Apparently, in deference to the animals, there would be no music or dancing that evening. It wasn't as though Lachlan had been looking forward to that, particularly, but it had proven an escape from the small talk he was now expected to make.

He was glad to have Robby there as a second ally, since they'd been seated with a not-altogether-very interesting group, none of whom were the people Michaela needed to speak with that night—nor were they particularly pleased to be sitting with her, either. It occurred to him that this was how it would have gone down a week ago, too, had Seamus not interceded.

In spite of her position with a powerful and well-endowed foundation, Michaela still had to fight to get to the table, so to speak. It was infuriating.

Robby seemed to think so, too.

"Let's go visit my parents, shall we?" he asked, rising to his feet and reaching for Michaela's hand. "Do excuse us," he murmured deferentially to the rest of the table.

Lachlan stayed seated, a curl of panic in his gut at the

prospect of being left alone. At the very least, he knew that with Michaela there she'd kick his shin if he started freaking out, or going down the wrong conversational path.

"You, too," Robby announced, pulling Lachlan from his chair.

Michaela put her hand out, and he lifted his elbow for her to take.

"I wouldn't have left you," she said quietly.

"Nor would have I," Robby promised.

Lachlan looked at Michaela. "Did you tell him?"

She shook her head minutely.

"Tell me what?" Robby asked.

"Nothing," Lachlan said quickly. "So, why wouldn't you leave me? I'm hardly likely to be of interest to your parents."

"I think you underestimate your charms, Dr. Morrison. I've watched the papers and followed her closely over the years. I haven't seen the princess's *real* smile in a long time."

Michaela blushed and Lachlan had no fucking idea what to say to that, though he liked the idea that he was responsible.

"Well, then, let's go meet your parents. Again."

He held out his other elbow to Robby, who eyed it suspiciously for a moment, then a big smile bloomed on his face. He hooked his hand through Lachlan's arm. "My, my. It's like you don't even know the rules," he said gleefully.

"I don't. And I don't care," Lachlan said firmly, walking in the direction Robby indicated.

People didn't even attempt to hide their stares. A contraband flash went off and Lachlan blinked, but held his smile—he was well-trained now—and sailed through the crowd. He glanced at Michaela to see she was smiling, too. The real one, he thought. Just as Robby had said.

Robby chuckled and murmured under the din of the party. "Oh my god, do you see the look on my mother's face?"

Lachlan did and it made him hesitate. Michaela and Robby, though, didn't, forcing him to continue or risk falling on his face.

"Mother," Robby said, grinning ear-to-ear. "I understand you've already said hello to Michaela and been introduced to Lachlan, but I thought you might like to spend some more time getting reacquainted. Michaela is doing such wonderful things with the Price Foundation."

Lachlan was painfully aware that at least fifty people were watching this exchange with ill-concealed fascination. The number grew as others drifted closer.

They were, it seemed, the entertainment for the night. Lachlan had a terrible suspicion that this didn't fall within the acceptable limits of *Michaela's Rules for Managing the Public*.

Mrs. Wigglesworth looked as though she rather wished the floor would open up and swallow her whole. Mr. Wigglesworth scowled, but rose to his feet and nodded to Lachlan and Michaela before turning a stern look on his son.

"Robert, you were meant to sit with us this evening."

Robby shrugged. "I wanted to catch up with an old friend, instead."

"We invited the Lidens to sit with us specifically so that you could get to know their daughter, Jessica," his father hissed.

Lachlan watched Robby's smile harden into something fierce and unhappy. On pure instinct, Lachlan tucked his elbow in to pull Robby closer.

"Mr. and Mrs. Wigglesworth," Michaela said in a smooth voice. "I would love an opportunity to speak with you about possibly working together on a project."

Mrs. Wigglesworth frowned. "Perhaps. We tend to focus more on the *family*."

Which was code for "not LGBT", Lachlan could guess, even without Michaela and Robby digging their fingers into his arms so hard he was beginning to lose feeling in both his hands.

Michaela opened her mouth to respond, but Lachlan was talking before he could stop himself.

"I should think, given your own family, that your priorities would align well with the Price Foundation," he said.

This was met with a startled silence, and not just from his immediate audience. Even the eavesdroppers were apparently stunned. Everyone turned to look at him and he swallowed, keeping his focus on Mrs. Wigglesworth.

Lachlan prayed he wasn't about to put his foot in it.

"I'm sure you're aware that over 1.6 million children go homeless in this country every year, but did you also know that while only five to ten percent of this country's young people identify as LGBT, they make up over forty percent of the homeless youth population? This is, in large part, because over sixty percent of them have been rejected by their families. Can you imagine that?"

Mrs. Wigglesworth appeared to have nothing to say. Mr. Wigglesworth appeared mildly ill.

"More alarming," Lachlan continued ruthlessly, "are the suicide rates."

At this, Mr. Wigglesworth positively blanched. Michaela was looking at Lachlan as if she'd never seen him before.

He'd done a lot of reading over the past week about homelessness and the issues facing homeless kids in this country. He was ashamed to admit he hadn't really known much more about it than what he'd read in the papers, and it turned out they weren't nearly as informative as he'd thought.

He plowed on. "Homeless or not, gay kids whose families have rejected them are more likely to commit suicide than those whose families accept them. They're also more likely to experience depression, use illicit drugs, or engage in unprotected sex. I'm sure you'll agree these statistics are appalling," he said, staring Robby's mother down.

Mrs. Wigglesworth looked increasingly discomfited the longer he waited for her reply.

"Yes, of course," she finally blurted. And she did appear sincere, which was something.

"This is what Michaela and the Price Foundation are working with, only the children they are supporting have all of that to contend with *and* are homeless. Their only families are often each other and the people in the shelters that support them. Many don't have access to those, but the Price Foundation would like to change that."

Mrs. Wigglesworth nodded vaguely in the way of people who can't quite believe what is happening to them.

"Given your focus on the family, perhaps you'd interested in helping those LGBT children who haven't been rejected by their families, or have been but weren't forced into homelessness. As members of families ourselves, I'm sure we can all appreciate the importance of that as a support structure and the need to bolster those within it, as well as those who are forced to go without."

"Yes, that's very important," she said meekly.

"I'm glad you agree," he said, perfectly aware he'd just railroaded an answer from her. He couldn't even pretend it would actually make a difference, but it felt good that he'd made her say it, at least.

His heart ached to see Robby watching his parents with an unbearably sad look on his face.

"Perhaps," Michaela said softly to the fairly stunned Wigglesworths, "I could call you this week and arrange a time for us to meet. If you're not interested in working with the Price Foundation, I might be able to suggest other organizations that align with your family focus."

Lachlan almost smiled at Michaela's clever and diplomatic phrasing.

"Yes," Mr. Wigglesworth said, startling Lachlan by speaking for the first time since Lachlan's heavy-handed lecture had begun. He was answering Michaela, but his eyes were on his son. "I'd like that."

Mrs. Wigglesworth frowned, her brows drawn in severely, and looked at her husband.

Mr. Wigglesworth glared back. "Come along, Priscilla. I think I see the Lidens looking for us."

He drew his wife away before she could speak, leaving the

three of them in the center of a silenced crowd.

Suddenly, conversation burst to life around them. Before Lachlan could think what he should do now, Robby was dragging him, and therefore Michaela, away from the party and up the spiral ramp around the main fish tank, weaving through a few sparsely scattered guests who had also escaped the crush below, until they reached a quiet spot out of sight from everyone.

Then Robby hugged him, fiercely, and started to laugh, though it sounded a little damp against Lachlan's lapel.

Lachlan hugged him back. "Sorry," he muttered, the weight of what he'd done and its possible repercussions sinking in.

"Shut up," Robby said, still clinging to him.

Michaela smiled up at Lachlan. "You are such a fucking troublemaker."

Robby stepped back. "You really are. I cannot believe you just schooled my mother in front of me."

"And about half the party, I think," Lachlan added regretfully. He looked at Michaela. "I broke the rules, didn't I?"

"You did," she said, though her smile didn't match the chastising tone. "I can't say it wasn't worth it, though."

"It was totally worth it," Robby declared. "I was one of those kids. If it hadn't been for my friends, I would have been a statistic. But my family was at boarding school, not at home. Friends like the princess here, and even Blake-the-epic-asshat, were my support network."

Michaela threaded her fingers through Robby's and squeezed.

"Now," Robby said, "let's get the fuck out of here. I think we've given enough of a show for tonight, and I need a real drink and less company."

That sounded like an outstanding idea to Lachlan.

They started back down the ramp toward the main floor, and Lachlan smiled as he'd been taught and ignored the number of eyes on them. He gazed at the exit covetously—so focused on it, in fact, that he didn't realize Robby and Michaela had stopped short until he was jerked to a halt between them.

"Mickey!" cried a man charging toward them from the midst of the crowd, who parted eagerly, clearing a path directly to them.

Mickey? Lachlan turned, arrested by the horrified look on Michaela's face before she quickly pasted on a wan smile.

"Blake," she said, her voice monotone.

Lachlan's heart stopped.

"So much for not putting on another show," Robby muttered, dropping Lachlan's arm and taking a step forward.
Blake practically jogged up the ramp toward them, but before he could say another word, Robby punched him in the face.

Chapter Seventeen

The next day, Michaela snuck through the door of the massive Starbucks in the heart of Harvard Square, the same one she'd come to with Lachlan countless times. This time, though, she bypassed the line in favor of zipping up the stairs to the large seating space above.

She immediately spotted her study group sitting in the corner by the big windows looking out over the Square and sighed.

This was going to be another disaster.

They'd met three times this week already, but it had always been in a study room in the campus library. This morning, Sadie had declared via text message she couldn't spend another minute in that room, let alone on a Sunday, and suggested that they meet here so they could enjoy some coffee and just relax.

Michaela was decidedly *not* relaxed.

"Hi," she said when she reached them, smiling tentatively.

"Hey," Sadie returned, looking at Michaela's empty hands curiously. "Do you want to go get a coffee?"

"Uh, no. I'm fine." She hovered by the group, not moving.

Tanner, who had long recovered from his embarrassment over his roommates' stunt, craned his neck to look at her over his shoulder. "You gonna stand there all day?"

"Yeah. I mean, no. But, um...Do you mind if I take this seat?" she asked, gesturing at the one Tanner was currently slouched into, looking extremely comfortable and not at all like he had any plans to move.

He frowned at her. Michaela fought back the urge to just turn around and leave.

Sadie, though, was quicker on the uptake. She leaned over to look beyond Michaela and rolled her eyes at whatever she saw.

"Get up, Tanner. Let her sit there."

"Why?" he said, clearly irritated.

Sadie glared at him. "How about you not be an asshole and try paying attention to the world around you?"

He stood. "What the fuck does that mean?"

"I can just go," Michaela said quietly, taking a small step back.

Tanner turned to look at her, following her hand as she gestured toward the exit. His eyes widened as they scanned the room.

"No, you sit here. Sorry," he muttered, grabbing his stuff and collapsing into the seat that faced the roughly one hundred other occupants of the room. His eyes narrowed at something—Michaela was sure she didn't want to know what.

She perched on the chair Tanner had vacated. "No, I'm sorry. Thank you for moving. If it's easier, I can just leave my stuff and you guys can meet without me today."

"No," Eric said, "you should stay."

She smiled gratefully. "Okay. Thanks." She pulled out copies of the abstracts she'd written for today's meeting and passed them around. The others did the same.

The third time Eric flinched, Michaela sighed in defeat. "Do I want to know?" she asked, still refusing to look behind her.

He frowned down at the papers in his lap. "Pictures," he mumbled.

Sadie and Tanner simultaneously glared at something or someone over Michaela's shoulder.

"I'll go," Michaela said, gathering her things as she rose to her feet. "I'm sorry this didn't work out."

"Sit. *Down*," Tanner snapped.

Michaela did. Quickly. Eric looked between them with wide eyes. Sadie kept glaring at whatever was going on behind Michaela.

"Is there somewhere else we can meet that's not the library, and not liable to require crowd control?" Tanner asked irritably.

"I'd offer my place, but my roommates are slobs," Sadie said.

"I'd offer mine, but I live in the 'burbs with my parents," Eric added.

Tanner's smirk was smirkier than usual. "I'm not even going to propose we go to my house. I'm pretty sure you don't want to meet my roommates again, and now they have your picture on their walls."

Michaela suppressed shudder, then noticed they were all looking at *her*.

"I bet *you* don't have a roommate," Tanner said leadingly.

"Oh. Right. Uh, you guys could all come to my place, if you wanted? It's not far."

Had she really just said that out loud?

Sadie stood before Michaela could take it back. "Let's get the fuck out of here."

Everyone hastily packed up their stuff, grabbed their coffee, and made a beeline for the stairs. Michaela followed them out of the café in a daze, only pointing them in the direction of her building when they reached the sidewalk and the others looked at her expectantly.

She'd just invited people she barely knew to her home. No one but Lachlan had set foot in it. No one but Callum and her family had ever come to her place in Denver. She hadn't had people over, an actual *group of people*, since…

She couldn't even remember when. She hadn't even been old enough to have her own space when the shit hit the fan. So this—this was definitely a first.

And weird. Holy shit, was she about to *entertain?* Did she even know *how*?

They walked down Mass Ave in a close group, no one trying to pretend they weren't with her, and all studiously ignoring any looks they received. Michaela was impressed with their composure. They were doing way better with this than she ever would have imagined, though it was fair to say they weren't exactly loving it, either.

Which, oddly, was also good.

Unfortunately, she was so focused on her companions, she didn't notice the tight cluster of people outside her building until it was too late.

"*Michaela! Can you give us a statement about the fight last night?*" someone cried from half a block away.

Michaela jerked to a stop and stared at the cameras pointed in their direction. She saw Mike hovering by the door and he looked absolutely furious.

"*Michaela, can you confirm that Lachlan Morrison is your boyfriend now?*" someone else shouted.

Her stomach dropped to around her knees. She turned to look at her study group in horror.

"I'm so sorry," she said sincerely, though it was totally inadequate.

Eric looked petrified. Sadie grabbed his arm, steadying him. "What do you want us to do?" Sadie asked.

"*Run,*" Michaela said desperately, because how was that not obvious to everyone?

"What?" Sadie asked.

"You should run. Now. Before they get here," Michaela said urgently, nudging Tanner's arm to try to get him moving.

"Fuck that," Tanner said sharply, shaking off her hand. "We'll never get this fucking work done if we keep having to move around. How do we get past them?" Tanner asked.

What the hell was he talking about? They needed to just leave her. Run in the other direction.

Go.

She could hear the vultures getting closer. Soon they would circle. "It's too late to go to the back door, and there are probably more of them there," she tried to explain. "I'm going to have go through them."

"Do we say anything?" Sadie asked.

"What?" Michaela asked, utterly bewildered.

"Do we say anything? Or do we just, I don't know, *plow*

through them?"

"But. You can't. I—"

"Just plow through them," Tanner announced decisively, like he had any fucking idea what he was talking about. "None of us should say a word. Eric, you walk on her right. I've got the left. Sadie, you good with going first?"

Sadie's smile was wolfish—all teeth and no humor. "Sure," she said. Then she turned and marched toward Michaela's front door.

And the others *followed.* What was wrong with all of these people? Had they lost their minds?

Michaela jerked into motion. She had no choice but to keep up, even if every instinct told her to grab them and run the other way. Eric was frighteningly pale, and she wanted desperately to take his hand—for her own comfort as much as to save the coffee that appeared to be slipping from his fingers—but that would only drag him further into her fucked-up mess of a life. And into the press.

Fuck, they'd left Starbucks because she'd wanted to protect them. Shield them from all this. And instead, they were diving in, head first, and she couldn't do anything to stop it.

A moment before they were surrounded, she blurted out, "They can't touch you. That would be assault. Just keep moving. And no matter how tempted you are, don't throw your coffee at them."

Tanner actually smiled at that last bit.

Eric flinched when a man shouted at them as if they weren't a mere three feet away, "Michaela, what started the brawl last night?"

She barely resisted the urge to roll her eyes, keeping her face carefully blank instead. Brawl? What brawl? Robby had punched Blake right on the nose and then they'd left.

Tanner sent her a speaking side-long look, and she wished, desperately, that she'd had time to train the others on how to handle this.

Which was totally ridiculous. Why the hell should they have to handle anything? Studying with her shouldn't come with required trainings.

Flashes went off like fireworks all around them, but Sadie didn't hesitate, and she didn't run, just marched on in a determined line toward Mike, who held the door for them.

He looked remarkably composed now that the cameras had swung in his direction.

"You okay, Ms. Price?" he asked quietly as they ducked past him into the building.

"I'm okay, Mike. And it's *Michaela*." She looked helplessly at his grin—he was so *stubborn*—as he closed the door firmly in the face of the press.

She quickly introduced everyone and assured Mike that if any of them should come by again, they should be allowed up to her floor. It was scary to say, but god knew, they'd earned it in the last two minutes alone. And, hey, maybe next time they wouldn't be harangued by the press on their way over.

In her experience, a punch in the nose wouldn't hold anyone's attention for long. Things would die down by Tuesday. Wednesday at the latest.

She turned to Sadie, Eric, and Tanner. "Thank you. Really. That was way above and beyond what you should have to deal with."

Tanner frowned. "I'm not even going to say you're welcome, because that shit is just bizarre."

Michaela winced. "I'm really sorry. I had no idea the press would pick up on what happened last night."

"What did happen last night?" Sadie asked curiously.

Michaela grimaced. "I'll tell you about it later. When they" — she tilted her head toward the pack of idiots jammed up against the lobby windows, which now appeared to include both the press and curious passersby— "aren't where they can see me."

"Fair enough," Sadie agreed easily, then let out a deep breath, as if shaking off whatever the hell had just happened.

"Shall we head upstairs? We still have a lot of work to do."

Eric, glanced over his shoulder at the door then shook his head. "I think I'm just going to head home," he said quietly.

Michaela felt miserable. "Okay. Let me get my car keys. I'll drive you."

"What? No. I can get home on my own."

And now she wanted to cry. "You can't walk out of this building. Not for a while. They just saw you with me and they'll follow you, asking questions."

Eric's already pale complexion went waxy. "What the fuck," he muttered.

She turned to Mike. "The back door?"

Mike looked at the screen on his podium and shook his head sadly. "No dice. They've got it covered, too. Your best way out is in a car through the garage."

"No, it's okay," Eric said, quietly resigned. "Let's just go upstairs and work."

The walk to the elevator, and then down her hallway, felt more like a death march, but Michaela led them to her door without breaking the silence.

The moment her key touched the lock, Fang greeted them with ecstatic barks.

Eric lifted his head for the first time since the lobby, his eyes getting noticeably brighter. "You have a dog?"

She opened the door and let her little monster barrel into the hallway. "This is Fang. He's very friendly, as you will see."

Eric dropped to his knees and Fang immediately tried to climb into his lap. Eric smiled and helped him up, letting the dog plant his feet on his chest and rubbing their faces together.

"*Fang?*" Tanner repeated incredulously. "What the hell is he, a Tribble?"

Eric shot Tanner a surprised look. "Nerd!" he accused gleefully. "*Star Trek nerd!*"

"Come on inside," Michaela said, opening the door wider and

leading the way.

Sadie stopped in Michaela's foyer and looked around. "Holy crap."

"Nice digs," Tanner said with a low whistle.

Michaela felt like she should apologize, which was stupid. Then she thought about offering a tour, but that felt even *more* stupid. Instead she hovered awkwardly in the hallway.

At least Eric didn't seem to care about her apartment. He'd already crossed into the living room and thrown down his bag so he could cuddle with Fang on the couch.

At a loss, she tried to remember what her mother always did when company came over.

"Can I get anyone a drink?" she asked.

All three of them turned to look at her, their coffee cups still in hand.

"Uh, right. Well, let me know if you want anything. I'll just go get myself a water."

Sadie almost looked sorry for her. "We'll get set up. Where do you want us?"

"The living room is good," she said, nodding to where Eric was already making himself at home, somehow managing to unpack his bag while still holding his new best friend, Fang.

When Michaela returned from the kitchen, she found Fang making the rounds, taking turns wriggling around on everyone's laps on the floor and sofa, and spending a few minutes being adored by each person before moving on to the next victim.

Everyone laughed at the look on Tanner's face when Fang tried to give him some enthusiastic kisses. Fang was a lot like one of those cats that always went to the person who was the most allergic, only Fang was drawn to anyone who loved Rottweilers.

It took a while, but eventually everyone settled in, the incident out front not forgotten, surely, but put aside so they could focus on their work. Michaela finally took a real breath.

It was almost two hours later when Tanner declared he was starving. "Do you have any food?"

Michaela shrugged. "Not really?" It wasn't like she'd been expecting company. Ever. "But I can get pizza delivered."

Eric sat up, looking enthusiastic. "Yes! I like black olives and anchovies on mine."

They all stared at him.

"What is *wrong* with you?" Sadie asked.

"You get your own pie," Michaela said firmly.

Tanner's gaze narrowed on Eric. "Which is precisely why he chose that."

Eric smiled innocently.

"Okay, so clearly we need at least two pizzas. What else do you guys want? I'll treat," Michaela said as she stood to get the menu.

Tanner scowled. "No. You won't."

Michaela froze. "Oh, I didn't mean. I'm not saying you can't afford to—"

"He didn't mean it like that," Sadie said quickly with a dirty look for Tanner.

"Actually, you're right. I didn't," Tanner said. "What I meant was, if we're going to do this, and we're going to invite ourselves over—which, by the way, we are, because hell, no, I'm not going out in public with you on a regular basis—I think it would be better if there was no question about whether any of us are interested in freeloading off your rich ass. Is that clear enough?"

A sharp laugh burst from Michaela. "Yeah, that was pretty clear."

"Jesus, Tanner," Eric muttered.

"No, it's okay," Michaela said quickly. "He's right. I mean, I didn't think that, but Tanner has a point."

"Excellent. Thank you," Tanner said, clearly not expecting the support. "Now, what do you want? I bet you like fancy shit, right?"

"Actually, my *rich ass* likes pepperoni."

Tanner grinned. "Excellent, so does my student-loaned-up-to-my-ass ass."

Sadie flopped back on the couch. "There sure are a lot of asses in this room," she muttered darkly.

Lachlan spent his Sunday as he often did, catching up on his work and his reading. His little house was a refuge, quiet and away from people and students and noise.

The night before had ended up a total shit show—thanks to Robby's surprisingly effective right hook—so after calling his parents for their weekly phone call, he gave himself permission to turn off his phone and take a break from the rest of the world.

He was still kind of pissed Robby had punched the douchebag. Not because he didn't deserve it, but because Lachlan had wanted to be the one to introduce his fist to that asshole's face.

Though, either way, the fallout was likely going to suck for Michaela. Robby had sent them fleeing to their car as soon as it happened, well before the press outside had figured out what was going on inside the aquarium. Robby had stayed behind to handle the clean-up, which apparently hadn't been as bad as Lachlan would have guessed, since Robby had called Michaela's cell before they'd even arrived home, promising that Blake wasn't going to press charges and that Robby would make sure everyone was clear Michaela had no part in any of his actions.

Which, of course, was a lie. Robby had absolutely punched Blake because of Michaela. And Lachlan now considered Robby a lifelong friend because of it. He was good people. The best kind of people. The only thing Lachlan couldn't understand, for the life of him, is why every single one of Michaela's friends hadn't lined up to take a shot at Blake *before* now.

He didn't necessarily mean violently, either—though that was extremely satisfying, even just to witness. Why hadn't people condemned Blake Whelton? To the press, to his friends and associates. The man should be a pariah for what he'd done, but instead, Michaela had to live in the midst of a circus she'd had no part in creating, while Blake got off scot free.

The whole thing just *sucked*.

Lachlan worried how Michaela was coping today, but he knew she was with her study group for most of the day and he didn't want to bother her. And he really didn't want to talk to the rest of his family today, when his choices would be to lie and say nothing was new—being at the center of a fight at a fancy party was definitely new for Lachlan—or tell them what had happened and having to field endless questions.

His time would be better spent with a few hours of peace and quiet while he worked his way through his freshmen class's biographies on philosophers of their choosing. He smiled when he discovered one kid had balls big enough to title his paper "Everyone Loves Bacon" and tried to decide if he was allowed to give him extra points for that. Probably not, but hopefully it meant the kid at least put some effort into the assignment.

Ten hours later, Lachlan was feeling decidedly less optimistic about the potential for this group of freshmen to actually graduate, let alone write an engaging paper about people who should have made that easy, at least with Lachlan as their audience. He'd worked through lunch and dinner with the reward of being done in time to turn on the game. Rhian was on fire, and spending a couple hours hollering at the television was the perfect end to Lachlan's day.

He staggered to bed—hockey games went way too late when he had an early class the next day, but it was *still* worth it—and crashed.

It wasn't until he was walking across campus the next morning that he realized he'd made a mistake. He really should have turned his phone back on yesterday.

He saw the gaggle of people on the steps to the building where his class was to be held, and wouldn't have thought anything of it had they not been surrounded by campus security, who were very clearly, and very *loudly*, telling them they had to leave the university property immediately.

What was that all about?

Then he saw Anna striding toward him, almost running, her shoulders up around her ears and her wide eyes pinned on him. She was mouthing something, but he couldn't tell what until she was almost within ear shot.

Turn around!

"What?"

Anna looked over her shoulder, then finally broke into a run. Lachlan watched with alarm as she bore down on him and grabbed his elbow.

"Turn around. And walk *fast*."

He did as she'd asked, alarmed. "What the hell is going on?"

"Campus security will get rid of them, but you don't want them to see you."

"See me? See who? What are you talking about?"

Anna looked up at him incredulously but said nothing until she'd dragged him around the corner of a building and out of sight.

"That, I believe, is what you call the paparazzi."

"The what?" Lachlan asked, his heart sinking.

"The press. Reporters, photographers. And they are *not* nice people."

"Were they rude to you?" he asked, concerned and furious.

Anna smiled at him, and he felt uncomfortable at how fond she looked. "No, they weren't rude to me. I mean, other than being in my way when I was trying to get to class. But then I figured it would be better to walk away and try to find you before you got there."

She peeked around the corner of the building they were hiding behind.

"Are they still there?" he asked, cold dread congealing in his gut.

"Yeah, but security apparently brought in the big guns. Cambridge's finest will get them out of here soon enough."

Lachlan slumped against the rough brick wall. "Shit. The police are involved?"

"The university is private property," Anna said with a shrug, perfectly matter-of-fact. "They can't be here without permission—which they definitely do not have."

Lachlan groaned. "I am so screwed. How did this happen?"

"Just guessing, but it was probably the brawl," Anna said dryly.

"Brawl? *What* brawl?" he cried, dismayed at how high his voice had gone. This was ridiculous. There hadn't been any brawl. He hadn't even played hockey this weekend.

Anna looked concerned. "Oh, boy. Please, tell me you know what's going on."

"I obviously have no idea," he said, trying not to lose his patience. Why hadn't anyone told him something was going on, and maybe explained how the fuck he had anything to do with it? Then he remembered. "Oh, shit. My phone."

With no small amount of trepidation, he fished it from his pocket and turned it on. It lit up like Christmas.

"Wow. Two hundred and forty seven missed text messages," Anna said with quiet awe as she peered over his shoulder.

"And almost as many unread emails," Lachlan muttered. He was overwhelmed at the idea of wading through all that. Then he looked at the time and happily shoved the phone back in pocket. "I'll deal with that later. Right now, we're going to be late for class."

"You're actually going to teach today?"

"Yes," he said firmly. "I'm going to be in enough trouble when Dick gets wind of this. I'd better at least show up for class."

"Good point." Anna checked around the corner. "Okay, ready to run for it?"

Lachlan grimaced and muttered, "Jesus Christ." Anna just

raised her eyebrows. He sighed and held out his hand. "Lead on."

She hadn't been kidding about the running part, either.

Michaela stared down at her phone, reading again the texts from Robby apologizing profusely and repeatedly. She'd already told him to let it go, but he was determined to fret. She considered asking him to come over after her class later, but she was hesitant to make any plans. Not to mention, if the press saw him, it would seriously undermine Robby's assertion that he hadn't hit Blake for any reason to do with her.

The phone buzzed in her palm and she quickly checked to see if it was...no, it was just her brother.

She should be studying. Or getting in her morning workout. God knew, her stress level was high enough to demand she do *something* to take her mind off of things. Instead, she just sat on the couch, Fang curled at her side gazing up at her with transparent worry, and waited to hear from Lachlan.

After twenty-four hours, she should possibly accept she wasn't going to. Probably not ever again.

Chapter Eighteen

Lachlan had a problem. Actually, he had a hell of a lot more than one of them right now, but there was really only one thing in particular that he could focus on at the moment.

Michaela wasn't answering his texts. Or his calls.

He had managed to teach his class that morning, thanks only to Anna's knowledge of the utility door into the basement of the building—which he was absolutely going to ask her about some day. It had actually gone pretty well, if he ignored the way his students were all staring at him like he was someone they'd never seen before. After that, he hadn't been willing to push his luck and had cancelled his office hours for later in the morning, partly because he figured it could be a madhouse, but mostly because he was a total coward and avoiding Dick by any means necessary.

Now it was mid-day, and he was trapped in his house. He paced around his living room, actively resisting the urge to look out the front windows to be sure he hadn't hallucinated what was currently happening out on the sidewalk.

It turned out he'd been damn lucky up to this point. The press hadn't found him yesterday because he made a point of not listing his contact and address information publicly. When you're a university professor living near campus, it was better if your students couldn't find you. Late night visits to beg for leniency, or a better grade, or, on one memorable occasion, to be told that if he didn't pass the student who'd had the balls to show up at his door, drunk, at one in the morning, the student's father would see that Lachlan lost his job.

He'd always wondered where that kid had ended up finishing school.

Anyway, for better or worse, he'd made it through yesterday unmolested at home. He probably could have done with a warning before this morning, but then again, he probably wouldn't have dared leave the house to get to class. Just like *now*, since he refused to crack his front door for any reason, knowing there were a half dozen cameras and at least four times as many neighbors, waiting for a show. Hell, the grad students across the street had actually set up a row of beach chairs on their lawn and were working their way through a cooler of cheap beer with front row seats to the freak show that was now Lachlan's life.

He jumped when his phone buzzed in his hand and he looked down quickly, disappointed to see it wasn't Michaela. But then again, maybe Callum was a good next option.

"Hello?" he said carefully. It wasn't like spoofing a number for Caller ID was unheard of.

"Dude, this fake dating thing doesn't seem to be working out for you. Did you really punch the douchebag in the face?"

Lachlan sighed. "No, but I wish I had." For all the trouble it had caused, he would have liked to at least have had that satisfaction.

"So, there was no fight?"

"Robby punched him, not me. I was just an innocent bystander."

"Damn," Callum murmured. "I gotta buy that guy a drink."

"Get in line."

Callum laughed. "So, how's it going? You okay?"

"Not really," Lachlan muttered. "I'm trapped in my house and Michaela isn't speaking to me."

"That's not what I hear," Callum said, the laughter gone from his voice.

"What the hell does that mean?"

"It means she tried to reach you all day yesterday and again this morning, and you've been blowing her off. I know this isn't what you signed up for when you agreed to show her around school and shit, but leaving her high and dry right now is really fucking uncool, man."

Lachlan cringed. Then he explained about his phone, finishing with, "I thought she'd be busy all day with her study group and then studying on her own. I wasn't expecting to hear from her until today. And I definitely wasn't expecting *all this*" — he waved his hand at the front of his house, even though Callum couldn't see him— "to happen."

Callum harrumphed, but Lachlan knew that was his brother's grumpy way of accepting what he'd said as the truth. And possibly reasonable.

"Go ahead and send the text," Callum said.

"What?"

"I was talking to my husband," Callum explained, which clarified nothing.

Suddenly there was a great melee in front of his house. Lachlan could hear people shouting questions and ran to his front windows, peeking out a curtain to see the press moving down the block.

Smiling for the cameras for all he was worth, Rhian strode down the street, making his way toward Lachlan's door.

"What the hell is Rhian doing here?"

"He's doing you a huge favor, that's what. He'll stall out there for a while, giving non-answers. I prepped him. Go unlock your back door. And if your fence gate is locked, go undo that, too. *Hurry.*"

Lachlan ran into his kitchen and threw the deadbolt, then yanked open the door to find Savannah, Garrick, and Michaela ducking into his back yard from the private alley that ran behind all the houses on his block. They quickly shut the gate behind them. He had never been happier to have a six foot privacy fence, but he still waved madly for them to get their asses into the house as quickly as possible. He didn't know if one of his neighbors could see them from a second story window, and he had no idea which of them might have sold him up the river by giving his address to the press.

He slammed the door and locked it as soon as they were inside.

Savannah shoved at him before he could so much as say

hello. "Go, save Rhian."

"What do I do?" he asked wildly.

Michaela looked absolutely miserable. "Just crack the door. He'll come inside as soon as you do."

Lachlan desperately wanted to pull her into his arms and apologize profusely, but his sister was going to dislocate his shoulder if he didn't get moving.

He paused at his front door and took a deep breath before unlocking it. He knew the press wasn't allowed on his front porch without his permission, since he'd asked them to leave, but he wouldn't be surprised if someone tried something stupid anyway.

The moment he released the lock, the knob turned. Lachlan raised his hands, ready to slam it shut, just in case. Rhian slipped through the door before Lachlan could smash it into his face.

"Easy there, killer," Rhian said quietly, locking up behind him. He hugged Lachlan fiercely. "You doing okay?"

Lachlan held on, all but sagging against his friend. "I'm all right."

He sighed when he was enveloped by his sister and Garrick, too, letting himself enjoy the comfort of his family, their fierce embrace smoothing his jagged edges.

Michaela didn't come any closer, standing alone in the kitchen and watching them, her shoulders slumped and her face miserable.

"Come here," he said, holding out a hand.

She shook her head after barely a second of eye contract. Lachlan frowned and let his arm drop. When he pulled away from the others, they all turned toward Michaela. She shifted uncomfortably, not looking at any of them.

"Come on," Lachlan said, walking to her and wrapping his fingers around her delicate wrist. She didn't resist when he pulled her from the kitchen and through the living room. "We'll be right back," he said to their audience, ignoring the various looks of concern, which morphed into smirks when he went for the stairs.

His house wasn't very big, and he wasn't going to have this conversation within earshot of his sister and de facto brothers-in-law unless he wanted the rest of the family to know everything that was said by sunset.

Michaela followed him, uncharacteristically meek and silent. Her smile was sad when she saw the framed photos lining his stairs, mostly of his family and his various youth hockey teams, ending with the huge shot of his team at Harvard when they'd won the championship.

Once upstairs, he tugged her into his bedroom and closed the door. She hovered there, not looking at him, and for the first time in a long while, he wasn't sure what to say to her.

"So," she said quietly, "we finally made it into a room with a bed."

Lachlan huffed out a laugh. She always knew how to put him at ease. "Sorry we can't make good use of it," he said sincerely.

Her smile was sad. "I'm sure the last thing you want is to be with me...like that...right now."

Lachlan frowned and brushed his hand down her arm. "That's not true," he admitted. "I pretty much always want to be with you *like that*."

"You don't mean that."

He did. Absolutely. But he didn't know how to convince her of the truth. Not with words. So instead, he slid his hand slowly up over her shoulder and behind her neck. Her eyes widened as he slipped his fingers into her hair and cupped the back of her head.

He held her close, not captive, and studied her face. He wasn't good at reading most people. But he could often figure out his family. And maybe he'd gotten to know Michaela well enough.

Then again, the disbelief on her face was probably obvious to anyone. He could guess what she'd thought would happen. What she thought *should* happen in the face of all the attention they were getting today.

And, if he were honest, the thought of running away had a certain appeal. The press wasn't exactly something he wanted in his life. But that desire to flee was crushed beneath the ache that formed in his chest when he considered not spending time with Michaela.

"I'm sorry I'm an idiot. I swear I wasn't avoiding you. I just turned off my phone and I didn't know anything was happening until this morning."

Her mouth curled up on one side. "I know. I got your texts and Savannah spent the entire trip here swearing it was just like you to do something so flakey."

"*Hey*," he protested, though his heart wasn't in it. He'd have to thank Savannah later for her defense of him, even if it had been insulting. "So, do you believe me?"

Because that was the real issue, he realized. Not whether or not she knew the truth, but if she would believe that he hadn't abandoned her when she'd needed him. Not on purpose. Not like so many other people had in the past.

He kept his eyes on hers and let her really look at him, hoping she'd see the truth. He didn't realize he'd been holding his breath until she smiled.

"Yes, I believe you."

He sighed with relief and pulled her close, wrapping his arms around her for a long hug. She sagged against him, and he held tight, trying to communicate as best he could that he was there. Still her friend. Still her...whatever the hell they were.

When she lifted her head, he kissed her. She curled her fingers into the front of his shirt, holding tight, and kissed him back.

He didn't pull away until he felt her sway, and even then he couldn't resist tasting her sweet, full lips a few more times before he pressed his lips to the top of her head and held her tightly again.

"I'm sorry," she murmured quietly into his chest.

"It's okay," he said.

"You should be mad at me, you know."

"It's not your fault."

"Yes, it is," she said insistently.

"No, it's not," he said right back in the same tone. "It *might* be a little bit Robby's fault, but I'm not mad at him, either."

His heart did something weird and sort of treacherous in his chest when she chuckled, the sound almost muffled by his shirt.

He nudged her back and was discouraged to see that, in spite of the hint of a smile and the color in her cheeks, she still looked sad. He cupped her face in one hand and ran his thumb over her cheekbone. "Tell me why you're upset."

"Oh, I don't know, maybe because I'm ruining your *life*," she said.

And Lachlan couldn't help it—he burst into laughter.

She scrunched up her nose, clearly annoyed, but he didn't let her move away, his arm still curled around her.

"It's not funny," she said tersely. "There's a pack of reporters on your front lawn."

He got himself under control. "I'm sorry. You're right. It's not funny that my house is under siege. But my life is not ruined. And you're neither so arrogant, nor enough of a drama queen, to get away with saying shit like that, or believing that it's your fault."

"If I hadn't dragged you to those parties, you wouldn't have been standing there, *as my date*, when Robby decided to defend my honor after all these years."

"He packs a lot of punch for a little guy."

She smiled, grudgingly. "He does, bless him."

"That's my girl," he said, giving her a little shake. "Blake needed punching. I'm just sorry I didn't get a chance to do it myself."

"Don't you *dare*," Michaela said sternly. "That would be a *gross* violation of *Michaela's Rules for Managing the Public*. If you think being a sideshow in this circus is a pain in the ass, you really wouldn't enjoy being the main event."

Lachlan wished he could disagree, but he was already living with the constant dread of going to his office and facing down Dick. The fallout from this was going to be ugly enough as it was, though he had no intention of sharing that with Michaela.

"So, how badly did I break the rules," he asked, turning the subject, "when I took Robby's parents to task?"

Michaela's smile widened into the full-blown toothy grin.

Lachlan blinked down at her as some weird, sexy version of the fight or flight instinct kicked up in his belly. When she smiled like that, he wanted to tear her clothes off. And for some reason, *that* made him want to run away, as fast and as far as he could.

Maybe that was the fuck or flight instinct? He didn't think that really existed, but it was real enough to him.

He really needed to think about what was really going on here. It hadn't escaped his notice that today was the first time he'd kissed Michaela when it wasn't a prelude to sex. And that it had seemed like a perfectly natural thing to do. Just as pulling her into a hug had been.

That had to mean something. Something that didn't quite fall under the heading of friends with benefits.

Though none of that seemed nearly as important, right now, as kissing her again.

Michaela slid her tongue along Lachlan's and tried to just enjoy being held, being kissed, even if part of her brain was still trying to make sense of the fact that he was willing to speak with her at all, let alone kiss her.

Before the debacle this past weekend, she'd been looking forward to coming here someday, seeing where and how Lachlan lived. She'd never imagined it would be under these circumstances. Though, when Lachlan was kissing her like this, she wasn't sure she cared *how* she got here, she was just glad she'd arrived.

A loud horn and someone yelling out front jolted them apart.

She took a deep, steadying breath and let it out slowly. Right. This was not the time. "Unless you plan on explaining why we didn't come back downstairs for a really, really long time, we should probably stop kissing," she said, clearing her throat to ease the husky timbre in her voice.

Lachlan's cheeks pinked up. "Good point. I'm pretty sure Callum would be on my doorstep within hours."

She winced. "You didn't tell him?"

"Did you?" he asked with an arched brow.

"No," she said with a reluctant smile. "I don't want him on my doorstep either. And god fucking save us both if he thinks he can take credit or something. He'd be insufferable."

Lachlan shuddered, making Michaela laugh. She very carefully didn't elaborate on what Callum might think he was taking credit for, in any case.

They went back downstairs, pausing on the stairway, ostensibly to look at adorable pictures of the Morrison Clan, but mostly so that Michaela could smooth Lachlan's hair back into place.

Based on the looks they received upon returning to the living room, no one was convinced their trip upstairs had been purely platonic. The grin on Savannah's face, in particular, was a little alarming.

Michaela made a mental note to warn Mike and the other doormen that Callum could show up unexpectedly.

They ordered lunch to be delivered, pooling their cash to be sure they could offer a tip of epic proportions to the poor kid who had to muscle his way onto the porch. Hanging out should have been weird, but everyone was acting like this was just a typical get-together, ribbing Rhian about his big goal the night before, teasing Lachlan for having woefully little in the way of beverage options, and fighting over who would get the last can of Moxie.

Michaela graciously bowed out of that argument and tried

not to gag when Savannah took her first sip. When her phone rang, she stepped into the kitchen to answer. It wasn't like she could avoid her parents forever.

"Hi, Mom," she said cheerfully, still chuckling over Rhian calling Garrick an old man for falling asleep on the couch as soon as his game was over.

"Darling, how could you get caught up in that mess over the weekend?"

Michaela closed her eyes, whatever joy she'd felt to just be with friends draining from her in an instant. She sucked in a fortifying breath, and very quickly and succinctly told her mother, who then relayed to her father, the real story.

"I'm shocked at Robert's behavior," her mother announced. "Perhaps he isn't someone you should be hanging around with."

A dull pain throbbed against Michaela's forehead and she rubbed her fingers there, hard. "Robby was just doing what he thought was right, Mom." *And I'm grateful.* "I'm sure it won't happen again."

"Well, I should hope not," said her mother.

Michaela couldn't get off the phone fast enough after that. As soon as she hung up, she went back into the living room and collapsed onto the loveseat next to Lachlan, since Savannah, Rhian, and Garrick had conveniently taken up the entire couch.

"You okay?" Lachlan asked in a low voice.

Before she could answer, the doorbell rang and everyone leaped to their feet, as if ready for an attack. Thankfully, it was just the severely harassed-looking delivery guy.

Michaela ignored the headache still building behind her eyes as they sat down to eat, telling herself firmly to shake off the call from her parents. There was nothing she could do about it now, and it would likely fade into one more on the long list of things she'd done to embarrass them.

She cringed when Lachlan's phone rang and he announced it was his parents. He probably didn't have a list of embarrassments—at least, not before he met her. She glanced at the back door and wondered if she could get clear if she made a break for it. Then she looked at Savannah and realized she didn't have a hope in hell.

Lachlan answered his phone by putting his parents on speaker, explaining of who was in the room with him and putting his phone down in the middle of the coffee table.

"Michaela, darling, how are you holding up?" Mary Morrison asked as soon as everyone had said hello.

"Oh. Uh...fine?" Why was Lachlan's mom talking to her first? "I mean, I feel so awful about all this. I didn't mean—"

"Don't be ridiculous. You didn't do anything. And Lachlan's made of sterner stuff than that. I'm sure he's hardly been bothered. Don't let his introverted ways fool you."

It was probably a good thing Mary Morrison couldn't see Lachlan's put-upon expression, or the grins on everyone else's faces.

"Thank you, Mother, for the vote of confidence," he said dryly.

"You know I'm right," Mary said in the voice only a mother could pull off—warm and totally dismissive at the same time. "Now, tell me what's been going on. I hear you were in a brawl? Did he deserve it?"

Michaela stared at the phone while Lachlan explained what had happened the night before, just as she had with her parents, only this time it was with wildly different results. She answered questions when asked directly, but mostly she sat listening and trying to understand what was wrong with everyone. They seemed hell-bent in their belief she was in no way culpable.

She listened to Mary gloss over the whole thing and for the first time in years thought maybe she should have stuck up for herself a little more when she'd spoken to her parents. It wasn't like she'd had any idea Robby would do that. Hell, she hadn't even known Robby would be there, let alone *Blake*.

Otherwise, obviously, *she* wouldn't have been there. And she certainly wouldn't have dragged Lachlan into it. But she was sort

224

of glad about the way it had turned out. It had been a long, long time since anyone had defended her publicly. In fact, she couldn't think of another example that was quite so dramatic.

Which was just like Robby. She was more grateful than ever that she had him back in her life.

Her phone buzzed and she looked down to see a text message from Sadie, addressed to their study group.

Michaela, are you going to make it to class today? If not, I can type up my notes and email them.

It was a kind offer and a fair question to ask, if you didn't know Michaela that well.

I'm going.

Sadie immediately replied with, *Meet us at the Mass Ave gate @ 2pm. We can all walk together.*

Michaela sighed. *You really, really don't have to do that.*

We know. From Eric.

Fuck that. From Tanner.

Sadie sent the eye-roll emoji.

I thought you didn't want to go out in public with me, Tanner?

I was kidding! Mostly. At least Tanner was honest. *And the press isn't allowed on campus, so I'm hardly being all that brave.*

Michaela grinned at her phone.

She startled when Lachlan bumped his shoulder against hers. "Good news?" he asked quietly, so as not to be heard over Mary and Bruce congratulating Rhian on his season so far.

She smiled at him. "I think maybe you were right. The study group is a good idea."

Chapter Nineteen

Lachlan stood in front of a packed classroom and wondered if he'd stumbled into the wrong building. Or possibly the wrong reality. Because there was no way this was his Thursday morning Introduction to Philosophy course.

He gaped at the dozens of freshmen staring at him with rapt attention. More than one of them had their phones out, perhaps convinced that they were being discreet as they took his picture.

At least half of the kids present weren't even registered for his class, which was intensely annoying as well as disruptive. He couldn't do shit about it, though, because he hadn't seen most of his students often enough to be sure who was legitimately supposed to be there and who wasn't, so he wasn't able to throw *any* of them out.

He glanced at Anna, who looked as confused and distressed as he felt but shrugged and turned on the projector anyway.

What choice did they have?

The presentation today was about morality, of all things, and the assigned readings were from Aristotle, Kant, and Nietzsche. Lachlan would eat his decade-old jock strap if even ten percent of the kids in front of him had read the assignment, let alone absorbed any of its meaning, clearly, since they were all here in a blatant attempt to gossip and gawk, rather than learn.

Lachlan thought about that for a moment, then smiled.

Perhaps today was the *perfect* day for a lecture on morality and ethics.

With a loud clap, he brought the room to order and dove head first into his first ever unplanned, untested lecture. It was terrifying and a bit disorganized and totally exhilarating. An hour and fifteen minutes later, he actually had to cut short a lively discussion on the ethical significance of tabloid reporting with the promise that they would pick it up again the next time this class met.

He traded grins with Anna, who'd given up on the projector

and the intended slides for the day about ten minutes in and had just sat back to watch the show. Goddamn, that had been fun. He practically chuckled with glee as a group of students filed past him, having returned to the argument about whether there should be an expected standard of behavior for sports stars, given they'd willingly and knowingly put themselves in the public eye, and should that standard be any different than regular people's.

Lachlan sighed happily and turned to gather his belongings as the last of the students left.

"A bit on the nose, don't you think, Dr. Morrison?"

Lachlan froze, his eyes locked with Anna's as they bulged with alarm.

Shit. When had Dick arrived? And how much had he heard?

Turning to face his boss, who he had managed to avoid for most of the week thanks to Dick traveling to a conference in Anaheim. Now Lachlan saw his scowl and almost cringed. Then he heard Michaela's voice in his head.

Head up, smile on, don't blink.

"Good morning, Dick," Lachlan said pleasantly, ignoring Dick's snide remark entirely. "What are you doing in our neck of the woods?"

Dick turned to Anna. "Would you please excuse us?"

She nodded quickly and hightailed it for the door, throwing a sympathetic look over her shoulder from behind Dick's back.

"Close the door on your way out, please," Dick called after her.

Lachlan's bland smile almost wavered, but he held firm. If he could get through being groped by horny octogenarians at charity balls, Dick Chomelsky wasn't going to break him.

"Lachlan," Dick began the moment the door shut behind Anna, "just what on earth do you think you're doing?"

Now Lachlan let his smile drop. He had always respected his boss, but it didn't sound like the feeling was mutual right then, and Lachlan had done nothing to deserve that. He studied Dick's mottled complexion and the sour twist to his mouth, and felt judged. Poorly.

"I'm teaching freshman about ethics, Dick."

Dick's scowl grew darker. "You were pandering to their salacious curiosity."

"No, I was not. I was faced with a group of fine young minds who'd been sucked in by the media and had come to my class for all the wrong reasons. I took that as an opportunity to help them *learn*. I cannot imagine a group that was more ripe for the picking, as far as lectures on ethics go. And if you listened to them, heard the discussions, then you know that my message got across."

"At the expense of our department's reputation!"

"I *hardly* think that's the case," Lachlan said severely, ignoring the thump of his heart against his ribs. "Unless it somehow tarnishes our reputation to promote critical thinking about right and wrong as it pertains to which news sources they select as ethical and reliable, or the impact of the celebrity culture on society."

"And that seems appropriate to you? For you, of all people, to be lecturing on that?" Dick spoke to him in a tone Lachlan had never heard him use with anyone but the most troublesome students.

"Yes, that seems appropriate. And I'm *exactly* who should be lecturing on this," Lachlan said sharply, his hands curling into fists at his side. "And I don't understand why you wouldn't agree. You're always telling us we need to help these young people see how philosophy can help them in life, and have real meaning to them, and I just did that. More than any other lecture I've given, I'm convinced those kids *heard me* and learned something they can apply to their day-to-day thinking. I also believe that more than one of them will come back to hear more, even when the fervor over my relationship with Michaela dies down."

"And just what *is* your relationship with Michaela Price?"

"You know what it is? *None of your damn business.*"

228

Dick's shoulders jerked back, his spine ramrod straight, absolutely radiating shock at being spoken to that way. To be fair, Lachlan was pretty damned stunned he'd said it, too, but he didn't give a fucking inch as he stared Dick down.

"Dr. Morrison, I don't know what you—"

"No, *Dick*," Lachlan said, ruthlessly cutting him off. "You don't get to ask me that. My private affairs are just that—*private*. I've thought of you as a friend for some years now and I'm sorry if this offends you or makes your job harder, but you don't get to come into my classroom and dress me down for who I spend my free time with. If you have an issue with the lecture I just gave, then I will be glad to discuss that with you. Anything else, you'll have to take your concerns to the administration and see what they make of them, because I've done nothing wrong."

It was terrifying to say it, to call Dick's bluff. Lachlan could feel his heartbeat all the way down in his fingertips now, but he flexed his hands and held firm. He knew he was right. The administration couldn't and wouldn't go near this.

Dick apparently knew it, too. "I'm sorry you feel that way."

"I'm sorry, too, Dick. It was never my intention to cause a stir when I formed a friendship with Michaela, but my own sense of right and wrong won't allow me to abandon a friend simply because it would make your job easier. She's a good person. A victim of circumstances outside her control. For this, at least, you should now have some sympathy."

Dick sniffed dismissively. "I hardly think one of my professors being fodder for the tabloid press is akin to her starring in a pornographic video."

And that was just *low*.

"Really, Dick? Because it seems to me it's pretty much exactly the same. Neither of you knew it was going to happen, and you both got fucked."

Dick's jaw dropped open and hung there, apparently speechless.

"What matters now," Lachlan said, plowing on, "is what you

229

do with it. You could hide and hope it all goes away, or you can do what I just did, and try to turn the unprecedented attention we're getting into something positive. You have an opportunity here, Dick, if you can see past what's been comfortable for years and embrace what comes next."

Lachlan grabbed his bag and threw it over his shoulder while his boss stared at him with something like awe and horror and a whole lot of bewilderment.

"You can add that to the list of things I would be happy to discuss with you," Lachlan said, far more gently. "I'd like to see our department benefit from this interest, because you're right. These kids want to know how the world works, and we can help them figure that out. But no matter how much Kierkegaard we ask them to read, there will always be the *Weekly Inquisitor*, tempting them from the newsstand. Finding a way to make those two things relevant to each other might just be the ticket to drawing more of these bright, promising students into a discipline that so few have an interest in anymore."

The clamp around Lachlan's chest eased a little when Dick actually gave a slow, thoughtful nod.

"Think about it," Lachlan said at last, patting Dick's shoulder because he just looked so overwhelmed. "You know where to find me."

Michaela was supposed to be studying, but instead she was reading Lachlan's text message discreetly on her phone.

Come over?

Michaela smiled. *When?*

Want you now.

Michaela's pulse spiked. She had no idea if that was an expression of his desire for her to visit, or of his desire for *her*. Either way, it was an exceptionally bad idea for him to put shit like that in writing. And an even worse idea for her to like it so much.

230

But she hadn't seen him in days, and she wanted him, too. *I'll be there as soon as I can.*

I'll be here.

"Whatcha got there?" Sadie asked with a sly smile.

Michaela immediately erased whatever look was on her face and tucked her phone back under her leg on the couch. "Nothing."

"Is that your *boyyyyyfriend*?"

Michaela was appalled to feel her cheeks heat up. She swore she wouldn't have blushed if it had been Sadie who asked. Or Tanner.

But that was *Eric.*

"Don't have a boyfriend," she mumbled so quickly it practically came out as a single word.

Eric grinned. "Is that the story you're going with?"

"What? No," Michaela said. "I mean, yes. I mean, it's not a story." She cast Eric a baleful look.

"You sure about that?" Tanner asked with a smirk—of course.

"*Yes.* We're just friends."

Tanner put his finger on his page to hold his place and closed his book, carefully setting it aside so as not to disturb Fang, who was sound asleep, belly-up, in Tanner's lap.

"I assume you're talking about the infamous Dr. Morrison, who has been squiring you around to all your fancy events?"

Everyone looked at Tanner.

"*Squiring*?" Sadie asked with an incredulous giggle.

"What, like you didn't read some of those articles after we were attacked out front?" Tanner defended. Michaela cringed and Tanner had the grace to look apologetic. "Sorry, but when your mother calls screeching about how she was standing in line at the grocery store and there you are on the cover of the *Weekly Inquisition*, I defy any of you not to look. Well," he said, waving at Michaela, "except you."

"As a matter of fact, my mother calls me screeching about that all the time. And yes, I also look." She laughed at their surprised expressions.

"You do?" Eric asked curiously.

They all looked genuinely interested, so Michaela admitted the horrible truth.

"This is actually embarrassing, but I pay a company to keep track of anywhere I show up in print or on TV. I get a weekly report, unless the shit is hitting the fan, then I get a call right away."

"That's..." Sadie seemed unable to find the word.

"Awful?" Michaela suggested.

"No, I wasn't going to say that. I was going to say *fucking weird.*"

Michaela let out a huff of laughter. "Welcome to my world."

"But why do that to yourself?" Tanner asked, proving he wasn't nearly as callous as he liked to pretend, and that he was perfectly aware of the awful shit people liked to write about her.

She didn't know how to make him understand without telling the unvarnished, brutal truth. "Imagine one day waking up to that screeching phone call, only it's your best friend, and she's telling you that her bother just watched you have sex on the internet."

All three of them stared at her in silent, unblinking horror.

"Right. Anyway," she said, trying to get this conversation back in any direction that didn't involve her sex-tape, "I don't always read it all, but I did check out the latest stuff, just so I would know what they were saying about Lachlan." She was sort of appalled at how affectionate she sounded when she said his name.

Sadie didn't miss it, either. "*Lachlan*, huh?"

Michaela arched one brow. "Well, you don't think I call him Dr. Morrison while he's squiring me, do you?"

"Oh, is that what we're calling it now?" Eric asked with a

grin.

Michaela laughed and pointed a finger at Eric. "You're a troublemaker. You hide it well with shyness, but underneath, you're an anchovy-and-olive-pizza-hogging troll."

His grin didn't dim in the slightest, nor did he deny it.

"Can I ask you something?" Sadie said.

"Sure," Michaela agreed, trying to remember the last time someone prefaced a question like that and she didn't feel at least a little dread. Now, though, she was struck by how not-worried she was. It wasn't that she didn't think the question would be personal, it was just that she probably wouldn't mind answering it.

"Is he okay with all this?" Sadie waved her pencil around, as if to indicate Michaela's apartment, but obviously meaning so much more.

Michaela sighed. "I don't really know."

"You haven't talked about it?"

"No, we have. He says it's cool, the press and stuff? But he was trapped in his house on Monday, and...I don't know. It's only going to get worse. I don't think he realizes that."

"Will the school give him shit?" asked Tanner.

That was a really good question, and a perceptive one. She realized she should probably ask Lachlan about it, but she dreaded hearing the answer.

"They can't," Eric said firmly. "There's no fraternization rules about you dating, since he's never going to be your professor."

Tanner grimaced. "I hope it's that simple."

So did Michaela, but she felt as skeptical as Tanner appeared to be.

They returned to their work, studying for an upcoming exam and sharing ideas about what the questions would be, but part of Michaela's brain was always on Lachlan. She was almost twitching with the need to see him, to talk to him, and to try to figure out what would happen next.

It was supposed to be simple. Friends. Or friends with benefits. But no one, least of all Lachlan, would see the paparazzi camped on one's front lawn as a benefit. She was afraid that the best answer would be that he stop going out to these events with her. Maybe then, if they were careful, they could still be friends and no one would be the wiser.

If staying friends with her was what he wanted at all. She didn't kid herself. It would be ten times easier for Lachlan if he were to just cut ties. And who could blame him? But, for the first time in longer than she cared to remember, Michaela wanted to cling to a friend. To a precious friendship. She could live without the company when she was out stumping for the Foundation. And she could learn to go without the sex she was already craving all the time.

But there was no way in hell she was giving up those hugs without a fight.

After another hour or so, the others packed up, agreeing to meet again the next day for a final review before the actual exam. As soon as they left, Michaela pulled out her phone.

I'm coming.

You will be.

Michaela shuddered and ran out her door.

Adrenaline was a funny thing. Lachlan was well used to experiencing the thrill of it on the ice, but this was the first time he'd ever gotten such a solid dose of the stuff because of his *work*.

He'd more or less chosen his field because it was so unlikely to produce the heady rush he was experiencing. Not on purpose, per se, but because he liked the predictability of his job. The quiet discourse and hours of reading and distilling texts and ideas.

Today was nothing like that, and it was a disorienting. His blood pumped like he'd just scored in the last seconds before the buzzer, but instead, he was walking across campus. His hands twitched, as if eager to fire a shot right into the back of the net, but instead, he was fumbling with his keys before finally getting his damn door open.

Adrenaline usually made him feel alert. Alive. His brain singing with it and full of ideas. But today it wasn't going like that. No, today, for some damn reason, it seemed to be channeling his energy in a single, different, direction.

His pants.

He was not now, nor had he ever been, a horndog—and he would gleefully strangle his brother Kieran for putting that term into his head to begin with. He knew plenty of guys—hell, he was *related to* several—who had this reaction to any kind of excitement. Who needed the outlet. He was just as happy, both before and now that he was experiencing it firsthand, that he had never been that guy.

That didn't stop him from texting Michaela and practically begging her to come over.

He paced around his house, jumping at every sound from the street and waiting. The chemicals were wearing off, thank god, and he was beginning to feel hot in the face from embarrassment, rather than need. It was completely unlike him to send dirty text messages. He should probably apologize. God help them both if the press ever got into one of their phones.

The idea was starting to make him sweat when he heard a gentle knock on his back door. Startled, his head snapped around, on full alert, then his intellect conquered whatever lizard brain had taken over and reminded him that Michaela couldn't very well waltz right up the street unnoticed.

He ran into the kitchen and threw open the door.

All thoughts of apologizing for his ill-conceived text messages went right out the proverbial window, the lizard brain once more in charge as he reached for Michaela and she dove for him. Their lips met before he could even slam and lock the door behind her. He managed it, eventually, and then they were stumbling toward the stairs.

He paused in the living room, eyeing his couch longingly because the bedroom just seemed *so fucking far away*, but good sense reasserted itself, barely, and he realized that they shouldn't do any of the things he was thinking about doing within view of any windows, even if the curtains were drawn.

Their climb up the stairs started out strong, but quickly devolved when Michaela caught a heel while trying to go backwards and Lachlan barely caught her before her back could hit the risers. He eased her down until her ass was perched on a stair and dove in for another kiss.

"Are you okay?" he managed when they briefly paused for air.

She hummed against his lips, and wrapped her long legs around his waist.

He was just going to take that as a yes.

For a long time they stayed like that, their lips locked, Michaela sprawled on his steps with him hovering above her, supporting her head in one hand and his weight with the other arm. His hips pushed into hers and she groaned, pushing back, using her arms and legs to pull him close.

He shifted forward, desperate to press his dick against *anything* and find some fucking relief.

"Ow," came the soft whimper.

Lifting his head, he groaned as need made his muscles tremble and he tried to suck enough oxygen into his lungs to get his brain functioning again.

What the hell were they doing? It had to be a miracle they hadn't slid right back down to the front foyer.

He straightened up and she came with him, clinging to him like a limpet. Which, actually, worked just fine. Curling one arm around her, he grasped the bannister in a death grip with his other hand and stood with Michaela wrapped around him.

Goddamn, he was going to feel that in his quads tomorrow.

"You know," Michaela whispered against his ear, her voice sexy and low, "that would have been super fucking hot if you

236

hadn't groaned like it was killing you when you stood up."

Lachlan chuckled and started up the stairs. "Forgive me?"

Michaela sucked his earlobe between her lips and bit. Lachlan almost tripped on the top stair, clutching her desperately to his chest as he regained his footing and sprinted down the hall to his bedroom.

He threw her to the middle of his bed, where she landed with a bounce and a shriek of laughter.

"Dr. Morrison!" she cried as if scandalized. "What are you doing?"

He grinned down at her, propped on her elbows, miles of legs spread open across his bed and her skirt flipped up to reveal tiny, tight lace shorts that hid nothing.
He reached over his shoulders to grab a fistful of his shirt and yanked it off over his head.

Chapter Twenty

Michaela stared up at Lachlan, her heart thumping against her ribs as he systematically stripped off his clothes and tossed them across the room without a care for where they landed. She giggled when he almost took out the reading lamp in the corner with a sneaker.

If only the *Crimson Gossip* could see Dr. Snorrison now.

His eyes never left her face, but she couldn't help but draw her eyes downward, darting her gaze over his broad shoulders and nicely delineated pectorals. Peeking at flat nipples, just a shade less pink and more cinnamon than his lips.

He didn't hesitate to bare himself, and that confidence was as singularly attractive as any one feature or part. Not that he had reason to be shy. Far from it. She licked her lips as her eyes traced over his cock, standing erect and pointed towards her.

It was an invitation she could not resist.

Sitting up, she reached for him, fingers almost brushing the flushed shaft that promised to be deliciously firm and warm and heavy, but Lachlan wrapped a hand around her wrist and stopped her.

"Oh, no, you don't," he admonished.

Her heart skipped a few beats when he grabbed her ankle and dragged her across the bed until she was perched on the edge of the mattress.

And now *her* clothes were flying around the room. She laughed, delighted, then got down to the business of helping him, because this was all she wanted. To be rid of any restrictions and to feel the press of all that bare skin against hers.

He hooked his fingers into the elasticized lace running over her hips and tugged, and she lifted her butt with the idea of helping him get the tight boy shorts off. She wasn't expecting him to grasp her hips and flip her over.

Her shriek was cut off with a huff as she landed on her

stomach, her legs hanging half off the bed. Dizzy with happiness and the startling thrill, she was momentarily disoriented. Then his big hands landed on the backs of her thighs, trailing upwards, and reality came pouring back in with the huge gulp of air she sucked into her lungs.

God, he was killing her. She shook with a low chuckle as she imagined what Tanner, Eric, and Sadie would think of Lachlan's *squiring* now. She should probably feel guilty about lying to them, but then, she hadn't, really. He wasn't her boyfriend.

But calling them "just friends" wasn't exactly an accurate representation either. She'd thought she'd known what friends with benefits was, but she hadn't ever pictured this.

Pushing up onto her elbows, she looked over her shoulder at Lachlan standing between her legs, hovering above her. Not that he noticed the look she sent him. His entire focus was narrowed down to one thing.

Her ass.

Yes, this *definitely* wasn't like any kind of friendship she'd had before. And it didn't feel like scratching an itch. Itches were on the surface, superficial. Her feelings for Lachlan went a whole lot deeper than that.

A long, delicious shiver worked up her spine as she took in his dark eyes, a ring of bright green barely visible around his dilated pupils. His tongue poked out, wetting his lower lip, and he might as well have traced it across her skin. Warmth bloomed low in her belly, and she wanted more. More of this laser focus. More of whatever the hell he had in mind for the next few hours, before she had to go meet Robby for dinner.

"God, you're spectacular," he murmured softly.

She wondered if she should be insulted that he appeared to be talking to her ass. In other circumstances, she might have come back with the classic, "My eyes are up here, asshole." But honestly, she couldn't be bothered. Not when she knew he respected so much more than the work she put into staying fit. Not when she knew he respected her mind and would treat her as his equal always.

Not when he was looking at her like *that.*

She swore he wanted to eat her alive. Or, better yet, fuck her senseless.

His hands slid further up her thighs until his calloused, hockey-rough palms cupped her cheeks below the high cut of her shorts. How many Harvard professors had hands like this? He obviously worked hard at his hockey. Both during the games and with his own training. His hands were as tough as any she'd shaken while she'd been "dating" Callum and had met the rest of his team. Those men played and practiced for hours every day and their hands were just like this.

And not one of them was a PhD.

It was hard to decide which was sexier on its own, but the combination was, without question, the sexiest thing she could imagine.

His hands pushed up and out and she pushed back against them, until lace caught up against countless eager nerve endings from the base of her spine down to her clit, teasing the already swollen nub. She rolled her hips back again and pushed into his grip, utterly shameless.

She had no idea where this was going, but she wasn't worried. In fact, she was decidedly on board with the direction they appeared to be headed, and was more than a little curious to see what he would do next. She was so amped up with anticipation, she jumped, groaning, when his lips brushed her waist, pressing moist warmth along the top of her panties, a trace of cool left in his wake. She hummed happily until he got to one side, then she squirmed, giggling, because goddamn she was ticklish there.

"Lachlan, please," she begged, though for what she didn't even know. To stop tickling her? To get down to business—in whatever form that would take?

He seemed to understand fine, though, and lifted his head to finally tug off the last scrap of her clothing. The cool air felt good against her flushed skin, prickling so much she could feel the negative spaces between where the lace had left its imprint.

She jumped again when his stubbled cheek rubbed across one cheek, nuzzling her ass like a cat would rub its face against a hand held out to stroke it. Lachlan did it again, this time on the other side, his lips catching on freshly abraded skin. He wasn't kissing her, but skimming across the fire left by his coarse beard.

Soon his cheek and chin and lips had rubbed over every inch of her backside. She felt as though he worshipped every inch of skin he touched as he nuzzled and caressed her with only his face, which, really, should have been strange, maybe even ridiculous, but it wasn't. At all.

She hummed and dropped her head, her forehead touching the mattress, her eyes closed. Like this, she could feel each of the thousands of coarse beard bristles as they dragged along increasingly sensitized skin. The comforter smelled faintly of detergent, but over that she could detect a hint of Lachlan. That something that clung to his skin, a scent that would forever make her pulse spike and her toes curl. His soap? Deodorant? Aftershave? Some combination of the three, perhaps, layered over the musk and sweat and salt of his skin.

Whatever it was, she knew no man would ever come close to replicating it. And she would miss it, horribly, when it was no longer hers to enjoy.

He distracted her from her wandering thoughts when he began to roll his head, this way and that, and now there *were* kisses. Quick pecks that left behind cool dots in delicious contrast to the heat of the beard burn he'd just spread all over. On one roll, his nose dipped between the globes of her ass, slowing and pressing in for a moment. She squirmed against him as a flush worked up her neck and into her face, burning as hot as any beard burn could. She'd had fantasies, lots of them, but this was shockingly more intimate than she'd imagined, and all he was doing was holding still, letting his breath ghost over delicate skin.

She jerked when she felt the cool press of lips and a quick flick of tongue, every muscle in her body going taut for one delicious moment. Then he was gone and she was left panting,

241

sprawled face down on his bed, ready for almost anything and not having the faintest idea what might come next.

She lay there, utterly pliant, and tried to absorb the shock and heat and aching need he'd stoked in her. His long fingers encircled her thighs and slowly pushed them open, and she moaned, spreading her legs until she had to lift up and plant her knees on the edge of the bed. Her ass hovered in the air, exposed, which she never had guessed would be as delicious as it was.

He resumed his slow torture, rubbing his face down the backs of her thighs, until his nose was pressed into the creases at her knees and he left gentle kisses there. Then back up, trailing along the thin skin of her inner thighs which lit up against his stubble even as she spread her legs further, encouraging him.

The first brush of his lips against her pussy was so gentle, she wondered if it had been on purpose, or just a happy accident on the way to the next long rub along her legs. Then it was there again, and she hummed, pressing her chest lower to the mattress and canting her hips back as far as she could, wantonly offering herself up.

His fingers sank into her legs, holding her steady, and her heart dropped before she felt the quick flick of his tongue along her labia. Once, twice.

Then he was gone.

"Please, Lachlan," she moaned, unbearably aware of the slow slide of liquid arousal slicking her folds for his tongue and touch. She couldn't see him, but she felt the press of his shoulders to her thighs.

And then, finally, he was there. She shuddered with the fast and hard rhythm of his tongue against her clit. The electric zings radiating through her made her cry out and push back against his face. If the obscene noises he made in response were anything to go by, he didn't mind.

His tongue was dexterous and maddening, dragging her higher until she was panting, her hands fisted in the sheets as tremors wracked her. She was so close, so fucking *close*, when he left her clit to lick and delve further.

Another long moan rose up out of her as she writhed against the mattress, and perhaps embarrassingly, against his face, but nothing stopped him in his quest to tease and tug and thrust and tickle. Her moans and sighs bled into one another, until all that was left was to leave her mouth hanging open, pressed to the comforter that couldn't live up to its name and offer her any relief. The tension in her back and legs ratcheted higher, making her shake, as Lachlan took her apart with his mouth and lips and tongue.

The first crest hovered and he shifted again, the broad flat of his tongue sliding back, right over the tightly clenched and wildly sensitive knot of muscles guarding the entrance to her ass.

"Oh my god," she whispered, momentarily stilled by a combination of shock and raw, unbridled *want.*

"Yes?" he asked quietly, so close she could feel the word as his lips pressed it into her skin.

She'd thought about this. Wished and wondered what it would be like to have someone do this, and then packed that away along with all the others things she would never know or only ever do to herself, since she could never trust anyone else to do them for her. With her.

Until now.

"Yes," she whispered, her throat tight with so much more than simple anticipation.

His tongue immediately slid over her again, and again, warming and wetting and pressing at tight muscles. The sensations were utterly foreign, completely unlike the touch of her fingers covered in lube or the thrust of one of her toys.

She could feel her body responding, opening little by little as he kissed and sucked and nibbled along the thin strip of electrified skin and over the tight furl of muscles. She moaned into the bedding, her chest aching at the intimacy of the act, even as her head swam with how good it felt. Not just what he was doing with his tongue and lips, but how freeing it was to be completely without concern about video cameras and the press and the potential fallout if something like *this* were ever to hit the internet.

Those concerns had no place here. This was for her and Lachlan, and she trusted that he understood and believed that in all the same ways she did.

She sighed, not an ounce of tension left anywhere in her. Her legs slid further across the mattress, leaving her exposed and vulnerable and utterly safe.

His finger slipped into her without a hint of resistance, and she hummed low in her throat.

"Is that good?"

She tried to say, "That's great," but was pretty sure it got lost in the translation from her mouth, through the comforter, and on to Lachlan's ear.

He chuckled, even as his tongue was licking around the finger lodged inside her, stabbing in beside it.

Michaela wasn't really sure *what* kind of noises she was making now. Her brain had gone to static, lost to the waves of pleasure coursing through her.

Lachlan didn't pause, thrusting and licking, nibbling and sucking until he could wedge a second finger in next to the first. Her thighs quivered as pleasure rolled through her like thunder and rain, waiting for lightening to strike.

Michaela cried out, his name bouncing off the walls of his bedroom. She was beautiful like this, completely without inhibition, gamely jumping into this wild idea without pause.

Which, actually, gave *him* pause. He finally dragged his mouth away from her body to ask, "Is this okay?"

Because as much as she *sounded* like she was having a good time, he had to be sure. This wasn't exactly a recipe from the vanilla cookbook.

"It was until you stopped," she groused, and he chuckled, already pressing back against her skin, into her body, letting her feel the shake of his shoulders from his laughter when his mouth was otherwise occupied. God, she had a way of undoing him. Making him talk when he'd always been silent. Making him laugh at moments he would have sworn he never would.

He reached out an unsteady hand and yanked open the drawer by his hip. Saliva was working for him so far, but he wanted to take this further and wasn't going to take any risks along that road.

The lube bottle felt cold in the room air, and positively frigid compared to her skin. He contemplated tucking it under her shoulder to warm it, but was loath to do anything that might distract her. So instead he wedged it high between his thighs, bracing for the shock of cold—though the only shock ended up being how little his body reacted to the chilly plastic tucked up against his nuts. He could probably jam an ice pack in there and it wouldn't dim him arousal at this point. Not when he was looking down at Michaela, spread out for him. Coming apart in his hands and on his tongue. He felt like he'd been hard for hours, his cock aching from being ignored.

He used one hand to draw her own slick back, easing the passage of his fingers as he scissored and thrust. Her body gave, opening beautifully, and while Lachlan didn't have a whole hell of a lot of experience in these things, he thought he was either extraordinarily lucky or his guess about her previous experiences were way off.

"You've done this before," he gasped, intending it as a question and wincing when it didn't come out that way.

"No." *So, lucky?* She moaned when his fingers spread wider. "Not with anyone else."

His hand, his whole body, hell, his *brain* stuttered for a moment.

"By yourself?" he hazarded.

He watched, amazed, as color seeped up her neck and into the cheek he could see—the one not pressed against the bed. When she didn't seem inclined to answer, he stopped moving. Which was probably cruel, but—

"Yes," she gasped, and he rewarded her with a deep stroke of his fingers. His head spun a little at the sounds she was making. The images she was provoking in his already over-heated imagination.

"Ms. Price," Lachlan said in a mock stern and sincerely intrigued tone of voice, "you never cease to amaze me. Care to elaborate?"

"No," she muttered.

He laughed, twisting his hand on a withdrawal and watching how her eyes fluttered shut. The muscles low in his belly clenched tight at the sight, his knees wobbling a little embarrassingly. Not that she noticed, thank goodness.

"Do you finger yourself?" he asked, his throat going hot and tight just picturing it and making his voice come out like gravel.

She nodded quickly, her mouth dropping open to suck in more air. He wasn't the only one who got hot thinking about it.

"Toys?" he questioned.

"Lots," she whispered, so quietly he wasn't certain he'd heard her correctly.

"Lots?" he asked as he fumbled with the lube and got the lid open. Jesus Christ, he'd started asking these questions so that he would have needed information, and now he'd managed to turn *himself* on so fucking much that he was about to lose it.

Which he absolutely refused to do before he was locked inside the promise of her tight, hot ass.

She sighed, and it sounded less perturbed than aroused and relieved. "I have a whole box of them. Locked up tight under my bed. I use them and I think about..."

He paused in the process of pouring lube over his fingers, probably applying way too much as he hung there, waiting for her to finish that thought and unable to function while so many ideas settled in and took root.

"What do you think about?" he asked hoarsely when it didn't seem she would say more.

She let out a long, almost painful-sounding groan. "You,

Lachlan. Lately, all I can think about is you," she admitted, her voice little more than a whisper.

The bottle of lube hit the floor with a dull thud, having slipped from his nerveless fingers. A bead of precome pearled on the tip of his cock.

She groaned as his other hand resumed moving, going faster, their passage made a thousand times easier by his—slightly excessive—application of lubricant.

"You—" He swallowed hard, his mouth gone dry. "You fuck yourself with a toy and—"

"Wish it was you. Yes," she gasped. "All the time since this started. All I can think about is how I want *you* to do these things to me. To fill me up with your cock and toys and fuck me properly."

And now Lachlan was groaning because, fuck, she was *killing him*. If his heart pumped this hard during a game, he'd bench himself until he could pull it together. Now, though, he went all in, plunging his fingers deeper, thrusting harder and watching how her muscles eased. He slipped a third finger in next to the others, pushing in and holding still as a long, keening cry locked in her throat.

"Please, Lachlan," she whispered.

He could do nothing but give whatever she asked of him.

Carefully, he eased his fingers from her body and scrabbled for a condom in the drawer. He hadn't felt this desperate and uncoordinated since he'd been a late-blooming teenager in college about to lose his virginity to his Philosophy TA from the semester before.

The image of Anna and one of the children in his current classes flashed through his mind and he shuddered. *Ew.* He forced the thought aside for another...never. It did, though, serve to restore a modicum of his control.

He managed to get the condom on quickly, if not particularly gracefully, and retrieve the lube from the floor to slick himself up. He took a deep breath to center himself but it was an utterly wasted effort the moment he looked down and saw her there, waiting for him.

"Ready?" he asked, pleased he didn't sound nearly as undone as he felt.

Her answer was to rock back, forcing the head of his cock past the tight ring of muscles and locking him inside her.

He swayed, immediately realizing far too late that he should have pushed them both up on the bed. How the hell was he supposed to stay on his feet when she kept sweeping his legs right out from under him?

He gripped her hips hard, his fingers digging in as he tried to ground himself and prevent her from going any farther. Not that he minded her enthusiasm—hell no, he did not—he just needed a moment, damn it. Even as his body was clamoring at him to *hurry up,* he wanted to wallow in the ecstasy that was pressure ringing the crown of his cock, his head spinning at the contrast of the cool air on his shaft, and the warm ache in his chest as he stared down at her face.

Shit, he was in so much trouble. And he'd thought his knees felt weak before?

Michaela shifted beneath him, impatient, and Lachlan forced aside the alarming realizations forming in his head in favor of honing in on the only thing that really mattered right now—getting this right.

He'd sort out the rest of it later. Maybe.

He thrust forward gently, keeping hold of her hips as he eased farther into her body, mesmerized by how she stretched around his shaft, how hot and tight she felt around it. He listened carefully as she made the most amazing noises, as if the air were forced from her lungs with each roll of his hips.

When his hips came to settle against the firm, soft skin of her ass, he stopped, sucking in deep breaths as he tried to absorb the heat, the *clench* of her body. Michaela arched her back, and he stared down at the long, smooth slope of it, trailing his eyes up her spine until he saw her face. The smile on her lips was arresting.

"You are so fucking beautiful," he said hoarsely, the words sent from his addled mind to spring honestly from his lips with no filter in between.

She blinked, her smile growing. "So are you."

He huffed at that, ignoring the way it stirred up that ache in his chest even more, and concentrating on how the motion shifted him inside her body. He shifted again and her eyes fluttered closed, while his made a run for the back of his head.

There was no way he could stop, setting up a steady grind, listening to how she moaned and cried beneath him until he couldn't take it anymore and pulled back, easing himself from her until only the head of his cock was trapped inside her body.

Then he thrust back in. Carefully. Slowly. Battling for control.

Control that within a few thrusts was gone, torn from his grasp by her cries that he go faster, harder. And, once, telling him to "hurry the fuck up."

He couldn't remember a time he'd laughed so much, so often, while having sex, let alone sex so blindingly good he feared he'd lose consciousness when he finally, *finally* could come.

She lifted onto her elbows, her hands fisted in the comforter to anchor her as she met and matched each thrust, pushing back into him until their bodies met with a solid smack that shook through his body and tore more cries from her throat.

He pounded into her, per her demands, and clenched his teeth against the coil of tension curling in his gut. His balls were tight and full and aching, each thrust forcing them against her wet, warm skin, until he had to stay there, grinding deep and close.

He curled an arm around her hip and attacked her clit with his fingers.

"Oh. God. Yes. That!" she shouted at him and he laughed again, resuming his thrusts, even more powerfully than before, until bright white stars hovered on the edge of his vision and he resigned himself to begging her forgiveness later, when he'd recovered enough to make it right, but there was no way he was going to be able to hold off for much longer.

He was startled by her hand grasping his, shoving his fingers back until he could sink them into her body.

"I got this," she gasped, and he could feel her take up his steady rhythm over her clit. He groaned, because Jesus fucking Christ, that was hot. How she took what she wanted. Needed. And told him how to help.

He wasn't nearly sufficiently coordinated, nor did he have enough room, to fuck her properly with his hand right then, but he curled his fingers as deep as he could manage and let the motion of their bodies do the rest.

It didn't take long. Three, four thrusts later she threw her head back and screamed, muscles clamping around his fingers and cock, holding him inside her body when he shoved forward one last time, dragging him over the edge.

"Fuck!" he barked. His face pressed between her shoulder blades as his orgasm crashed over him, bright lights exploding behind his eyelids and his spine bowing as he tried to get as deep and as far into her as he could.

Awareness returned when Michaela slid forward, taking him with her until they were both laid flat. He knew he should get some of his weight off her, but he hadn't quite regained the ability to control his limbs.

"Holy crap," Michaela muttered, her face hidden beneath the wild disarray of her hair.

Lachlan grinned and pressed a kiss to her shoulder, very carefully not saying any of the words rattling around in his brain. For now, *holy crap* covered just about all of it, anyway.

Two hours later, Michaela carefully lowered herself into the chair across from Robby's in the swanky South End restaurant, Valentine's.

He took one look at her and burst into laughter.

Chapter Twenty-One

The next week was a blur of exams and papers, suitably accompanied by torrential downpours and a cold, wet wind that made everything feel raw. The study group met almost every moment they weren't sleeping or in class, and Michaela's apartment was constantly filled with people and food and laughter and frustrated groans.

There was a distinct possibility that Fang might actually explode with happiness at having all this company, and Michaela had to admit she was pretty content with it, too.

The only thing missing was Lachlan.

He'd been texting her throughout the week, they'd talked on the phone a few times, and they'd tried to find a time for a meal, or even just a cup of coffee, but between her study schedule and all the work he was putting into revamping his lectures for his new and expanded audience, there hadn't been a way to make it work.

Tonight he was at his hockey game, and she had the crew over for another round of studying for their last—*thank god*—exam until finals kicked in at the end of the semester. She'd actually contemplated trying to convince the rest of her group to study in the stands at the ice rink so she could keep one eye on Lachlan's game, but hadn't dared voice the idea. They already liked to make moony eyes and bat their eyelashes whenever Lachlan came up.

It was ridiculous. And sort of awesome.

Tonight, they were in her kitchen, sitting around the table and in the midst of a heated debate about what new form of torture their professor would subject them to on the exam, when her phone buzzed.

"The boyfriend again?" Eric asked with a smirk.

Michaela sent him a dirty look, the effect somewhat diminished by the fact that she could see that the message *was* from Lachlan and she couldn't stop her lips from curling, just a little.

Tanner made a gagging noise. "You're sort of disgusting, you know that?"

"Leave her alone," Sadie said, but she, too, was silently laughing at Michaela.

"He's not my boyfriend," Michaela said for what might have been the thousandth time.

Eric snorted. "Okay."

She picked up her phone and typed out a quick message to Lachlan, explaining that the exam prep was still going strong and that they were thinking about ordering dinner so they could keep going for a while longer. As tempting as it was, she wouldn't be able to sneak out to McGinty's for a drink.

She didn't think too much about it when he didn't write back, figuring he was getting dressed and heading out with some of his teammates. She was deep into reviewing their readings when, an hour later, there was the sound of a key in her front door and Fang took off running, barking his head off.

Michaela looked over her shoulder from her seat in the kitchen and watched Lachlan come through her door. She tried very hard to ignore the way her heart sped up at just the sight of him.

He scooped up Fang with a fond smile and tucked him under one arm, allowing the little dog to lick his chin enthusiastically. His briefcase hung from one shoulder, and two very full plastic bags that smelled suspiciously like the Indian food they'd ordered swung from the fingers of one hand.

"He has a *key*?" Tanner asked under his breath.

Michaela ignored him. She'd left the key for Lachlan earlier in the week when she'd known she would be tied up at the library for long hours and he'd offered to come let Fang out for her.

She'd been grateful for the help, and scolded herself not to dwell on how ridiculously sweet he was.

"What are you doing here?" she asked, hoping her smile

didn't look as big and happy and stupid as she suspected it did.

He came into the kitchen and deposited the food onto the table. "Mike sent this up with me," he said, as if that answered the question. He bent to press a kiss to her cheek and smiled at the rest of the table. "How's it going here?"

If Lachlan thought it at all odd that her study group was, to a member, grinning up at him like he was the greatest thing they'd ever seen, he didn't show it. Michaela quickly took care of the introductions, praying none of them would embarrass her, and went to get everyone plates and utensils. Sadie, Tanner, and Eric chatted with Lachlan easily, insisting they had more than enough to share as they divvied up the dishes and made him a plate.

Sadie slid her chair to the side, away from Michaela. "Here. Have a seat."

Lachlan smiled gratefully. "I don't want to interrupt." He looked at Michaela. "I have a ton of work to do, too, and my hip is killing me from the game. Are you okay if I take this into the bedroom so I can stretch out and get some work done?"

The study group monsters were grinning again.

"Sure," she said, as casually as she could manage, holding still as he bent to kiss her again. Her heart gave a treacherous lurch as his warm lips pressed to her forehead.

She didn't dare attempt to meet anyone else's eyes, instead keeping her gaze fixed on Lachlan as he went down her hallway, Fang trotting happily at his heels, and disappeared into the bedroom. A moment later, the door shut gently.

She didn't suppose she could get away with not turning around again *ever*.

Probably not.

As expected, all three of them were staring at her, eyes wide and unblinking. Eventually, Eric couldn't contain a slightly hysterical giggle.

"Not your boyfriend, huh?" Sadie asked dryly. At least she kept her voice down.

"He's just a friend," Michaela said, sounding desperate even to her own ears. "We've only known each other for a couple months."

Eric stopped laughing. "When I fell in love, it only took two weeks."

Everyone looked at him, but he glanced down at his books, as if he hadn't just said something important. Eric was single, they knew that much. And they knew that the reasons for that were not something he was interested in discussing.

Tanner cleared his throat, uncharacteristically tactful in drawing the attention off Eric, who clearly didn't want it. "He has a key."

"He lets Fang out for me sometimes."

"And your doorman, who is more protective than a mother bear with her cub, gave him our food."

"They've gotten to know each other pretty well."

Tanner looked unimpressed with this admittedly poor counterargument.

"He's hanging out in your bedroom," Tanner added with a pointed tilt of his head.

"He doesn't want to disturb us. He's really considerate. He knows how hard we're working."

"*And* he's really considerate," Sadie said, throwing Michaela's own words back at her.

"Well, I'm not dating every considerate man I know, am I?" Michaela tried desperately. "Although, that would certainly exclude the two of you if I were," she added with dirty looks for Tanner and Eric.

Eric grinned. "You're not my type," he assured her blithely before going in for the kill. "Also, *he kissed your forehead.*"

And, well, that had been particularly sweet. Michaela sat silently and tried not to think about what it meant that she really, really *wanted* Lachlan to be her boyfriend.

Which was so stupid. She was too old to have a freaking boyfriend, first of all. She wanted a partner. A *significant other.*

Which had been a turn of phrase that had always seemed kind of weird to her before, but now she understood completely.

None of which mattered, of course, because it wasn't going to happen. She was all wrong for him. They were totally ill-suited. He hated the attention, the press, the social commitments, and the constant rumors and speculation. He would never *want* to be her boyfriend, because he was smart and knew himself well enough to know that it would make him miserable.

He deserved better.

"Michaela," Tanner said with his customary smirk, "*I* am your friend."

She smiled helplessly at him, because that was nice to hear. And even better, it was *true*. He *was* her friend. They all were, and she wasn't even sure when it had happened, but it was kind of amazing and great.

If there was any way she could express that without sounding like an insecure second grader who'd just discovered their first BFF, she would have done it.

As it was, Tanner was studying the dopey look on her face with something like alarm.

"Oh. Um. Yes. Thank you?" she said, going all-out on the award for Most Awkward in a bid to get him to continue.

He acknowledged that with a nod, kindly refraining from pointing out that she was a complete dork. "And I'm never going to kiss your forehead, okay?"

"Me, either," Eric added helpfully.

"Nor I," from Sadie.

Michaela rolled her eyes, even if her heart did skip a little as hope crept in. "You're all reading too much into this because you want it to be true."

Tanner continued, undeterred. "The only foreheads I ever kiss are my sister's and my grandmother's. Is that how it is with you and Lachlan? Do you think he thinks of you like his sister?"

Which, *ew.* No. That was just wrong on a lot of levels, which she was sure was written all over her face. She stared fixedly down at her kitchen table and suddenly pictured Lachlan eating her out on top of it before fucking her senseless in the chair that, if she weren't mistaken, Tanner was currently sitting in.

Swallowing back a hysterical giggle, she glared at her books and wished furiously that she could blame the vindaloo for the heat searing her cheeks and neck.

"*Oh, ho!*" cried Sadie gleefully as all three of them burst into laughter.

Michaela buried her face in her hands.

"Definitely not his sister, then," Eric gasped between guffaws.

Michaela locked the door behind her departing study group and slumped against the wall. They were definitely as ready as they could be for the exam, but it had taken longer than any of them had predicted to cover all the possible material.

It was well past midnight and she was ready for *bed*. Dragging herself down the hallway, she opened her bedroom door and smiled.

Lachlan was asleep, propped up against the headboard with books and papers scattered around him and his laptop on his legs. Fang was curled up on Lachlan's chest, with one of Lachlan's big hands curled protectively around him to prevent him from sliding off.

Moving as quietly as she could, she gathered up Lachlan's work and set it on her dresser, then plucked Fang off Lachlan and popped him outside to his patch of grass. When they returned, she found Lachlan blinking at her blearily.

"I'm sorry I woke you," she said softly.

"No, it's good. My back would never forgive me if I slept like this," he mumbled back, slowly sitting up and putting his feet on the floor. He groaned as he stretched his arms above his head.

She padded around the bed to stand in front of him, using

257

his distraction and raised arms to start tugging his shirt up and off. He looked up at her curiously, his hair going in every direction once he was freed from the shirt.

"I can go home, if you want?"

"No."

He smiled faintly and stood, shucking his pants and socks. She stripped down to a t-shirt and her underwear and crawled under the covers. Lachlan slid in on the other side, Fang surfing the shifting covers with a disgruntled look before jumping to safety on Michaela's side of the bed.

As soon as her head hit the pillow, Michaela felt the need for sleep evaporate. This was...awkward, actually. She hadn't slept in the same bed with someone in years. And she probably shouldn't be doing it now. That wasn't what this was supposed to be.

Not that Lachlan seemed the least bit bothered as he shut off the remaining light and rolled over, scooting up behind her and throwing an arm around her waist. Before she could say anything, like, "What the fuck are we really doing here?" he tugged her back against him.

"This okay?" he murmured. He sounded half asleep.

She nodded quickly, instinctively curling back into his warmth. God, this was nice. She liked how their breathing synced up, growing deep as she forgot all about her concerns and the tension bled from her shoulders, the heat radiating from Lachlan's body seeping into hers.

Lachlan's hand on her belly jerked when Fang pawed at it and he reached out to snag the little menace and pull him in against her chest, a third very, very small addition to their set of spoons. She snuggled back even more and watched Lachlan's thumb stroke over Fang's bulbous little head in long, slow sweeps.

The dog fell utterly under Lachlan's spell.

He wasn't the only one.

The following week was Halloween. In honor of the holiday, and in a bid to raise money for a local organization helping orphaned refugee children find new homes in the area, Seamus Lynch was throwing a party at his house.

As far as Lachlan could tell, what Seamus was *actually* doing that evening was cementing his support for Michaela, and forcibly entrenching her into Boston society with the clear message that she would be welcome, *or else.*

Michaela had responded eagerly when Seamus had sent along his invitation, but looked genuinely alarmed when the wily old man anchored her to his arm the moment they passed through the door. She looked at Lachlan with wide eyes, and he realized she was worried, in part, about him. He waved her off with as reassuring a smile as he could manage.

Tonight, at least, she wasn't his only ally in the crowd. His sister and her partners were here. Somewhere.

It took a distressingly long time to find any of them in the enormous mansion perched at the top of Beacon Hill. Lachlan was proud, though, that he managed to greet some people he'd met before, be introduced to others, and politely extract himself again without any help.

Now he stood in a quiet corner of the intimidatingly large living room—or was it a parlor when it was this fancy? A salon?—and looked out over the crowd of elegantly dressed guests. Seamus, ever happy to exert his power, had declared that the fete would be black tie, and that everyone should endeavor to wear only black, white, or orange.

Michaela looked fucking amazing in orange, as it turned out. But then, she'd probably look fucking amazing in a mud-brown sack.

Rhian, also pretty amazingly good-looking in his tux, stood at Lachlan's side, champagne glass clenched in his fist, frowning fiercely.

"Chill," Lachlan said mildly, without looking at his friend.

259

Rhian snorted. "Since when have you become so Zen about these things? You used to hate parties."

"I still do," Lachlan said automatically, but as soon as the words left his mouth, they felt like a lie. "Okay, I don't hate them as much as I used to. But, the point is, you're supposed to be the one with superior social skills here, and you're freaking out."

"I shouldn't have come to this thing," Rhian said. "What if someone recognizes me?"

"You're a professional hockey player in Boston. There is a very good chance someone is going to recognize you."

"That's not what I mean. What if...what if someone thinks I look like Seamus? Or Chelsea?" Rhian lifted his hand to indicate his sister on the other side of the room, chatting happily with another guest—one who perhaps should have reconsidered wearing orange, as now she appeared as though she was in liver failure.

Rhian and Chelsea did look a lot alike, but no one here knew they were related. As far as the rest of the world was concerned, Seamus, a well-known hockey fanatic, had befriended Rhian when he'd come to Boston to play.

"No one will figure it out," Lachlan said soothingly.

"How do you know?"

Lachlan glanced at Michaela across the room. *Michaela's Rules for Managing the Public.* People only see what they want to see. What they expect. If you don't give them a reason to wonder, they won't."

Rhian followed Lachlan's gaze. "Is that what Grandfa— *Seamus* is doing with Michaela? Giving everyone a reason to doubt their preconceived notions about her?"

Lachlan smiled. "Yes. That's exactly what he's doing."

As if she could feel their eyes on her, Michaela looked over her shoulder and smiled at Lachlan. His heart skipped a beat. Or four.

"*Oh*," Rhian said, staring at Lachlan's face as if someone had just handed him an unexpected gift.

260

"Shut up," Lachlan muttered. "It's not what you think."

"What's not what he thinks?" Savannah asked, coming up behind them, her arm threaded though Garrick's.

"Nothing," Lachlan said quickly, turning to his sister. "I was just saying that this kind of party was a lot easier than some of the other things Michaela has dragged me to."

Garrick pursed his lips. "Maybe for you," he said darkly, his hand subtly brushing the back of Rhian's.

Officially, Garrick and Savannah were here as a couple, and Rhian was here stag. It sucked for everyone involved, but given Rhian's high-profile career, no one questioned the wisdom of the charade.

"Fair enough," Lachlan said with a frown. He was distracted from dark thoughts about how everyone should just mind their own business and let people live however they wished by the arrival of a waiter.

"Drinks?" he asked politely.

Garrick and Lachlan both requested a glass of wine and Rhian asked for a water, since he had a game the next day. Savannah gave no reason for her ginger ale, but perhaps the game tomorrow was keeping her from indulging, too. She was, after all, the team's trainer.

Though that didn't explain why Garrick and Rhian were smiling like that.

"Are you all having a nice evening?" asked Seamus as he wandered over to them, Michaela still on his arm.

Lachlan figured he might as well resign himself to being without her for the entire night.

"It's a very nice party," Savannah said politely.

Seamus's eyes narrowed. "What happened?"

"What? Nothing," Savannah said with her best wide-eyed innocent look, the one any member of their family could see through in an instant. Including, apparently, Seamus.

"My sweet girl, you will tell me or I will hound you for the rest of the night."

Savannah leaned in close and whispered furiously, "Grandfather, you cannot go fighting all my battles for me. It's fine."

Seamus frowned. "Spill it, young lady."

Garrick sighed gustily, caving way faster than Savannah. "Some snotty old lady declared that it wasn't appropriate for women to work in a locker room full of those—and I quote—*sweaty, smelly men covered in tattoos.*"

Rhian grinned. "Hey, I don't have any tattoos."

"But you are pretty smelly," Garrick returned. "And sweaty, sometimes," he added, his grin turning sly.

"Anyway!" Savannah said quickly before the conversation went in directions none of their family members wanted to go. "It's fine. She's just old fashioned."

"Who was it?" Seamus demanded.

"Wiggle-something?" Garrick said. "I don't know, it didn't even sound like a real name."

Lachlan and Michaela's eyes met, and in unison they said, "Wigglesworth."

Seamus's eyebrows went up. "You know her, I assume?"

"Her son Robby is a close friend of mine," Michaela explained. "And Lachlan had the pleasure of being introduced to them the other night."

Lachlan refrained from commenting on Michaela's definition of "pleasure" in this case. Instead, he turned to Rhian. "I have an idea. Care to join me for a stroll around the party?"

"Uh, sure?" Rhian said. "Where are we going?"

"Just follow me," Lachlan said as he cut through the crowd toward the room Savannah had indicated, looking back to confirm Rhian followed in his wake.

It only took a minute to find the Wigglesworths. He'd done his homework on these two since that night at the aquarium, and now he felt a thrill remarkably similar to the moment before lining up for a tough face-off. He slapped on a big smile and sailed right up to them. Mr. Wigglesworth actually looked almost pleased to see him, but Mrs. Wigglesworth couldn't hide her distaste. Or her alarm when Rhian pulled up to stand next to Lachlan.

"James, Priscilla," Lachlan said, greeting them cheerfully.

"Dr. Morrison," Priscilla Wigglesworth returned repressively. "What a surprise."

"Is it? Seamus is a good friend of mine, so I wouldn't miss this for the world," he returned blithely. He thought Robby's mother actually paled a little. "I'd like to introduce you to another dear friend of mine." He held his hand out toward Rhian. "This is Rhian Savage. You may have heard of him. He and my sister, Savannah, work together. I believe you met her earlier?"

Lachlan was certain Mrs. Wigglesworth would not have been amused to see the smile twitching to life on her husband's lips.

Rhian shook their hands briskly, nodding to each of them. Lachlan then launched into a detailed and exhausting description for Rhian about how Lachlan had come to meet Robby—omitting the fact that he'd grabbed Lachlan's ass repeatedly—and then went on to expound on Robby's many, many fine qualities. Rhian did a marginal job of not looking at Lachlan like he'd lost his mind.

It was possible Rhian had never heard him speak so many words in a row.

Michaela, Seamus, Garrick, and Savannah were gathered in the doorway behind the Wigglesworths, blatantly eavesdropping. Seamus smiled proudly when he caught Lachlan's eye, while Michaela and Savannah kept their heads bent together as their shoulders shook with ill-concealed mirth.

When Lachlan ran out of wonderful things to say about Robby, he moved on to Rhian, and Savannah, and how hard they worked to reach the very highest levels in their professions. He made sure to ask Mrs. Wigglesworth if she was aware that *two* of his brothers were professional hockey players. Which, of course, led to a description of how much physical strength, discipline, and mental acuity was needed to attain these heights.

Rhian actually blushed a little at the effusive praise, and Lachlan had to look away before he broke down laughing. Mrs. Wigglesworth now looked mildly ill.

Mission accomplished. It turned out knowing how to make people staggeringly uncomfortable in social situations *was* a useful skill.

The only issue now was how the hell Lachlan was going to get *out* of this conversation after having dug himself in so deep.

His savior arrived in the form of Seamus, with Michaela in tow. "Lachlan, son, forgive me for interrupting. I can see that you've quite captivated your audience, and I hate to pull them away, but I must." He turned to the Wigglesworths. "Priscilla, James, I hoped we could speak? Michaela here has some wonderful ideas I thought we could discuss."

Priscilla Wigglesworth had probably never been so glad to lay eyes on Michaela, nodding so quickly she almost dislodged her coiffure. Seamus smiled benignly and led them away toward a discreet door in the corner. Lachlan wondered cheerfully what torture Seamus had in store next. Whatever it was, they probably deserved it.

Michaela winked at him before disappearing. As soon as the door shut behind them, Rhian burst into laughter. "Oh my god," he gasped. "That was awesome."

Lachlan grinned, delighted to have amused his friend and relieved when the waiter and their drinks arrived. He was parched. He routinely gave one-hour lectures that required him to speak less than he'd just done. He looked around the room, interested to see who else he recognized, and trying to remember if any of them were on Michaela's radar. He suddenly understood the appeal Seamus found in making everyone learn how wrong they were about Michaela.

He was pleased to pick out a few more familiar faces that would be likely candidates for a chat. It was clear these particular social circles weren't that big. He was considering the couple in the corner, whose names he couldn't remember, but he clearly recalled they needed more convincing about a shelter project somewhere, when someone literally bounced off his side.

"Oh, forgive me," said a high, breathless voice at his elbow.

Lachlan smiled down at the petite blonde as she curled a hand around his elbow under the guise of steadying him. It was ridiculous, of course, since she was tiny and he had been hit at full speed by two-hundred-and-fifty-pound defensemen while wearing skates on a regular basis for years.

Speaking of defensemen, he saw Rhian shift out of the corner of his eye, no doubt coming to save him.

"It's no trouble," Lachlan said, waving a hand to still Rhian, and putting on what he now thought of as his "parent's weekend and press" smile. When she didn't blink, or look away, *or* release his arm, he raised one eyebrow. "Can I help you with something?"

"Oh. Um, no. I mean, hi. I'm Amanda."

Her hand wandered up his arm. Subtle, she was not.

"And I'm Lachlan. It's nice to meet you." He kept his voice neutral. Not rude. Not interested.

"Care to join me for a drink?"

"I'm sorry, I can't. But it's kind of you to ask," he replied, pulling out one of Michaela's favorite send offs.

"Oh, well, maybe later?"

He smiled enigmatically. "Maybe." *Never.*

After a long look, she wandered away. Lachlan turned back to Rhian, who was staring at him with a wide-eyed, wondrous expression.

"Who the hell are you, and what did you do with Lachlan Morrison?"

"What?" he said defensively.

"That was...you just..." Rhian shook his head as if to clear it, then searched Lachlan's face for god knew what. "Is that what Michaela's been teaching you?"

"No. Well, yes. But to be honest, I'm not sure she taught me all that much. I mean, I always knew how to be polite—you've met my mother, right?—I just couldn't employ it when I was freaked out."

"But that didn't freak you out," Rhian stated, though there was a hint of a question there, too. "I mean, I'm pretty sure that would have freaked you out, before. Right?"

"Yes, probably." Lachlan shrugged. "But not anymore, I guess."

"Because you're no longer nervous around woman you're attracted to?"

"No...not exactly," Lachlan said, looking over to where Michaela and Seamus had reentered the room and were holding court in the corner. "I think it's more that now there's only one women I'm attracted to."

Rhian grinned. "Well, I'll be damned."

Chapter Twenty-Two

Lachlan was acting weird.

Michaela had no idea what was going on in that big old brain of his, but something was bouncing around in there, and he couldn't seem to stop chewing on it. Maybe it was some great philosophical question. Or logistics for the hockey league's next season. But whatever it was, he wasn't inclined to tell her, and it seemed to necessitate him staring at her a lot.

Which she didn't mind so much, as a rule. If anyone were going to stare at her, she'd rather it were Lachlan. But often these deep thoughts came with a frown that made her worry. Maybe he was already beginning to tire of the insanity that surrounded her life. God knew she was sick to death of it.

For the first time in years, she was giving serious consideration to the idea of hiring someone to help her run the Foundation. Someone who could split the duties of attending events and going to meetings and dealing with the administration. Not another project manager or accountant. But a director.

It would take a while to find someone she could work with that closely. Who she could trust. But in the meantime, even if she couldn't save herself from the constant grind of fundraisers and dinners, she could save Lachlan. Seamus's party the other night had been perfect, since it had been small and private. There would be plenty more like it in the coming months, now that she was getting to know some of the players in Boston. She could still spend time with Lachlan and help him with his social skills without subjecting him to the full onslaught of her miserable life.

"You're busy this weekend, right?" Lachlan asked, as if he were reading her mind. They sat at her kitchen table with their work spread out before them. They'd promised themselves and each other they'd get it done before doing anything else.

"Yes, I have a thing this weekend. In New York."

Lachlan cocked his head, studying her far more intently than was warranted. "You do?"

"Oh, yeah, it's the annual gala for the Price Foundation," she explained, trying to make it sound far less traumatic than it was. "I didn't mention it because I know you don't want to deal with all that."

His eyes narrowed. "I don't mind."

She smiled, hoping it didn't look as sad as it felt. "You would mind, I think, in this case. There will be about a hundred times more press at this thing than at anything we've been to together."

Lachlan shuddered, proving her point.

"Yeah it's...*big*," she agreed. "They'll make a huge deal out of us dating, and won't believe it if we tell them otherwise. I'd just as soon not give them the fodder they'll need for articles about how I've been dumped by multiple Morrisons when you're not around to help me out anymore."

"I'm not going anywhere."

Yet, she thought. Though hearing him say it did make her feel a little better. She suspected, though, that nothing would end their arrangement faster than exposing Lachlan to the full extent of the bedlam surrounding this event.

Lachlan's scowl grew darker the longer he sat there watching her.

"Do *you* have to go?" he asked at last.

Michaela wished she didn't, but admitted, "Yes, it's pretty much a command performance for the Chairwoman of the Board."

"Right. Of course. I'm sorry?"

She smiled, genuinely, at that. She didn't know when she'd started to think of New York as enemy territory. It had been her home most of her life. She should be looking forward to her visit, but mostly she was already looking forward to coming back to her life here in Cambridge. She was hardly anonymous, but she felt...safe, and cared for, in a way she hadn't ever in her adult life.

Shaking off that thought, she focused back on Lachlan.

"For the record," she said, "it won't be nearly as much fun without you there."

He rolled his eyes. "Right, because being my social chaperone is so much fun for you."

"I was hardly your chaperone at Seamus's. You took that place by storm while I was off in another room with Boston's elite being forced to pretend they liked me."

"If Seamus is pushing too hard, I can talk to him."

She laughed. "No, I'm enjoying it, to be honest. I've never had a champion like him before. It's really nice, knowing there is someone on your side. Someone who would protect you."

Lachlan opened his mouth to say something, then seemed to think better of it.

She didn't question it. She was too busy picturing her parents and realizing how much she wished they'd done the same. How disappointed she was that they hadn't. At the time, she hadn't blamed them for forcing her to face down the demons she'd unleashed. They'd stood by her, at least, but they hadn't leaped to her defense. Not like Seamus. She'd never once questioned whether it had been an option, until now.

"Let's take a break," Lachlan said suddenly, standing and pulling her from her chair.

She rose with a reluctant look back at her books as he led her from the kitchen, her hand in his. Her eyebrows went up when he walked through her bedroom door.

She'd been hoping, of course, that they would end up here eventually, but figured it would be after their work was done and they'd gone out to eat. That had been the vague plan, anyway.

As Lachlan bent to kiss her, she decided she liked this plan much better.

Her hands went for his shirt, working open the buttons while his cruised up and down her back, soothing her while they kissed. It was, perhaps, a wasted effort, since just the feel of his lips against hers worked her up. Thoughts of her parents, of

269

champions and people who would stand by her no matter what going by wayside in favor of focusing all her attention on one person only. Lachlan.

He shrugged his shirt to the floor the moment she got it completely open, and her shirt soon followed. They stripped quickly, hands everywhere, palms rubbing over warm skin to search out the sensitive spots with quick, knowing fingers.

She gasped when he tweaked her nipple, pinching it hard and unexpectedly. Blood rushed to that point the moment he released her, and she curled her hands into his hair, her tongue wrapping around his in a show of appreciation.

He did it again. And again. Stopping only when they had to break apart so she could climb on the bed or risk dissolving to the floor.

She rolled to her back and raised her arms to pull him over her, but he was already there, pressing her into the mattress, his cock slipping between their bodies. Her breath sounded loud in the dark room, each little noise he teased from her with the roll of his hips and his questing, curious, *devious* fingers, burst like a shout into the silence.

His hands skimmed up her thigh and she lifted her legs, wrapping them around his ribs, her hands clenched in his hair, holding him close. Her lips buzzed, feeling swollen and bruised from their long, avid kisses. He rocked against her harder, his cock nudging between her legs to run through the slick where her body ached, hollow and needy.

She was aware, distantly, that this was different. The part of her brain not lost to the slow, powerful thrust of his cock along her clit and the dance of his tongue in her mouth understood that they hadn't had sex like this before.

One reason why popped into her head and she laughed, abruptly forcing their mouths apart at last.

He pulled back a little, his nose brushing along hers sweetly. "What?"

"We finally made it to a bed."

He grinned. "That okay?"

"No. Yes. This is great."

His smile turned softer and she leaned up to meet his descending lips eagerly, feeling that smile and letting it warm all the places in her heart she'd sworn she would never be able to open to anyone.

Lachlan smiled and kissed Michaela, letting himself sink into every physical sensation, accepting every strange new feeling, and enjoying how she responded to every touch. Every kiss.

He'd been thinking about that a lot over the past few days. About how he felt when he was with her. How *he* responded to *her* touch and kisses. How his stomach did somersaults every time she smiled at him, or the way his heart would skip beats when she laughed.

Needless to say, he'd drawn some fairly obvious conclusions about where his head and heart were in all this. But, sadly, that didn't mean she felt the same way. The lack of invitation to New York made that clear enough.

He was astounded to find that his feelings were a little hurt that he hadn't been invited to a party. This was, as a rule, the kind of thing that had flooded him with relief whenever it had happened in the past.

But it wasn't the party he was interested in. It was the company. He wanted to spend any time he could with the beautiful woman and friend who at this very moment writhed beneath him as he ran the length of his shaft along her clit. He bit his cheek, hard, to keep his head screwed on straight and the words from spilling out while he teased her, and himself, his dick aching with the need to be inside her.

He threw an arm out to search for the condom he'd tossed on the bed a moment before discarding his pants, whimpering in relief when his fingers closed around the foil packet.

"Here," she said, plucking it from his grasp. "Let me."

271

He watched her tear it open with her bright, sharp teeth just pinching the corner of the square. The moment it popped free and into her hand, he pulled away just far enough for her to reach between them and roll it down his shaft.

"*Fuck*," he muttered, squirming at the feel of her long, hot fingers running along his length.

"Yes," she sighed, wrapping her forever-long legs back around him and pulling him close.

Surging forward, he plunged into her, buried to the hilt in one long, heavy thrust.

The hairs on the back of his neck stood up, every muscle shuddering as he was swamped with the desire to thrust, to seek out more of this perfection. He pressed their foreheads together while they attempted—and failed—to catch their shared breaths. The tight, hot clench around his cock was amazing, but it was nothing compared to the smile in her eyes as she looked up at him, the slow stroke of her fingers over the goosebumps along his spine.

He felt connected to her in a way that he'd never experienced before. And it had nothing to do with the physical.

Though the physical was good, too. Jesus fucking Christ, was it good.

He rolled his hips, rubbing his cock along her clinging walls and swallowing her moans with his lips. When he couldn't stand it any longer, he withdrew, slowly, stopping when just the head of his cock hovered inside her body, before pushing just as slowly back in.

He tortured them both with a slow climb, until her hands went from soothing strokes to a hard grip around his ribs, and her hips rose to meet his on every stroke. His kissed her through it all, trying to capture every touch and scent and sound. To figure out how the fuck something as simple as this could feel more powerful, more intimate, than anything they'd done before.

"Please, Lachlan. I need..." she writhed beneath him, her words lost and her eyes vague.

He nodded, possibly stupidly, because he wasn't really sure what he needed either. He knew what his body wanted. What clamored for release in the tingle at the base of his spine and the heat pooling low in his belly. But it felt bigger than that. That he needed to do something *more.*

He didn't want to take his hands from under and around her shoulders, where they'd caught in her hair and the silk of it slipped between his fingers. He didn't want to lose the feeling of her long, strong body pressed from chest to hips with his, or the warmth of her thighs along his sides.

Instead he picked up speed, each thrust coming a little faster than the last. He pressed his cheek to hers, so that her lips carried her cries directly to his ear, the moment their bodies met forcing a loud staccato burst of pleasure up from her throat. His knees slid across the bed, anchoring him so that he could shift lower and thrust harder.

She arched beneath him, her fingers ten perfect points of pain against his ribs, and cried out. She was close, so close. He didn't stop. Didn't hesitate. His rhythm relentless, his balls drawing up tight, so that he struggled to force his orgasm back. She wasn't there yet.

She looked wrecked, her cheeks bright pink and her breathing hectic. Her hair a tangled mess spread across his bed.

He wanted to tell her how beautiful she was. Pour out all the words in his heart, but he didn't dare. Even half out of his mind, he knew such a declaration made within moments of orgasm would be a mistake. Too easily dismissed or discounted.

He kept going back to what she'd said about Seamus, and how she'd never had someone like him help her before. Her tone had said she hadn't ever expected one either. And that just seemed so *wrong.* He wanted to be her champion. To protect her no matter what.

His ears rang with Michaela's loud shout, cut off when their mouths met and she gasped against him, shaking, her tight sheath clamped down around him. The tension coiled at the base of his spine rolled up and out, washing over him, pouring from his body into hers, whiting out anything but the joy of having her in his arms, wrapped around him, sobbing in his ear. He bucked against her, again and again, until there was nothing left of him but quivering muscles and a full, aching heart.

His hips finally came to rest against hers and he clung to her, indulging in long, lingering kisses that didn't begin to communicate what needed to be said, but which eased his mind from dizzying heights to a warm, post-coital haze he wanted to wallow in forever.

Work and dinner and the rest of the world forgotten, he barely separated from her long enough to dispose of the condom before rolling them both under the covers and holding her close, her face pressed to his throat, their legs tangled together, as they drifted off to sleep.

Chapter Twenty-Three

Lachlan couldn't remember the last time he'd been more reluctant to answer the phone—and that was saying something, since he was pretty much *always* reluctant to answer the phone.

As usual, though, the guilt of ignoring anyone in his family got the better of him.

"Hey, Callum."

"Hey! Can Michaela hear me?"

Lachlan frowned at his empty living room and wondered if his brother had lost his mind.

"Uh, no? Why would she be able to hear you? You called *my* phone."

"Okay. Good. So she's not right there or anything, right?"

Honestly, his brother was a mystery to Lachlan a lot of the time, but today he seemed extra-specially weird. Maybe he'd lost track of the date? Lachlan knew Michaela had invited Callum and Rupert—*unlike Lachlan*—to the Price Foundation thing in New York, even though they couldn't make it this year. But the hockey season could get disorienting for the people who were caught in the constant pull and push of travel and games. Sometimes it felt like they didn't know which way was up until April, or, if they were lucky, June.

"No?" Lachlan said. "She's not here, Callum. She's in—"

"Look, I just want to say this quickly, before she comes back, because she'll totally know I'm telling on her, but I had to get in touch before tonight."

Lachlan was sufficiently intrigued by his brother's rambling to stop trying to correct him and remain silent.

"This thing. Tonight? It's the worst. She *hates* it. Last year she was shaking so hard, Rupert resorted to getting her drunk before we hit the red carpet. I mean, not loaded or anything, but a good buzz. It barely helped. Though, you might try it."

"What the hell are you talking about?" Lachlan asked,

bewildered and alarmed, the idea of Michaela shaking over anything making his stomach churn.

"Did she not tell you?" Callum asked, then muttered, "Of course she didn't tell you. Okay. Look, tonight is a big deal. The Price Foundation Gala is attended by everyone in New York who donates, and a whole bunch of people who don't, but turn up every year like an entire bank vault's worth of bad pennies. The asshole friends who turned their backs on her, the press, and of course, the douchebag."

Lachlan stood abruptly. "Blake Whelton will be there tonight?"

"*Yes*," Callum said with blatant exasperation. "That's what I'm telling you!"

"Why?"

"Why what? Why am I telling you or why will the douchebag be there?"

Lachlan had a terrible suspicion about the first answer, but he focused on the second. "Why would the Price Foundation invite him?"

Callum's sigh spoke volumes, none of which Lachlan wanted to believe but needed to hear anyway. "Her parents invite his entire family because they insist on remaining good friends with his parents."

"They *what?*"

"I know, it sucks. I've tried talking to her about it, but she doesn't see it the way I do. The way you maybe do, too. Her parents dealt with the scandal by pretending nothing was wrong."

"By pretending their daughter's boyfriend hadn't betrayed her trust and exploited the family's reputation and her good looks and fame in order to exact revenge for being dumped and possibly for some twisted, prurient gratification or to further his own career?"

"Okay, apparently we see it the exact same way."

"Fuck."

"Yeah, I'm sorry to dump this one you, but Rupert and I can't be there, so you're on point tonight."

"*Fuuuck.*"

"It's going to be fine. Just stick by her side and be her friend, and accept that the press is going to have a field day with it, and you'll be fine." It sounded more like a question than a statement at the end.

"No, they're not going to have a field day at all."

"They're not?"

"No, because *I'm in fucking Boston*!"

There was a long, pregnant pause. "What?"

"I'm in Boston. To quote our dear friend, she'd just as soon not give the press any more reasons to say she'd been dumped by multiple Morrisons."

"*What?*"

"She didn't invite me, Cal. She went alone."

"Oh, damn," Callum said quietly, his bleak tone terrifying.

How bad was this going to be for her?

"I never even thought of that," Callum admitted. "She's fake dated two brothers now, and when you move on to a woman you're actually dating, she'll get raked over the coals again, won't she?"

"No, she won't."

"Right, because she's keeping you out of the press now."

"No, she won't get raked over the coals because I have *no intention of moving on.*"

This pause was shorter but no less pregnant than the last. "Pardon me?"

"You heard me. Also, in the spirit of full disclosure, we've been having lots of amazing sex."

It felt good to finally tell the truth, and even better to listen to Callum squawking like a protective and hilariously prudish brother on the other end of the line—not in defense of Lachlan's honor, of course, but for Michaela's.

"I'm going to fucking kill you!"

"Why? For caring? For wanting to be part of her life? For making your best friend *my* best friend?"

"No, you asshole! For letting her go to New York alone!"

Which brought Lachlan crashing back to reality. "She didn't invite me, Callum."

"Which means she cares, you idiot. It means she doesn't think you deserve to be dragged into the craziness. She thinks her life is a punishment she's somehow earned. If you know her at all, you know I'm right."

Callum was right. And Lachlan *hated* it. Her own parents made her parade in front of everybody with that fucking asshole right in the same room, stealing the foundation's thunder, distracting everyone from the amazing work she was doing.

And he'd let her leave him home. Let her think she was doing him a *favor*.

Lachlan was furious with himself. He'd told himself he wanted to be her champion, and the only way he could do that was if he was willing to stand up and be counted, no matter who was watching and how many cameras were pointed in his direction.

Even he was surprised to discover he was more than willing. This was no sacrifice. It was what he *needed* to do. What he was meant to do from the moment she found him on campus two months ago and forced him from his sheltered, small world into her big, bright, crazy one.

Now the only issue remaining was that it was noon, he was in Boston, and apparently, he had a date—a *real* date—in New York at six o'clock.

Oh, yeah, and his tux was at the dry cleaners.

Shit.

Michaela climbed gracefully from the limousine, the core tenets Lachlan had drawn from her foolish and arrogant jokes about *Michaela's Rules for Managing the Public* running though her head like a mantra.

Head up, smile on, don't blink.

Who was she to ever presume to tell anyone how to manage the public? Her life was managed *by* the public. She'd bent over backwards to accommodate the press and the gawkers and her parents, who, as always, stood at the doors at the far end of the red carpet, greeting their guests. For the first time since she'd been awoken by a friend's frantic phone call saying there were pictures of her having sex all over the internet, she let herself feel angry at them for leaving her out here alone.

Her parents had done the best they knew how with what they'd been dealt, but in the end, and at any point over the years, they could have done better. She'd *deserved* better. From a lot of people.

As if to prove her point, the one person in all this she'd always, rightly, been angry at, leaped from the very next car after hers, grinning from ear to ear. The explosion of flashbulbs was more than even Michaela could manage. Gritting her teeth, she turned her back to the cameras and watched, dismayed, as Blake strode right up to her.

The hollow feeling she'd been carrying around inside her chest all afternoon bloomed to something bigger and darker and almost overwhelming. God, she missed Lachlan. She hated that she was here alone. At the very least, she should have brought a friend. Maybe Robby. Blake wouldn't have had the balls to stride up and throw his arm around her shoulders if she hadn't been alone.

He did it to get his face in the papers. So people would laugh at his audaciousness and write witty photo captions about bygones apparently being bygones and help him land his next big role. He did it because he knew she wouldn't cause a scene, and it made him feel powerful.

Michaela gritted her teeth and watched Blake's parents

climb from the car. He always came with them, no doubt to ensure he'd be allowed in. Michaela wished that just this once, there would be an exception made. Glancing at her parents' frozen smiles as they watched the annual debacle unfold before them, Michaela let that hope go.

If she made a scene, if she finally threw Blake off and told him where he could shove it, she'd have to do it without anyone else's help. And when it was over and the pictures were splashed across every magazine cover and website imaginable, she'd be more alone than ever.

"Michaela!"

It was hard to pick one person out from the dozens shouting her name, Blake's name, but she swore she heard a familiar voice.

"Michaela!"

She turned back to the line of cars as a yellow cab pulled up, her mouth dropping open as the back door flew open and discharged Lachlan.

In a kilt.

A hysterical giggle bubbled up from her chest, a wide grin breaking across her face. Lachlan was obviously relieved when he saw it, holding her gaze and grinning back.

God, he was handsome in the formal bonnie Prince Charlie jacket, his knee socks perfectly folded and his sporran bouncing as he jogged toward them. His eyes narrowed on Blake's arm around her and even though Lachlan's smile was still in place, she thought he looked dangerous. Blake either didn't notice or didn't have the sense to care, totally unprepared when Lachlan planted his shoulder into the middle of Blake's chest and checked him back a good four feet. Lachlan's other hand grasped her elbow, ensuring Blake didn't take her with him.

The press went bananas.

Blake looked so bewildered by this turn of events, Michaela almost burst into a fit of laughter. Before he could come up with any kind of response, his parents reached his side and turned him toward the door.

"I don't think so," Lachlan said, his voice hard but low enough that the press wouldn't hear him. "You set foot through those doors, and I will spend the rest of the night making an absolute spectacle out of all three of you." Blake's parents' eyes bulged in alarm. Lachlan leaned closer and growled, "Do I make myself clear?"

"You...you *can't*," gasped Blake's mother. She turned to Michaela. "Your parents will never stand for this."

Michaela smiled grimly. "They won't have a choice."

For a moment they hovered there, Blake and his parents clearly uncertain what to do. At last, Blake's father guided his family back to the row of cars, only to discover theirs had long since departed to wherever their driver intended to pass the next few hours. Michaela watched Blake actually blush, possibly for the first time in his shameful life, before the three of them marched down the sidewalk away from the hotel, the street alight with flash strobes capturing their ignominious departure.

Michaela turned back to Lachlan, unsure how to even begin going about thanking him sufficiently. Before she could come up with the words, he took her hands in his and captured her gaze.

"I'd like this to be a real date," he said in a low, serious voice only she would hear over the melee beyond the red velvet ropes. "But if you just want us to be friends, that's okay, too. I'm going to stick by you, no matter what. From here on in, I'll be your champion, too."

"You...what?" she asked, her head spinning.

"I want this to be a real date. I want them all to be real dates. You're the bravest, most interesting, frustrating, and brilliant woman I know, and if it means I have to parade around in front of these yahoos every weekend for the rest of my life, it will be one hundred percent worth it, because I'll get to do it with you."

And, well, what the hell was she supposed to say to that? He'd left her speechless, but her smile must have been answer enough, because then he was kissing her, bending her over his arm and capturing her mouth right in front of god and country and the New York fucking Times. Her heart swelled, practically bursting with joy as her hands cupped his cheeks and she kissed him back.

With a final peck, he set her back on her feet, his cheeks bright pink and his eyes sparkling with laughter.

"*Wow,*" she said dazedly.

"I thought a more public declaration of intent was in order," he said mildly, as if he hadn't just blow her mind. "Should I apologize?"

"Apologize?" She gave a breathless laugh. "Don't you dare. Though I don't need to tell you that you've just broken every rule in *Michaela's Rules for Managing the Public.*"

"Yeah, sorry about that," he said, though he sounded utterly unapologetic. "It turns out a lot of that goes directly against *Lachlan's Manifesto on Protecting the People He Loves.*"

Her heart stopped in her chest, even as a smile bloomed on her face. "It's a manifesto, huh?"

Lachlan's gaze held her captive. "Well, I guess I have a lot to say on the subject."

"And I can't wait to hear it," she assured him. Then she tilted her head toward the source of the still-endless strobe lighting. "But maybe not while we have such an avid audience."

He glanced up at the hundreds of eyes and dozens of cameras fixed on them. "Good point."

She took his hand. "And for what it's worth, I love you, too."

"It's worth everything," he said quietly, threading his fingers through hers. "Now, come on. Introduce me to your parents. I'm pretty sure I didn't make a very good first impression."

She blinked innocently. "You think?"

"Well, it could have been worse," he said with mock defensiveness, tucking her hand in his elbow and turning toward her parents, "It *could* have been windy tonight."

Michaela stumbled, her mouth dropping open. "You didn't,"

she breathed. "You *aren't.*"

Lachlan grinned. "I am." He waggled his eyebrows at her. "Care to find a deserted coat room and conduct a proper kilt inspection later?"

"Oh, my god," she gasped. "I really do."
Then she looked at all the people around them and laughed, mouth open, head thrown back, eyes closed, and not giving one good goddamn what the pictures would look like in the morning.

About the Author

Samantha Wayland has always dreamed of being a novelist. She wrote her first book as an escape from the pressures of her day job. That fascinating piece of contemporary erotic mystery/suspense with elements of paranormal, international intrigue, and god only knows what else is safely tucked under her bed, where it will remain until hell freezes over. Since then, she's learned a lot about the craft and turned her attention to writing contemporary MM and MMF ménage erotic romance.

Sam lives with her family—of both the two and four-legged variety—outside of Boston. She used to spend her days toiling away in corporate nerdville but was recently sprung from that hell. Now when she's not locked away in her home office, she can generally be found tucked in the corner of the local Thai place with a few beloved friends (and fellow authors).

Her favorite things include mango martinis, tiny Chihuahuas with big attitude problems, and the Oxford comma.

Sam loves to hear from readers.

Email her at samantha@samanthawayland.com or find her on Facebook (Samantha Wayland) or Twitter (@SamWayland).

Fair Play

Hat Trick Book One

Savannah Morrison is the new athletic trainer for the Moncton Ice Cats, a professional hockey team in the wilds of New Brunswick. It's a good thing she's got plenty of knowledge and grit, because as the only woman trainer in the league, she has to work twice as hard to win the players' respect. The last thing on earth she would do is date one of them.

Twelve year hockey veteran Garrick LeBlanc isn't ready to hang up his skates, particularly since he hasn't figured out what the hell he's planning to do next. He needs the new trainer to keep him fit to play, and she's got the skills to do it. Too bad he lost his mind and hit on her the day they met. Now she hates his guts and he's made an art of ignoring her.

When the team is put up for sale, Garrick and Savannah have to work together to save their jobs and their team. Somewhere along the way, they discover Garrick isn't just a hockey player, Savannah isn't only passionate about her work, and just maybe they've got more in common than they thought.

Two Man Advantage

Hat Trick Book Two

Rhian is working his way up the ranks of professional hockey, with the dream of making it to the NHL getting closer every day. He's doing it alone—no family, no friends—and that's the way he likes it. Then he arrives in New Brunswick, and meets the Moncton Ice Cats. Suddenly, he's got friends—and even something that might be an honest-to-god crush.

Garrick is lonely and counting the days until his last season with the Ice Cats is over and he can move to Boston. When his girlfriend suggests he take a lover—as long that lover is a man and Garrick tells her all about it—he laughs it off. But damned if his buddy Rhian doesn't take on the starring role in his fantasies. Good thing Rhian is way too young—and straight—for what Garrick has in mind.

Rhian takes a chance when Garrick's increasingly confusing signals start making sense, and soon discovers he's bitten off more than he can chew. Sex with strangers is simple. Sex with his best friend? Complicated.

End Game

Hat Trick Book Three

Garrick LeBlanc never intended to fall in love with two people, but he has, and now he has to figure out what to do about it. He wants to make them happy, but is afraid he's doing just the opposite. To make matters worse, he's trapped in New Brunswick until the end of the hockey season, while his lovers are both in Boston.

Savannah Morrison has no one but herself to blame for practically shoving her lover into the arms of another man. After all, it was her idea that Garrick take a lover while they are separated for the season. She loves Garrick with all her heart, but how the hell is she going to share him with Rhian?

Rhian Savage used to have such a simple life. Now he's in love, his dreams of skating on an NHL team are coming true, and he keeps spotting a strangely familiar face in the crowds. To top it all off, he has to see Savannah every day. He knows she's Garrick's real future, but he doesn't have the balls to do the right thing for all of them and end it—until his life goes sideways. As usual.

Now Rhian is alone, Garrick is heartbroken, and Savannah—the one person Rhian figured would celebrate his departure—is beating down his door. What the hell is up with that?

Crashing the Net

Mike comes to Moncton wanting nothing more than to play for the Ice Cats and finally live on his own terms. He's broke, bruised, and covered from head to toe in cheap lube, but he isn't going to let that stop him. All he needs is a place to live and some time to figure out how to reconcile who he really is with who everyone wants him to be.

Dumping three gallons of lube on the new kid is just another day at the office for Alexei. He knows exactly who he is: a goalie on the ice, a prankster in the locker room, and a man who knows better than to share his private life with anyone. He's let people in before and it's taught him that if he can't have what he really wants, it's better to be alone.

Despite their apparent differences, an unlikely friendship grows. Neither of them could ever have guessed how much they really have in common.

Home & Away

You can build a team, but you have to find your home.

Rupert Smythe is fond of many things. Callum Morrison isn't one of them.

Rupert is a quiet, thoughtful business man and, sadly, a total wimp. Maybe not the ideal candidate to run a professional hockey team, but he signed on to do it anyway. As his life has reminded him on an almost daily basis since, this isn't the most brilliant idea he's ever had. And that was before Callum showed up.

Being in the spotlight is just part of being a professional athlete, but Callum needs a break. He arrives in Moncton unannounced, determined to help grow the team he just bought, and under the assumption he'd be welcome. Possibly he should have tried to make a better first impression.

Callum figures he can push through the rest of the summer, never expecting two kids, a host of friends, and his growing feelings for Rupert to derail everything he has ever believed about what he wanted, and what he could have.

www.ingramcontent.com/pod-product-compliance
Lightning Source LLC
Chambersburg PA
CBHW060542180626
46817CB00002B/687